The Uncoupling

The Uncoupling

MEG WOLITZER

RIVERHEAD BOOKS
A member of Penguin Group (USA) Inc.
New York
2011

RIVERHEAD BOOKS
Published by the Penguin Group
Penguin Group (USA) Inc., 375 Hudson Street, New York, New York 10014, USA •
Penguin Group (Canada), 90 Eglinton Avenue East, Suite 700, Toronto, Ontario M4P 2Y3,
Canada (a division of Pearson Penguin Canada Inc.) • Penguin Books Ltd,
80 Strand, London WC2R 0RL, England • Penguin Ireland, 25 St Stephen's Green,
Dublin 2, Ireland (a division of Penguin Books Ltd) • Penguin Group (Australia),
250 Camberwell Road, Camberwell, Victoria 3124, Australia (a division of
Pearson Australia Group Pty Ltd) • Penguin Books India Pvt Ltd, 11 Community
Centre, Panchsheel Park, New Delhi–110 017, India • Penguin Group (NZ),
67 Apollo Drive, Rosedale, North Shore 0632, New Zealand (a division of
Pearson New Zealand Ltd) • Penguin Books (South Africa) (Pty) Ltd,
24 Sturdee Avenue, Rosebank, Johannesburg 2196, South Africa

Penguin Books Ltd, Registered Offices: 80 Strand, London WC2R 0RL, England

Library of Congress Cataloging-in-Publication Data

Wolitzer, Meg.
The uncoupling / Meg Wolitzer.
p.   cm.
ISBN 978-1-59448-788-0
1. Women—Sexual behavior—Fiction.   2. Desire—Fiction.   3. Man-woman
relationships—Fiction.   I. Title.
PS3573.O564U63   2011   2010039495
813'.54—dc22

Printed in the United States of America
1   3   5   7   9   10   8   6   4   2

BOOK DESIGN BY AMANDA DEWEY

This is a work of fiction. Names, characters, places, and incidents either are
the product of the author's imagination or are used fictitiously, and any
resemblance to actual persons, living or dead, businesses, companies,
events, or locales is entirely coincidental.

While the author has made every effort to provide accurate telephone numbers and
Internet addresses at the time of publication, neither the publisher nor the author
assumes any responsibility for errors, or for changes that occur after publication.
Further, the publisher does not have any control over and does not assume any
responsibility for author or third-party websites or their content.

For Sarah McGrath

The
Uncoupling

I tell a tale of an unusual enchantment that made women turn away from their men. O Eros! This spell entranced the young ones, glued to their mirrors; the ones in the middle of life, glued to their duties; and the old ones, glued to air. Why did these gentle women withdraw so swiftly, without mercy? Do not cast judgment upon them—they knew not what they were doing, or what had been done to them. Their refusals were made in blindness, in innocence, and in bed after bed after bed.

Part One

1.

People like to warn you that by the time you reach the middle of your life, passion will begin to feel like a meal eaten long ago, which you remember with great tenderness. The bright points of silver. The butter in its oblong dish. The corpse of a chocolate cake. The leaning back in a chair at the end, slugged on the head and overcome. Dory Lang had always thought there was a little cruelty in such a warning. It was similar to how, when she had a baby, people always tried to clue her in on what they were sure would befall her. Once, long ago, Dory and her infant daughter were riding a bus in the city, when an old woman leaned over and said, "May I tell you something, dear?" She had a kind face full of valleys and faults. Dory imagined she was about to describe the baby's beauty—in particular, the curve of the mouth—and she made her own mouth assume a knowing, pleased modesty. But what the woman said, leaning even closer, was, "You will never have another day in your life that is free of anxiety."

There was a little private pleasure to be taken in the fact that that old woman, though she was of course correct, was now dead, and Dory was not. As for the warnings about the disappearance of passion, Dory recognized the sadism stitched into the words. Because the love lives of the women who said such things had gone soft and pulpy and tragic, they took a little comfort in telling as many women as they could that someday such a change would happen to them too.

Dory and Robby felt they were exempt from such an outcome, assuming that even when they were so old that they appeared interchangeable—even when his ankles were as narrow and hairless as hers, and her lips were as thin and collagenless as his, and their pubic hair could have belonged to Santa Claus; even when they resembled those dried-apple dolls sold in the gift shops of folk museums—they would sleep together frequently, happily, and not just gently, but with the same gruff, fierce purpose as always. Around them, in other houses in their neighborhood, there would be a terrible pile-up of non–sex-having couples, all bone and tendon and indifference and regret.

Warmly, hotly, tirelessly, in their own bed they would stay.

The Langs had been teaching English at Eleanor Roosevelt High School in Stellar Plains, New Jersey, for a decade and a half when everything changed. It had been an uneventful school year so far; there had been no deaths, neither student nor teacher, and not even any halfhearted, prankish bomb threats, which had become as common to suburban high schools as intramural sports.

Robby and Dory Lang began that year at Eleanor Roosevelt—Elro, everyone called it—with the same optimism that they almost always felt. It had grown tempered in recent years, since the economy

had tumbled, and certain concrete signs of optimism were no longer as central a part of the school experience: the smell of pencils,
for instance, with their suggestion of woodshop and campgrounds
and the promise of some precocious kid's standout in-class essay.
Pencils still lurked, fragrantly, but you had to look for them, and
they seemed outnumbered by all things with a keyboard. Still,
though, the Langs were hopeful; still, they thought it would be a
good year.

Together they were often spoken of in one breath by the other
faculty members as *Robby and Dory Lang*, or just *Robby and Dory*,
or by the students as *Mr. and Ms. L,* those two married, easygoing,
still fairly young English teachers who walked the halls with a
genial air. There were some teachers at Elro who lived to crack
down on the kids. "Where's your pass?" they would demand of a
boy with a mouth freshly wet and slack from the water fountain.
"Wha', wha'?" said the boy, stammering, dripping. But the kids
knew that Dory and Robby weren't out to get them. Even their pop
quizzes were humane.

At just past forty they were both good-natured, decent-looking,
tallish, and as dark-redheaded as Irish setters. Robby wore egghead
eyeglasses that had become fashionable in recent years. He had a
hard shield of a chest, and he rode a bike on weekends through the
smooth streets of the neighborhood. Each morning he unscrewed
one of the green glass canisters on the countertop and poured himself a dusty bleat of oat and twig, pious about his intake, wanting
to live a long time so he didn't miss a second with his wife or
daughter.

The Langs were young, but not too young; old, but not too
old. Girls often exclaimed over Dory's boots, which dated back to

her Brooklyn days and were the approximate color of caramel, narrowing to a subtle point—not quite the boots of a snarling female rocker, but not the boots of a hiker with bags of muesli swelling her pockets either. The girls also liked Robby's pale, much-laundered work shirts, which by third period he had invariably rolled up at the sleeves, revealing arms with a light spatter of goldenrod hair. Neither Robby nor Dory repelled or depressed the kids the way their parents tended to. Nor were they like the kids themselves, who had unfinished faces and piercings that punctured the most tender membranes of their bodies like buckshot—the kids with their energy drinks, their Xtreme sports injuries, and with their restless need to be in touch through some device, even if in real life they'd only been apart long enough to go to the bathroom:

"what r u up 2"
"peeing"
"when will u be back"
"look up i am back"

In the time that they'd spent in the English department at Eleanor Roosevelt, Robby and Dory had both been named Teacher of the Year with surprising frequency. Once in a while an art teacher with a head sprouting dreadlocks, or the unusually lenient Spanish teacher, Señor Mandelbaum, busted up the monopoly, but for years at a time husband and wife had predictably passed the honor from hand to hand.

It was as if they had each said to the other:

Okay, this year *you* be the better teacher. This year *you* be the one who remains in the classroom tacking up pictures of

J. D. Salinger and Maya Angelou, with captions like, "For Chrissakes, Jerry, You Were Never a Phony," or, "So Why *Does* It Sing, Maya?"

Meanwhile, *I'll* be the one who ducks out the moment school is over, telling the class over my shoulder, "Don't forget to check eSignment for tonight's homework. And for those of you who can't stand to wait, I'm asking you to read until the part where he sees Daisy Buchanan again."

"Wait, until who sees who?" someone would ask, but it was too late; their teacher was out of there, done, *gone.*

Robby and Dory gracefully and uncomplainingly took on those roles, and then, the following year, they switched. They had met at a hotel in Minneapolis during an education conference in the earliest, most know-nothing days of their teaching lives. Teachers flowed through the revolving doors, laughing, gesturing, using the words "curriculum" and "curricular." Robby Baskin, twenty-four years old then, an age when even not really being beautiful falls under the category of beautiful, was in the bar off the polished hotel lobby, sitting on a high stool with his long, weedy legs hanging down. He was talking with two female teachers, all their voices loose and careless, and Dory Millinger of Brooklyn, aged twenty-three, waded closer.

He was telling the women, "Here is a sentence that one of my students actually wrote: 'At the time that Virginia Woolf and James Joyce were writing, the world was very much as it is today, *though to a lesser extent.*'"

The women laughed as if he'd told them something uproarious and filthy. Dory thought that if she'd been sitting there she would've laughed a lot too, for she would have wanted him to like her. She'd seen him on a panel that afternoon called "Young Teacher as Mentor/Friend," and he'd been funny and courteous and *brief,* unlike the man sitting beside him, who'd held fast to the microphone. Robby Baskin among the women now seemed just as much at ease, and when she came closer and told him she'd liked what he'd said on the panel, that those were the same issues she thought about when she was teaching too, his face became vivid and alert.

"Oh, no, wait," he said as she turned to walk back into the crowd, and then he caught up with her, taking his drink and arching and angling among the other teachers, going past the stick-thin, Ichabod Crane types and the pigeon-breasted older females with their brooches (for some reason, teachers liked brooches). A table was free at the big picture window with its curtain of hanging metal beads, and they sat there alone, two young, neophyte high school teachers, one from Brooklyn, one from Pettier, Vermont, fingering the already fingered nuts in their little tin bowl.

Inevitably, on the last night of the conference, they slept together. There had been a closing party in the hospitality suite, and they stayed as long as they could, until finally they were pinned in a corner with a few other young teachers while an old, distinguished Southern education pioneer grew agitated about the state of the American high school. "Come," Robby said when the man went to get some cheese. Many flights up, in Dory's hotel room, she lay back with her head squarely on the pillow, and Robby Baskin sat above her, both of them smiling as if they'd won something. There, where the walls were covered with a twiney fabric that probably rendered them perfect vessels for sound transmittal, they discovered that their long, similar bodies worked well together. Robby was fervent, effective in bed. He buried himself in her; his heart worked so hard it seemed like a thing that might leap away. She thought that she could do this with him forever, watching as time and life slipped away, as other people went to jobs and made dinner and ironed and talked.

In bed, at first and then later, when he visited her in Brooklyn, and even much later, when he left Vermont for good and moved in with her, they shouted in big voices, or squeaked or hummed with industry and focus. They both noticed that they perspired roughly the same amount, and it was never overpowering, but instead more like a delicate broth. *Chickeny*, Robby commented once. *The bouillon of love.*

Robby was a quiet man, straightforward and reliable, and when the time came, he flexibly transformed himself into a good husband and father. None of it was much of a stretch. Together they decided to change their last names to something invented and new. They were casting off their old families, their old lives; why not cast off their names too? "Lang" was decided upon in the middle of the night. It was a neutral, appealing name; the single syllable seemed easygoing, much the way they imagined themselves. They free-associated to various good-sounding "lang" words: "*languid*," "*language*," even "*langoustines*," those tiny lobsters they both loved and had eaten by the bucket that summer. The name was chosen, and the old names fell away, just as their old, unattached selves did too.

At Elro, Dory Lang was looked up to and beamed at. Robby Lang was often asked to direct the high school play, and he also served as the faculty liaison for the literary magazine, *The New Deal*. Before school, he would sit and talk earnestly with the kids about their poems and stories and the lithographs of their grandmothers' hands. Students often confided in both of them, and so did other faculty members. Fifteen years passed, and everyone knew the kind of marriage the Langs had, the stability and reciprocity, the lack of sexism, the love and the passion.

Women admired the way Dory and her husband loved each other, and she knew this because they occasionally told her. Once, after seeing the Langs quickly kiss goodbye before Robby went off on an overnight field trip with his class, Dory's friend Bev Cutler, the guidance counselor, seemed to redden slightly. It was as if she had been caught observing the Langs in an explicit moment. Or maybe she had been caught longing for something of her own, explicitly. "Oh, you two; it's really something," was what she said. Everyone understood that, although the Langs were past forty, they still often wanted to do various elaborate things to each other. They were entirely free to do whatever they wanted, sensation hitting them, *pow, pow, pow*, like light hail popping against their bodies.

Unlike Bev and her hedge-fund manager husband Ed, Dory and Robby had a good amount to say to each other at the end of the day. Because they worked in the same building, in the same department, they always enjoyed the time at night when they could slowly go over all that had happened to them, beat by beat. "Tell me about lunch with Leanne," Robby would say as they arranged themselves in their bed, bodies close, and she'd tell him what she and her closest friend, Leanne Bannerjee, the school psychologist, had talked about.

"She's still threatening to leave and join a practice with her friend Jane in the city," Dory would tell him. "To become a teenologist."

"That is not a real word."

"I know, but they make a lot of money. They make house calls to 'talk to teens.' They go on reality TV as experts. It's pretty disgusting." Leanne was twenty-nine, almost absurdly beautiful, tiny, vulnerable but confident, and the girl students in particular desperately attached themselves to her.

"And what about McCleary? That's still going on?" Robby would ask quietly, as though afraid their teenaged daughter Willa might hear them and be given information that only they knew: that Leanne and the married, astonishingly stiff school principal, Gavin McCleary, had been involved since last spring.

"Yes," Dory would say. "Still going on. Also, that foreign-car dealer, Malcolm. And the bartender, Carlos, from Peppercorns. But yes, McCleary; she's still seeing McCleary."

"I see him in the halls," Robby would say, "and I think: *That's who she chooses?* These things are always such a mystery."

"Attractions."

He would nod. Sometimes when McCleary stood onstage to speak at an assembly, Dory imagined him in bed with Leanne. That same wooden, formal voice that said, "Girls' field hockey, Team B, will meet out front after school for team pictures," also certainly spoke intimate and startling phrases. She agreed with her husband about how mysterious it all was.

"Oh, and next topic," Dory would say to Robby. "What happened with *The Odyssey*? Did they respond at all to the part where Telemachus says that line . . . what is it exactly; I always get it wrong."

Robby would recite, "'*I am that father whom your boyhood*

lacked / and suffered pain for lack of.'" Then together they would finish it off: *"'I am he.'"*

They had these little routines, which were all part of the patter and rhythm of their full home life. Rounding it out was Willa, who, at the time, was a high school sophomore, self-involved, uncertain, spending her time noodling around on different websites, or frequently in the deep, cool, virtual landscapes of Farrest. The Langs lived in a small, pretty white Colonial on Tam o' Shanter Drive in Stellar Plains, with an upright piano and walls hung thick with artwork and photographs, and with their twelve-year-old yellow Labrador, Hazel, who had resolved the potential problem of loss of desire by lying curved on the front hall rug each day and licking the brambles of her underside until she was soaked and zonked. She needed no one else for love; she was satisfied by her own long and faithful self.

The Langs had waves of students who stayed in touch for years after they graduated ("A Shout-Out to Ms. Lang," they wrote as e-mail subject headings, or, "Yo, Mr. L!" they bellowed from across the parking lot at Greens and Grains). The students lurked on the edges of their teachers' lives for years, and brought bulletins from their own lives, which over time began to include lovers, ambitions, an upward trajectory. It was only when everything settled down for them and became permanent and maybe disappointing that their former teachers never heard from them again.

Robby and Dory were fixed in place themselves, but all was well. It might have gone on like this for a long, long time. It might never have changed. They might have remained one of those miracle couples who never stop, never quit, and whom everyone regards in head-shaking awe. They might have stayed at an impressive pitch, sexually, even after so much time had gone by. But one night in December, a school night, a strange and unnoticed but also undeniable spell was cast. At least, this was when the spell was cast upon Dory Lang, though of course she did not know it. And since she did not know it, she had no idea what had set it in motion either. Robby had shoveled the snow and Dory had made dinner, and then they'd sat down and eaten it with Willa. Dinner-table conversation ensued, then came to a natural close as they stood to clear the plates. Finally they said goodnight to their daughter, and then they climbed the stairs and got into bed.

For a while, under the pale gray duvet, they talked, murmured, coughed occasionally, made the kinds of remarks they always made, some tender, some dull. And then Robby put a hand on her shoulder to turn her toward him, as he often did, and what she felt was a stunning bolt of cold air strike her body. A formidable wind seemed to have flown in through the half-inch of open window, but had then immediately found its way under the duvet and under Dory Lang's old, thin, stretchy, skim-milk-colored nightgown.

It was the cold air of the spell, come to claim her. Other spells were far more dramatic, accompanied as they were by lightning, or a sizzling clang of thunderclap. This spell was more subtle, but still when it first came over a woman it was shocking, perhaps even grotesque, and she didn't have any idea that she was under it. Dory Lang simply felt as if she was freezing, and then she was aware of a mild disgust, no, even a mild horror at being touched. Certainly not pleasure; none of that for her anymore. Her body momentarily shook—a brief death rattle, a *death-of-sex* rattle, technically—and then stopped.

Robby turned her, and she faced him, and his hand was upon

her and his mouth was on her face, her neck, and instead of being drawn toward him as usual, all she knew was that she had to find a way out of this moment. Obviously, it wasn't the first time she'd ever wanted to say no, or had ever said no to him, in bed, but she thought it may have been the first time that she'd felt the need to lie.

Other times, entirely truthfully, she'd said:

I'm not in the mood.

Or:

I'm tired.

Or:

I'm coming down with something.

Or:

I've got that thing in the morning.

And all those times, she had been telling the truth. The excuses were real. If Dory Lang said she had a thing in the morning, then she certainly did; there would have been some legitimate event that she needed to rest up for.

Now, though, under the power of the spell, all Dory could think was that sleeping with your husband after so many years was not at all like sleeping with him when you were young. It was no longer effortless; it was *full of effort*, and now that she was aware of that effort, how could she ever ignore it again? She was irritated by the realization, and angry. Suddenly she wanted to shake everything up, to take the sweetness and constancy and even the conscientious effort that was apparently now a part of their love life, and throw it away. Destroy what they had.

Robby was touching her, and she was meant to touch him back, but she couldn't bear it. She had to say something to him, for he was patiently waiting. "I have that thing in the morning," she said to her sweet and lovely husband, who had done nothing different, nothing wrong. It was as if the words had been supplied to her by some hidden prompt.

"What thing?" he pressed, for he also didn't understand what was happening to his wife.

Dory paused for a moment. She actually did have something in the morning, she remembered with relief.

"That conference with Jen Heplauer and her mother," she said, settling into this alibi, making her voice serious and responsible. "The plagiarism thing."

They shifted in the bed, moving apart. All around Stellar Plains, the same low, hard wind was starting to blow in and out of bedrooms, under blankets, nightgowns, skin, and it would keep doing that for weeks, making its circuit, taking its time. That night and over the days and nights that followed, other women, newly enchanted, said to men, "I have that thing in the morning," or "Sorry, I'm kind of out of it," or "I can't see you anymore," or simply, *"We're done,"* or else they just turned away, giving their husbands or partners or boyfriends the long flat of the back like a door in the face.

Robby sighed and then scratched himself somewhere beneath the blanket; the timbre of the scratch made her think it was the inside of a thigh. It was true that Dory had a conference in the morning—though "conference" was a lofty word to apply to a brief and uncomfortable conversation that would be held in the classroom before school with Jen Heplauer and her mother. She pictured their hopeful, unimaginative Heplauer faces; the gap between Jen's front teeth, her hair still lying wet from a shower;

the mother's gum-colored pocketbook with all those buckles and knobs. Dory heard the daughter's defensive, rising voice, and the mother's echoes, and her own tolerant but ultimately insistent words, repeating herself as many times as it took: "Ms. Heplauer. Jen. Ms. Heplauer. Jen. Listen. I appreciate that you worked hard, Jen, I really do."

"I did work hard," the girl would say, her lower lip on vibrate. "You have no idea how hard I worked, Ms. L. I stayed in when everyone else was going out. I stayed in on a *Wednesday night.*"

"You don't have to keep saying that. I understand that you put in a lot of effort."

"And did footnotes," her mother would murmur.

"Yes. Footnotes," Jen would add, mother and daughter looking at each other and nodding, a unified front.

"That's not at issue," Dory would say, and she would try to get them to understand. Eventually they would give in, the way people always gave in to teachers, those bullies. She'd shepherd them from the classroom just as the first bell was ringing and the rest of the students began to gallop and flood toward her, wanting something, wanting everything.

In bed, Robby understood that this was what awaited his wife in the morning. It wasn't as if Dory needed to fall asleep immediately so that she could be in fighting shape for Jen Heplauer and her mother. It wasn't as if she needed to rest up for some kind of Ironman Challenge, and they both knew it.

He looked at her in slight confusion. "Oh, okay," he said, remembering. "The plagiarism thing." He was trying to figure out the link between the conference in the morning and the inadvisability of sex right now. He was stumped.

"She doesn't even understand that she plagiarized," Dory went on, using Jen Heplauer and her mother as a human shield. "She thinks that you can just go on Booxmartz and read a summary of the book, then read other people's analyses of it—other people's actual thoughts, the brainpower of strangers who you'll never meet—and write them down and hand them in. Because why actually just sit there with the book trying to come up with something of your own, right?"

"Right," he said.

"And you can take these little pieces of information that you read on these websites, as if you're building a nest or making paella," she continued with new conviction. "And suddenly it's *your* work. You actually tell yourself that you worked very hard. And you believe it. It's suddenly all yours. It's suddenly . . . *Jen Heplauer's*! I just can't get over it. She's like someone in a dream."

"Oh, sweetheart, they're all like someone in a dream," Robby said, and they grimly snickered together at the idea of a whole generation prodded by pixels and clicks, and link after link that sent them leapfrogging in search of something increasingly abstract that they thought they wanted. The generation that had information, but no context. Butter, but no bread. Craving, but no longing.

Dory thought of Jen Heplauer and her friends, and her daughter Willa and her friends, all of them constantly checking for news or non-news from one another. All of them lately logging onto Farrest, spending many hours in its puzzlingly simple mossy green groves, feeling as if they were getting an infusion of air and sunlight and vitamin D. She thought of Willa's avatar of choice on Farrest—a sleek purple ninja—and she imagined her daughter stalking silently across the grass to locate a patch that was untrampled by elves or dry-docked mermaids or big-eyed androids or various woodland animals. Dory could picture her daughter's ninja-self free of the little plantation of whiteheads that grew in a scatter at the hairline of her real self. She pictured Willa standing in one place, pulsating lightly, the way these animated creatures always seemed to do when they weren't in motion.

All of which forced real-life parents to make curdled and no doubt ignorant remarks about what their kids were missing, even as the parents themselves were drawn to their own screens, where they sat slack every night before a radiant blast. As the hours disappeared, sometimes they purchased slippers, or read about a newly discovered species of lizard, or about a disease they feared they had, or about the unmysterious wars that quietly continued in Iraq and Afghanistan, as unseen as fires burning underground. Leanne had recently remarked that if you wanted to get to know someone's unconscious, all you had to do was take a look at everything they had looked at and done on the Internet over the course of a couple of hours when they were all alone.

After a second or two now, Robby's hand fell away, open-palmed. He'd had to accept that there would be no touching tonight. The closeness of love had temporarily been replaced by the closeness of railing together, predictably, against this brave new world and all that was shallow or incomprehensible or life-frittering about it. Dory kissed his head in consolation, smelling the tang of the tea tree oil shampoo they both used.

She said, "I love you."

"Love you too," he said.

They did; they loved each other.

She moved farther away from him, as if there hadn't been the suggestion of sex at all. It was as if he had *made it up*, and it was all in his head like the desires of a man toward a woman he's never spoken to in his life, rather than toward a woman whose body he has been in and around so many times that it was staggering to them both. Once, driving home from a faculty potluck, probably a little too wine-headed, they had actually tried to figure out how many times they'd slept together. "Is it even a doable calculation?" Robby had wondered. "Wouldn't you have to have kept diaries about it over the years, like Pepys?" They attempted to count every sexual experience they'd shared, but by the time they arrived at their house they realized that somehow marriage itself had made it all uncountable. At first they'd been able to think of various episodes that had taken place before they'd gotten married, pinning them to different, specific events: sex the night they'd been to the Spanish place with those good, slippery olives; sex in front of the stuttering air conditioner during that heat wave. Then, though, the marriage began, and not too long after Willa was born the suburban years began. And though those years had still been layered with plea-sure and humor and joy, distinguishing one time from another was much more difficult.

Now, in bed, Dory imagined telling a couple of other women in the teachers' room tomorrow morning about what had hap-pened here tonight. "It's strange," Dory could have said to them. "In bed last night, when Robby touched me, my first thought was, *Please, please don't.*"

Had Dory admitted this, another teacher might have looked up from scraping the last of her yogurt with a plastic spoon, and said, "Funny. Same thing happened to me last night too." Across the room, by the coffee machine, still another female teacher might have looked up as she flattened and smoothed a filter, wondering if she should also join this conversation, because, interestingly, the exact same thing had happened to her within the past few days.

Dave Boyd, the biology teacher, might have watched from the side, not really relating to any of it. He was a gay man, and he would never be affected by the spell. Apparently he and his boyfriend Gordon, a landscape architect, would continue to throw themselves upon each other in their restored carriage house without any interruption. Only women were enchanted that winter—specifically, women who were in some way connected sexually to men. The men, it seemed, stayed the same, never changing, only responding to circumstances. But Dory didn't say a word to anyone in the teachers' room, and no one else did either. What she had done in bed was private. She had no idea that what was starting to happen to her would happen all around the high school, and that it would keep happening in waves. It happened mostly to middle-aged women, but also to ones who were older or, notably, younger. The spell touched some teenaged girls, who had so recently experienced the first shuddering illogic of love, only to find themselves sharply pulling back from it, leaving boys shocked and thoroughly undone.

"Really?" a boy might say to a girl, his voice splitting in the middle. "We can't do this anymore? *Never?*" How could he have been introduced to all that beauty, only to have it taken away?

Suddenly, the sex lives of these girls and women caved in and collapsed, just as the women had been warned they would someday; suddenly, they collapsed them. Dory knew she was obviously much too young for this moment to be considered the *someday* she had been warned about. She was still on her own upward trajectory. She was only just past forty, after all, and forty didn't mean sixty. Forty was still rapacious, viable, possibly fertile, in the mix. Forty was way too soon for this to happen. Forty didn't need to lie on the front hall rug in a patch of sun, licking itself into unconsciousness.

But the spell had started to come over all of them, seizing them in their separate beds, changing them in an instant. Starting that night, and continuing for quite a while afterward, the wind picked up and the temperature dropped and the windows shook like crazy in their frames, and all over that town, you could hear the word "no."

2.

Pre-enchantment, the only thing at all unusual so far that year was the fact that a drama teacher had joined the faculty of Eleanor Roosevelt. On the first day of school in September she had appeared, quietly and without much fanfare. The other faculty members were aware that she'd been hired, of course, for the principal had sent a memo the previous spring proudly stating that even in these budget-slashing times, money had been found to bring a drama teacher to Elro.

But everyone, as usual, was distracted and overextended on the first day of school. New teachers were just a part of life; for a few days after one arrived, squawks of interest were emitted from various corners, but then they died away as the teacher was absorbed like everyone else into the homogenizing vortex of 8-to-3 school-day life. Before you knew it, the fresh new ones seemed to have been teaching there forever, too, or else they didn't last very long, and were gone before you'd gotten to know them.

On that day in September, the new drama teacher, Fran Heller, stood in the doorway of the teachers' room, looking at her surroundings. Usually, nothing much happened in that room; it was a place of mildness, often dullness, and the arrival of a new teacher didn't seem as though it would change that. Dory knew that the students imagined the place to be a kind of first-class airport lounge, blocked off from their view while they were left in the dreary, waxy halls. They pictured soft lighting and one of those perpetual chocolate fountains, and perhaps a scatter of reclining chairs that performed acupressure massages on the necks and shoulders of faculty members during the interval between classes.

Once in a while when Dory Lang was in there, the door would open long enough for one of the kids in the hall to get a chance to see inside. One time the art teacher, carrying a few glazed, lumpy ceramic coffee mugs made by students, pushed open the door with her elbow and held it for a substitute teacher who ducked her head as she came in, unsure if she was even allowed in here. During that suspended moment, a snaggle-toothed eleventh-grader planted herself in the doorway in awe. When she saw Dory, she said in a low moan, "Holy crap, Ms. L, *this* is where you guys go?" as if in disbelief that this plain room was where some of her favorite teachers willingly collected—that this, astonishingly, was *it*.

"Yep, this is it!" Dory replied with false cheer, and as the door moved on its pneumatic cylinder and the view narrowed, she saw the girl's imperfect smile narrow too, for she had been betrayed. Now the girl would have to wonder: what, really, was there to look forward to in adulthood?

The teachers' room in Eleanor Roosevelt High School was painted the milky green of glow-in-the-dark stars when the lights are on. The chairs were apparently considered ultra-modern back in the Clinton years, when a truck carried them to the doors of the school and then drove off. There was a midsized refrigerator in which the faculty placed items from home, though sometimes it took on a decisive, acidic tang. ("Abby Means must be storing a vinegar douche in there again," Dave Boyd would whisper behind his cupped hand.) The occasional poisonous smell inside the refrigerator was evidence that something was silently transmogrifying at the rear of a shelf; that putrefaction was taking place behind the traffic of yogurts and soda bottles and plastic tubs that were brought in each day by Abby Means, a thin, ropy-necked math teacher in her late twenties who sometimes wore vintage poodle skirts and other affected consignment-shop finds, and who was generally disliked.

Once, Dave Boyd added, "Abby Means *is* a vinegar douche."

DO NOT TOUCH—PROPERTY OF ABBY MEANS, she wrote across the tape of her containers and bottles in block letters. Disliking Abby Means actually brought some of the teachers together in that room. Dory got to know not only Dave and his boyfriend Gordon through this connection, but also the new drama teacher. Fran Heller was small, arty, assertive, spiky-salt-and-pepper-headed, vehement, with hammered silver earrings that moved around her head like quotation marks when she spoke. You could picture her stalking the stage in the auditorium, or monkeying up a narrow metal ladder to change a gel.

While she was new, most of the others had long settled into their lives here. A few faculty members had come to the school after having been denied tenure at small colleges or universities.

Abby Means had actually filled in for an instructor in a section of a class at Harvard one semester, though Dave Boyd had more than once insisted, "Oh, she probably taught at a college called *Harver,* and she mumbles the name so we'll hear it wrong."

Robby and Dory had moved here when two positions in the English department had simultaneously opened up. They joked that there had been a suicide pact between the departing teachers who could no longer tolerate the soul-killing demands of suburban home ownership. The Langs were hesitant to leave Brooklyn at first, where they'd lived since Robby had moved from Vermont to be with her; but after they had Willa, they outgrew their small apartment with its burnt-looking wood trim. At the time, both Dory and Robby had teaching jobs in local city high schools. Supplies were scarce, and once in a while the schools went into semilockdown mode, with a whooping siren like at a prison. Then they saw the ad for the jobs in Stellar Plains.

Stellar Plains, New Jersey, was a town that got mentioned whenever there was an article called "The Fifty Most Livable Suburbs in America." Unlike most suburbs, this one was considered progressive. Though the turnpike that ran through it was punctuated by carpet-remnant outlets and tire wholesalers, and even an unsettling, windowless store no one had ever been to, advertising DVDS AND CHINESE SPECIALTY ITEMS, Main Street was quaint and New Englandy, with a cosmopolitan slant. There was an excellent bookstore, Chapter and Verse, at a moment when bookstores around the country were making way for cell-phone stores. (*"Make Way for Cell-Phone Stores,* a children's book by Robert McCloskey," said the wary owner.)

Everyone in town went out for dinner once in a while to Peppercorns. When the economy began to sputter and tank, the restaurant turned quiet, nearly empty, and Dory worried that it would close. She couldn't bear to lose Peppercorns, with its baskets of snowy, soft rolls and its long, looming salad bar that made you remember that there were choices in life. But then business picked up a bit, and everyone came to Peppercorns a little more frequently, sitting with tall, sturdy menus in front of their faces once again. Being a teacher at a restaurant in the town where you lived was a little like being a TV star, as opposed to a movie star, at a restaurant. A tenth-grade lacrosse player from Elro sitting with his parents might raise a hand from the next table, and his parents would glance over with shy smiles, and maybe the father would lift his glass of beer and say, "Here's to a teacher who deserves an A!" The son would be humiliated by his father's weird and pointless remark. But it had no doubt sprung from true emotion, for all that parents ever wanted, really, was for you to love their child the way they did.

Robby, Dory, and Willa Lang sometimes sat in the restaurant near the wood-burning oven in the back, and while the heat warmed their necks a little too strongly, and kitchen workers shoved flatbreads in and out on paddles, they traded anecdotes from the day at school. All around them, other families did the same. Later on, after they came home again, Robby and Dory would get undressed for the night. Every so often, maybe once or twice a week—not that Dory ever counted back then—one of them would turn to the other with sudden interest, or with the wish to create interest.

"You," Robby would say, "are just who I was looking for."

"Oh yeah. A wiped-out English teacher who's headed for peri-menopause in a bullet train."

Sometimes, if he was standing in his untucked work shirt and pants, she might grab his belt by its buckle and pull it through the loops. Then they'd find themselves on the bed with the light blazing and their daughter awake but preoccupied down the hall—doing her homework or in touch with friends, though rarely on e-mail, for that was too slow; and less and less frequently on the phone, for that form of communication was apparently fading away. Or maybe she was sending a text message or going to some random website or was off once again into the depths of good old Farrest, all the while floating in her ergonomic desk chair like a dental patient in space.

The new drama teacher Fran Heller had apparently come to Stellar Plains from a high school in the more conventional, mall-defined suburb of Cobalt, about twenty miles away. "I can't even get a new language lab," Señor Mandelbaum had complained when they first learned about the new hire, "and they bring in a drama teacher? I mean, come *on.*"

"Oh, Mandelbaum, stop," said Leanne Bannerjee.

"Leanne, aren't you supposed to want to hear my problems? Isn't that your job?"

"If you were an adolescent I would," she said. "But you're not. And don't you like being in a school that cares about the arts? Or do you want this place to be like so many other places in America? Do you want everybody here to be the same as they are all over the country?"

No one said what they were thinking, which was that, of

course, despite the semi-specialness of the town, you couldn't make people more unusual than they actually were. The teenagers here had a sameness about them that seemed universal. For one thing, this whole generation of kids had fully integrated sex into their lives. Until it was called to the attention of the principal, Leanne's secret lover Gavin McCleary, two girls had been wearing T-shirts to school that read SLUT I and SLUT II. When brought into McCleary's office, the girls insisted that the administration had failed to see the irony embedded in the word "slut." The principal asked them to explain it to him, but neither girl could. "No offense, Mr. McCleary, but why do you wear that tie?" asked one of them. "It has little boxes inside boxes on it," she pointed out. "What do you mean to say by that?"

He dismissed them quickly; the T-shirts never reappeared at school, and neither did the tie. Young people today, everyone was told, hooked up with one another—"*hooking up*," a phrase that, if put into quotation marks, made the person referring to it seem like an old, tragic loser whom the world had left behind—but if *not* put into quotation marks, made the person seem to have accepted the concept of hooking up fully and completely.

Bev Cutler, the fifty-two-year-old guidance counselor with the well-tended honeyed hair, expensive linen jackets, and appealing face, but, over time, the very large body, sometimes held court around the faculty cafeteria table. She discussed the subject of hooking up in a voice meant to impart something sorrowful, and several teachers would have much to add about "the way the world is now." This conversation usually was accompanied by meditative chewing, and a shaking of heads.

"In the past," Bev had said at lunch recently, "sex just seemed like it was so much more extracurricular. It was almost like Model U.N.—something that a number of them signed up to do after the school day was over. It served no actual purpose, but they enjoyed it: 'I'm Burma, and I object!' And that was fine, of course, except for the occasional pregnancy—remember Cami Fennig and Jason Manousis?"

Everyone nodded solemnly, including Dory. "God, them," said Mandelbaum. "I would never have thought of them again in my life if you hadn't mentioned them. It's been what, four years? Five? What happened to them?"

"They broke up after the baby was born," Bev Cutler said. "Jason Manousis joined the military and went to Afghanistan. He was blinded in one eye and sent home."

"Oh my God, that's right," said Dory.

"There was a fund for him," said Bev. "Ed and I contributed."

"I do remember this now. It's so sad," Mandelbaum said. "And what about the baby?"

"Joint custody, I heard," said Bev. "And I swear to you that this next part is true: they named the baby Trivet."

"Oh, they did not," said the music teacher, Ron di Canzio. "You are making it up, Bev. You are embellishing."

"Yes, they did," the guidance counselor insisted. "They apparently thought they were naming it Trevor, or Travis, but they got confused."

The teachers often talked in such a free-floating way about their teenaged charges. The students alternately compelled and appalled and bored them. Right now, on the first day of classes in September, there was nothing that needed to be said or done about any particular students, at least not yet. Class lists had been handed out, and all the teachers were busy with the clerical tasks of the new year. The spell would not hit any of the women until December. They went about their business during the day without knowing that at some point in the next couple of months, their sexual lives, their love lives, would be upended. They were as happy as they ever were, happy and preoccupied, simply doing what they were meant to do and not at all anxious or fearful that something important would be stolen from them.

When the new drama teacher appeared in the doorway of the teachers' room, Dory Lang got a good, long look at her. There had never been an actual drama teacher at Elro before; in the past, when Robby directed the play, he tended to choose works by Sam Shepard or David Mamet or other writers about whom the word "terse" was often used. Teenaged boys stood onstage in their fathers' boxy old double-breasted suit jackets, or red-and-black-checkered flannel jackets, scowling. Every time their heads moved, powder was tossed into the air like seasoning from a shaker. As the mothers of girls began to point out, there were never enough female parts, and this didn't seem fair, for girls were generally the ones who wanted to be in plays in the first place.

Many girls *lived* to be in plays—notably, Willa's friend Marissa Clayborn, a tall and beautiful African-American girl with the best posture and the best diction of anyone in the school. She was almost always given the biggest female part available. Marissa could both project and emote, and you found yourself tearing up a little when she spoke onstage, even if she seemed pretty much like an elevated, costumed version of herself. Boys, except for a few, had to be bribed or tricked to be in plays, but girls were forever standing with a prepared monologue in hand, their hair pulled back tight, their hearts pushing hard in the narrow birdcage of their chests as they strode out under the lights to audition.

After Robby was confronted by the unhappy mothers of girls, he picked *The Crucible*, and the high school stage became a sea of bobbing bonnets, with Marissa at the center of them all. But finally he was tired of directing. He said he wasn't particularly gifted at it, he had too many papers to grade, the compensation wasn't good, and he wanted to spend more time with Willa and Dory, so he told Gavin McCleary that he was done.

Now, on the first day of school, Fran Heller entered the teachers' room, then came right over to Dory, who, she had noticed, had been looking at her. "I'm Fran Heller," she said with a New Jersey accent.

"Dory Lang. Welcome." The drama teacher's hand was small and cold, with a few odd gemstone rings, the kind that you could buy—but mostly never did—from artisans at street fairs in the city. The rings pressed into Dory's hand briefly and a little painfully.

Fran, as though she'd been on faculty longer than five minutes, went to the fridge and peered in, then finally took out a bottle of diet soda and sat down beside Dory, twisting it open with a good ten seconds of air-release sibilance. It turned out that the Hellers—Fran and her son Eli, who was in Willa's grade—had just moved into a house at the other end of the Langs' long, straight street. Dory immediately knew which house it was: the one that had had the FOR SALE sign up for a long time, then the SOLD sign; and then, this summer, that had been painted in a Southwestern color scheme. The paint job was jaunty but too assertive. There were no adobes around here; the house just looked bohemian-pretentious. The drama teacher was married, but her husband Lowell, she explained, lived in Lansing, Michigan, where he was an accountant for small, struggling nonprofit companies.

"It works better for us this way," Fran Heller told Dory Lang. "It's not a separation; nothing like that at all. It's just a marriage, and a solid one. The only part that's less than ideal is that Eli misses his dad, and vice versa. But they're very close. When I tell people, they have a hard time wrapping their heads around it, but there you are. We're a pretty happy family, the three of us."

Dory said that this was very interesting; the two women talked lightly, and Dory asked her what play she was thinking of putting on that winter. Fran Heller murmured that she hadn't even begun to decide.

"I have to meet the kids first," Fran said. "When I see what kind of talent pool I've got to work with, then I'll have a better idea of what sort of play would be best."

Ambient chatter floated through the teachers' room. Fran was lifting the soda bottle to her lips when Abby Means appeared above them in one of her full-bodied skirts. She was like a skater who had silently glided over. "Hello," she said.

The new drama teacher looked up. "Hello," she said. "Fran Heller." She put out her hand again.

"That's my Diet Splurge."

There was a moment of bewilderment, then Fran looked at the drink in her hand in slow comprehension; the math teacher reached down and rotated the bottle so that the other side of the curve revealed a strip of masking tape, on which was written A. MEANS. The drama teacher had just assumed the refrigerator was communal and that anyone could take anything. That was the way she saw the world; that was the way she conducted herself in it.

"Sorry," Fran said neutrally.

"You know, I don't really ask for much," said Abby Means. "But the one thing I do expect is that when I reach into the fridge each day, my soda will actually be there. That no *wildebeests* or *hobos* have come and taken it away in the night."

All the teachers watched with open interest. By the copy machine, Dave Boyd laughed at Abby Means's latest outrageousness. The gym teacher Ruth Winik, a big strong blonde, sleepless from a nursing infant and twin toddlers at home, backed away silently, as if from the stirrings of a knife fight. Dory thought that if she herself were the new drama teacher and someone had criticized her like that, she might even have teared up a little bit in front of everyone. But Fran Heller said to Abby Means, "Oh, relax. I'm not a wildebeest and I'm not a hobo. You just like saying those words. I'm *new*. Cut me a little slack, and it will all be fine."

Everyone was surprised by the drama teacher's composure. In the background, other teachers murmured that Abby Means had gone over the top yet again. There were eye-rolls, and Ron di Canzio made the international crazy sign in the air, but Dory Lang was the one who decided to befriend Fran Heller.

"Come to dinner tomorrow night," she said. "You and your son."

"That's so nice of you. But I don't want to put you out. I know it's a school night and all."

"We'll do it early. We'll live dangerously," Dory said, and Fran smiled and nodded, and her earrings moved, and she accepted the invitation.

It was true that school nights were a big deal. There were

in-class exercises to grade, sex to have sometimes, car insurance forms to fill out, chicken breasts to marinate, standardized-test prep classes to drive a kid to, hours that had to be spent in the sheer unwind from the tight spool of the day. Feet had to go up on a footstool, eyes had to flicker and close. Everyone in Stellar Plains was embroiled in the way they lived.

On the day that Dory Lang met Fran Heller, she was struck by how the unflappable drama teacher had stood up to Abby Means—something that she herself would never have been able to do—so she insisted that Fran and her son Eli stroll down Tam o' Shanter Drive the next night, and that they bring nothing except themselves. That evening, at the kitchen table with Robby and Willa, Dory said, "The new drama teacher seems kind of great. Unconventional. Her husband lives in Michigan, but they're completely married. They live in that house up the street; you know which one I mean."

"Santa Fe, New Jersey?" said Robby.

"Exactly."

"Maybe you'll even try out for the play this year, Willa," said Dory.

"Not likely," said Willa, snorting.

"Did you just snort?" Robby asked her.

"Sort of. So?"

"It's not like your mom suggested you try out for the Nazi Party," he said.

Willa lightly shoved her father's arm across the table, and they both laughed. "I wonder what play she's going to pick," Dory went on. "Hope it's something good. Oh, and she has a boy in your grade—Eli. Know him?"

Her daughter looked up at her mid-milk; the fluid in the glass rocked as she shook her head. She finished drinking and said, "No, the grade's too big."

She was a slightly homely girl, with the suggestion of an over-bite that somehow years of braces and little translucent retainers hadn't corrected. In tenth grade Willa was very young for her age, inexperienced in life and love and pain. She was one of those red-heads whose skin was always in an uneven pink and white state, like a sky streaming with clouds. She played the flute, and though she wasn't a natural and was never chosen for solos in the orches-tra, her face always grew flushed with purpose and intensity when she practiced. Dory would sometimes discreetly watch from a doorway as Willa played, noticing how her red hair swung around her, her eyes closing and popping open and then closing again, as if she were flickering in and out of consciousness.

"Well, they're coming to dinner tomorrow," Dory said. "Be sure you're home on time."

"Dinner? Tomorrow?" Willa said in a voice of sudden emer-gency. "With this family we don't know? With this boy? Are you serious?"

3.

The night the Hellers came to dinner, Dory Lang wasn't thinking about sex, nor was she aware of its fairly imminent and
startling end. It was still fall then, and most days held on to their
summer warmth. The new school year had hardly begun, and
everything appeared possible, even probable. The economy was in
the process of being intermittently slapped back to life. The two
wars continued, and though almost everyone in Stellar Plains had
initially been against them, and still made disgusted noises about
them, over time the wars had become indistinct and blurred. Dory
was in family mode at dinner, hovering over the deep wooden
salad bowl at the dining room table, mixing the greens with a giant
spoon and fork.

"Willa made the vinaigrette," she said to the room, pointlessly,
and her daughter looked at her with cold horror. It was as if Dory
had said, "Now, Eli, here's an interesting fact: Willa got her first

period the day she turned thirteen." Her remark was apparently inappropriate; *she* was inappropriate.

Robby had had Eli in his second-period English class earlier that day, and even after a brief meeting with the students, he'd said that Eli had made an impression on him. He seemed very smart, Robby had told Dory. Eli was nearly grown-looking, but not entirely, his dark, clean hair worn down to his shoulders. Almost no boys had long hair anymore, Dory realized as she looked at Eli across the table, but whenever you saw one who did, you were immediately at least a little interested, because it brought up your own adolescence, when many boys had hair as long as girls'.

At the dining room table, Eli was awkward and appealing in a stretched-out maroon sweater, pulling his sleeves into the palms of his hands. He had a bright face, with a scattered interruption of mild acne and facial hair along his jaw. His whole head seemed to assert itself into the dining room like the head of a moose mounted on a piece of wood. As they ate together, Dory could feel how humiliated Willa was by the presence of parents. By the fact that these parents ate; that they had teeth and gums; that they *existed*. It was hard, Dory knew, when your parents were teachers at the school you attended, for of course there they were every day, lurking in hallways and at the panini-maker in the cafeteria, and sometimes actually even interacting with your friends, making boring and chummy remarks like "Well, hello there, Marissa. And hello to you too, Lucy. Are you girls enjoying your classes this year?" and generally being far too visible, and far too watchful.

But Dory hadn't seen the full burden of this for Willa until the evening the Hellers came to dinner. Willa was unresponsive and nearly catatonic during the meal, and Eli wasn't much more receptive toward her. The two of them were almost rude in their disregard of each other. Eli, while ignoring Willa, paid attention to Robby, asking him about the syllabus for his class.

"I've never had a student who wanted to chat about the syllabus," Robby said. "I'm going to guess you're a big reader." Eli said yes, he pretty much was, and he named a few writers he liked, all of whom Robby liked too. Delighted now, Robby said to Fran, "Bottle this kid. He's rare."

This was true; reading as a passion was fading away, and everyone knew it. Sometimes, when Dory took the train into the city for the day, she would see novels for sale on street corners, as if their owners were surrendering them in an act of radical housecleaning for the new century. The changes in reading were all bound up not only with technology, but love and sex too, though it was hard to tease it all apart.

You weren't supposed to think life was worse now; it was "different," everyone said. But Dory privately thought that mostly it was worse. The intimacy of reading had been traded in for the rapid absorption of information. And the intimacy of love, well, that had often been traded in for something far more public and open. What had happened to sexual shyness? she wondered, picturing herself in her parents' house in Brooklyn, knowing nothing, having never seen a naked man, and being shocked nearly to the point of aneurysm when a boy put her hand on his lap at a party. Sexual shyness and lack of information—they were gone. But was that so terrible? The world was different, *not* worse, her colleagues said to one another. *Different, not worse.* They told themselves this like a silent mantra as they walked down the hallways of the school, or navigated the wild and lush, brightly lit planet.

After dinner with the Hellers, Dory said that they'd have coffee in the living room, and that maybe Eli and Willa wanted to be free of them—which didn't mean that the kids wanted to be with each other, but they weren't given a choice. Eli trudged off upstairs along with an embarrassed Willa; soon came the frank thump of her favorite band, The Lungs, and then a crunching, heavy step as Eli probably walked around her calamine-pink carpet in his heavy work boots, examining the snow globes and friendship bracelets and seed packets and plastic containers of zero-calorie sweets that dotted the surfaces of her room.

He wouldn't be interested in talking to her, Dory thought; she was too recessive and conventional. And she would find him strange. "He's an odd one, Mom," Dory imagined her saying later. "All my friends would think so." Eli and Willa were likely sitting on the bed and the chair listening to The Lungs in oppressive silence.

"You have a great kid, and what's particularly great, as Robby said, is that he's a boy who reads," Dory said to Fran as she poured coffee. Robby brought in the flat-looking apple cake he'd hastily made after school. He had two standard dishes, and this was one of them; the other was a cheese bake, which always crusted and flowed over the lip of a square pan that they would take turns partially cleaning, then invariably leave to soak in the sink for days.

Dory sliced into the apple cake, which barely gave under the blade. "Yes, Eli definitely reads," Fran said, "but still he's always on that *thing* all the time, too. Robby, I can't believe you baked this. Or I guess I can believe it; my husband, Lowell, is the cook in our family. During the school year, poor Eli has to eat whatever I decide to put together. Last year I fell in love with extra-firm tofu; that became the theme of our meals. Choosing tofu is like choosing a mattress."

"What thing?" Dory asked. "What thing is Eli on?"

"Farrest," she said.

"Oh, Farrest. Yes." The three of them sat in silent contemplation of that green and—to their thinking—uninteresting virtual world. "I'm not against it," Dory said after a moment, "but I just don't understand why they love it so much. If they wanted a forest, a real forest spelled the normal way, we'd be happy to drive them to one. The nature preserve is only twenty minutes away, and they could bring a picnic lunch or something, and spend the entire day." She knew she sounded asinine even as she said this, but she couldn't stop herself. "I'm just not sure why they need it," Dory added. "I'm not a Luddite; I practically live on the Internet too. I love a lot of that stuff; it astonishes me to see what's out there. And I hear that little *ping* whenever an e-mail's just come in, and my heart speeds up. I actually get all excited, you know? What *is* that?"

"Endorphins," said Robby.

"But what do we think the e-mail's going to be?" Dory asked. This was a conversation they had had before, and it usually went the same way. "We act like it's going to change our lives," she said, "but it's rarely very interesting." In Dory's inbox at that very moment—she'd checked right before the Hellers arrived—was a message from a friend, signed "xoxox," like many e-mails between women. Even the most casual female acquaintances tossed around x's and o's in a promiscuous display of intimacy. "And half the time," said Dory, "if it isn't just a generic note, it's something to help you improve your penis size."

"Except they spell it 'penus,'" said Fran. "To slip through the spam filter."

"Yes, my *penus* size," Dory said, and they all laughed a little. "I sit there staring at my laptop every single day," she said. "Totally enmeshed. It's my constant companion, and I can't get enough of it."

"Well, it's the end of civilization, I guess," said Fran Heller. "And we all need to band together."

They quickly agreed that yes, they would certainly band together, but then they all added that of course they knew that civilization wasn't really ending; that in fact it was only beginning, it was in many ways *thrilling*, it was all cracking open, and in their lifetimes, which was so terrific. How wonderful to be there for the show. The problem, though, was that they themselves were getting outdated. They just couldn't remain as fluid as they needed to be in order to thrive and embrace the hulking, steaming heap of technology before them. Dory's laptop never seemed up-to-date; it was always too slow. Always, the little colored wheel spun and spun, and she actually felt herself tighten with tension in the thighs and crotch when this happened, as if she was doing those horrible Kegel exercises women were supposed to do after giving birth. She hated to wait excessively for a burst of information, but she often had to wait and wait.

Over recent years, the world had run roughshod over them, but it hadn't entirely left them behind. They were excited when new, seductive electronic inventions appeared; they updated their own computers and bought their own gadgets, which they carried everywhere, enjoying the reassuring feel of an object in a pocket, and the texture of its skin-tight protective case that made it seem like it was in a condom, pulsing and fully loaded and waiting. But some websites felt to them like the biggest waste of time in the world. "What about whatdotheylooklikenow.com?" Robby had recently said. The site where people posted photos of child stars from shitty old shows who were now bald and chinned and unemployable. The whole point was to *see* the ravages of time, even as you imagined time wasn't passing while you sat there wasting it yourself. And what about sexting? Fran wanted to know now. Did every new electronic activity need a clever name? Did a new word or phrase need to be coined for every single transitory preoccupation? Yes, was the answer; yes it did.

Not only that, but the Internet could be dangerous, deadly; about this, the three parents were all in agreement. "As you know," Dory sometimes said to Willa, "some of the social-networking sites you love are basically the equivalent of a public square, and so you're totally vulnerable to anyone who comes along." All parents made grand, threatening statements to their kids; they all used the term "public square."

The Langs and Fran Heller told one another what their kids' avatars were on Farrest: Willa was a ninja, and Eli was a centaur. Then they laughed at the absurdity of this, the grandiosity and yet the sweetness, and they each tried to figure out what their own avatars would possibly be, if they were forced to choose.

"Dory," said Robby, "would be a bird. Some big bird."

"Not flightless, I hope," Dory said. "I hope you don't think I'm that sedentary," she added in a jokey voice.

"No, no, you'd fly," he said. "But low to the ground." He wasn't trying to insult her; he just meant that she wasn't a risk-taker, that she was interested in life, but that she was also cautious and gentle. This was all true.

"And you," Dory said, "would never leave the ground. You'd be a dog. A long, sweet, loping dog."

"Yeah, that sounds about right," her husband said. They were in agreement about each other.

Fran Heller said that she would be a spider on Farrest. "The kind that *bites*," she said with a rapid laugh. "I know I tend to be a confrontational and impatient person. Eli and Lowell always tell me I've got to learn to ease up a little. 'Chill, Mom,' Eli says. But I just can't stand it when other people do things that seem to me shortsighted or self-destructive. I think I'd be a spider, because my instinct is to want to creep in and sort of scuttle around, figuring everything out and making it go the way I want it to."

Of course Fran had stood up to the other confrontational teacher, Abby Means, she of the swirling fifties skirts and Diet Splurges. Fran seemed to be one of those people who were born without the gene for fear, and who would say anything to anyone. Perhaps she had other kinds of brazenness too, Dory thought— sexual brazenness in particular. Unbidden, an image came to her of Fran with her generic husband Lowell, clicking handcuffs onto his hairy wrists and attaching them to the posts of a Southwestern-looking bed. Dory wondered again what Fran would pick for the play. Probably it would be something dark and provocative that no one could understand. The whole audience would sit in the auditorium feeling cheated, for all they had wanted was to laugh, to loosen up a little during the brief slice of time in which they had been forcibly released from their laptops and their cell phones, and now instead they had to listen to *this*.

Dory realized that she felt tired all of a sudden. The new drama teacher had worn her out; Fran Heller was a spider, spinning, and Dory understood, with disappointment, that she didn't really like her all that much.

When it was time for the Hellers to leave, Eli and Willa came downstairs together blank-faced, which Dory didn't recognize to be a studied state. Had she been looking carefully, she would have seen the way the pink mottling of her daughter's skin had rearranged itself again; the clouds had moved.

"What did you and Eli talk about up there?" Dory asked her later in the kitchen, the two of them loading the dishwasher while Robby pushed a sponge across the counter.

"Nothing."

"Nobody talks about nothing."

"People talk about nothing all day," said Robby.

"We listened to The Lungs," Willa finally said. "We compared schedules."

"Is he nice?" Dory asked.

"I don't know," Willa said, shrugging, peevish. She gooped a slug of green gel into the detergent maw of the dishwasher, then closed the door, letting the handle slap shut, which triggered the slow revving-up from inside. Two plates seemed to knock against each other in there, and would continue to do so for the next hour.

"He seems like an interesting kid," Robby said, and he happily picked at the edges of the half-eaten apple cake.

"Actually, I still have work to do," said Willa, wanting to leave this conversation immediately and forever—probably also wanting to leave the static comfort of the kitchen, in which a dishwasher churned and moaned, as if expressing all the effort it took to sustain family life. She would be leaving home in a couple of years. It was possible that her strongest desire to do so occurred in the kitchen that night.

4.

Over the following weeks, Willa and Eli seemed nearly bored around each other, barely looking up when the other spoke. In the evenings sometimes, Eli wandered down Tam o' Shanter, appearing on the Langs' doorstep, hoping to have a conversation with Robby about a novel he had just read, asking Robby questions about theme, character, motivation.

Willa, named for a writer, wasn't a big reader; her parents had long known this about her. She had loved *The Thunder of Hoofbeats* during her middle school unicorn phase, and then she'd loved Jane Austen, or more accurately Mr. Darcy, like many girls who imagined clinging to his mutton-chop sideburns the same way that they would have clung to the unicorn's mane. But then Darcy was replaced by the effeminate zombie love interest in a series of frankly stupid novels that Willa and her friends Marissa Clayborn and Carrie Petito and the two Lucys had read compulsively in seventh grade. The zombie had "glazed, oaken eyes and a mouth that was forever slightly open in want," and Dory remembered practically shouting at this prose when she read it. "Oaken!" she and Robby had cried, though much later Dory would recall the line and think that, to some extent, it was an accurate description of teenaged desire.

Robby and Dory didn't know then that this would be the height of Willa's pleasure reading. Had they known, they would have kept her supplied with books about alluring, oaken-eyed zombies. Instead they harangued her, and little by little she stopped reading altogether, except for what she'd been assigned at school. When Eli Heller came over to discuss novels with Robby, the two of them sat in the den for long stretches. Then finally Eli would stand and walk out into the front hallway, where Willa might be, and they would hardly acknowledge each other, and he would go home.

Eli could be seen in the school cafeteria most weekdays eating the high school's crude version of panini, his fingertips practically polished with oil. He was just one of many students Dory would smile at, say hello to, ask a bland question of about his classes. She almost never thought about him, and she had no idea she would ever need to. During a fire drill in the middle of November, all was revealed. Dory had been standing at the SMART Board talking about Stephen Crane, and her students were desperate in their boredom. She made a note to herself that she should lobby to remove Crane from the curriculum for next year; the kids could no longer read *The Red Badge of Courage*. It was an easy book—it used to be taught to seventh-graders, and she herself had read it when she was eleven—but as far as she could see, the students' brains had changed. Whether they'd evolved or devolved wasn't clear to her, for they also possessed that astonishing capacity for technology. They were distracted, their neurons pulled apart, and now their brains somehow magnetically repelled Stephen Crane. Though maybe this wasn't the worst thing in the world (after all, if she had to read Stephen Crane now, for the first time, would she actually find it exciting? She had a feeling she knew the answer), their distractedness still bothered her.

"You guys," Dory said in class on this day, "are keeping yourselves from a powerful reading experience. You have very little to say about the book we just read by Stephen Crane, who was so talented and died tragically young of tuberculosis. That alone should interest you. Yet I am certain you will have *tons* to say to one another tonight when you get home."

"That's not fair, Ms. L," Jeremy Stegner said, and Dory thought that he was right; it wasn't fair, she knew that, and she'd been speaking in a hectoring voice. But before she could say anything more, the fire alarm rang, and they all headed outside into the frozen morning, coatless. Dory saw Leanne usher a group of kids to their assigned part of the athletic field. The kids were lively, playful, taking this opportunity to stretch and preen and get a little exercise, forming packs and then breaking off into little clusters. Anything was possible for them; you could see this even at a casual glance during a fire drill. Leanne looked young and exotic, wrapped in some gold-threaded blouse that only she could "get away with," as people said. The principal, Dory saw, kept glancing in her direction.

Bev Cutler, over by the side, so overweight, stood with her hands pushed deep into her skirt pockets, as if about to scatter seed for birds. Though she was an experienced guidance counselor and in charge of helping the kids plan their futures, it seemed, increasingly, as if she was lost inside her swollen self.

Then, up ahead, Dory saw Robby surrounded by kids, as he always was, especially boys. He caught sight of his wife and waved, smiled, then returned to what he'd been saying to them. He liked holding court, making little speeches to small groups of kids, who always liked to listen. By a frozen tree, out of the side of her vision, Dory noticed one of the school's teenaged couples shivering and taking solace in their own embrace. Without really looking, she assumed it was Chloe Vincent and Max Holleran, eleventh-graders who, as the entire school knew, had been involved for years. The boy wrapped the girl into himself to keep her warm, and her head was ducked against him. Dory saw, from a distance, the way their breath sifted into the air, and also the flowering of the girl's golden red hair against the dark field of the boy's maroon sweater.

Immediately she felt multiple, clarifying shocks: first, that it was Willa, then, that it was someone with Willa in a somewhat sexual state. And then, of course, that it was Eli Heller, the boy Willa barely ever seemed to acknowledge.

Dory was now hot-faced in the cold. She turned to motion to Robby, as if to say, *Look*. But he had been spirited away. She stood alone beside the school and the emptying field, until one of her students came over and said, "Ms. L, everyone's going in."

Later, still agitated and still not even exactly aware of why, she went downstairs to Leanne's office, two doors down from the pool. LEANNE BANNERJEE, PH.D., read the metal sign on her door. Chlorine congested the little room; distantly, there were splashes and whistles, as teenagers pushed their seal-selves through water. Leanne had a stack of student folders on her lap with color-coded stickers on them. One folder was peppered with the full spectrum of stickers, foretelling a life of specialists and trouble. Dory Lang sat in the chair where the students usually sat, and Leanne leaned forward in her own chair, beneath a poster of a girl cutting herself.

"What's the deal?" Leanne asked.

"It's Willa. I saw her with Eli during the fire drill. They were intertwined, let's call it."

"Oh," said Leanne after a second. "Okay."

"You don't seem very surprised." Then Dory added, "Wait. Leanne, you knew?"

The school psychologist pushed back in her chair, as if wanting to escape from her good friend, but there was nowhere for her to go, and she backed into her desk. "I thought you knew too, Dory," she said. "I just thought you hadn't mentioned it to me."

"Well, no, I didn't know," Dory said. "Not at all."

"I knew pretty much immediately."

"You did?"

"Sure," said Leanne. "I spend so much time in here telling kids that I know their attractions are completely thrilling. Then, after we get that out of the way, I remind them that they don't want to screw up their lives like that teenage couple from Elro did a few years ago—the one everybody talks about, who had that baby named Trivet, right? I'm always sitting here, making these deadpan, supposedly nonjudgmental statements like, 'Oh yes, Jen, it's very interesting to me that you think blow jobs don't count as sex. Now how did you reach that conclusion?'"

"Jen? *Heplauer*?" Dory asked.

"I didn't say that. And they confess things to me that they can barely handle. A ninth-grade girl came into my office the other day and said, 'I am totally turned on by my best friend, and she'd die if she knew.' Another kid said he's been using J Juice every weekend, you know that drug? It's all over the place. I wouldn't want to be them for anything. I tell them I understand. That when I was in high school, there were times when I just got so lost in my own problems and couldn't find anything peaceful to think about. When it all seemed so ugly and hateful and pointless. I tell them how my parents only wanted me to marry a nice Indian boy. At night I'd come home from being with a secret boy who my parents would never have approved of, and I'd be filled with feeling, and I'd go past the living room where they were watching TV and balancing the checkbook. And there would be these atrocities on the news, and I'd feel everything so strongly—the good and the bad—and I was overwhelmed."

"I'm sorry, Leanne," Dory broke in, "but I don't understand what you're trying to tell me."

"I worry about these kids, Dory," Leanne said. "They are like little baby birds. But if I had a daughter like Willa, who was having her first relationship with someone like Eli, I think I'd feel that I'd done something right. I think I would feel happy." Both women took a moment to note, tacitly, that Dory did not feel happy. "You've got Robby," Leanne said, "and you've both figured out how to be. How to be with just one person. So let Willa have someone too, if she wants that. She's entitled."

That night, Dory decided to call Fran and tell her the news. As soon as she began to talk, she could hear that her own voice sounded slightly feverish. "Are you alone?" she asked the drama teacher.

"Of course," Fran said. "Eli is in his room with the door closed. Story of my life."

"He's probably talking to Willa. They're probably on Farrest together. Listen, Fran," Dory said. "I bring news from the front. Our kids seem to have developed a special thing between them."

"Excuse me?"

"They're involved."

"What are you talking about, Dory?"

"They're seeing each other. Boyfriend and girlfriend."

Fran was silent. "Well, I'm surprised," she finally said. "I've been so busy with the new job that I feel kind of blindsided." Both women agreed that this was definitely a new stage of life, and then they quickly said goodnight.

Dory had always assumed that when her daughter had a boy-friend, she would confide in her about him. After all, teenagers easily told one another everything. They didn't have to be force-fed truth serum in order to talk. Maybe a mother could be given a little information once in a while. One evening, when Dory and Willa were alone in the den and the TV was on, Dory managed to say, "I know this is awkward. But you and Eli, if this is relevant—and you don't have to tell me if it is—I just want to say that I hope you're protecting yourself. There's nothing more important."

Their bare feet were up on the coffee table, and Dory noticed that each of Willa's toes was painted a slightly different shade; she pictured Eli's big hand holding a miniature brush, dipping and re-dipping in five different bottles. Willa had finished her home-work for the night, and Dory had finished all her grading. Robby was already asleep in his *New Deal* T-shirt. It was a school night, and all of them were a little knocked out by life, but there were so few times when Dory was alone with her daughter anymore, and she wanted them to talk.

Willa just kept watching the screen, and then she said, "Oh God, Mom. You are seriously going to make us have this conversation?"

"You know I can't make you do anything."

Willa sighed, aggrieved, then seemed to consider her options. "Without getting into details about my own life," she finally said, "yes, I do know all about how to 'protect' myself. Without you," she added, stingingly. Then the commercial ended and the TV show came back on, and Willa turned her head back into profile on the couch. That face, the expressive mouth with the teeth slightly pushing through, suggesting their presence even when her lips were closed, wasn't for her mother any longer.

Dory Lang watched Eli and Willa every day from a distance. In the school hallway she would see a mess of long dark boy-hair and slightly shorter red girl-hair, and sometimes it would suddenly split apart as she or Robby or Fran came down the hall.

"Leave them alone," Leanne advised when Dory came back downstairs to her office a second time. A ninth-grade girl had just left, sniffling into her bare hand. The one attracted to her friend? Dory wondered. The tiny room felt surprisingly enveloping, and the English teacher looked up to the school psychologist soupily,

much the way some of the students did, and she felt just as confused and helpless as any of them. "Let them figure it out," said
Leanne. "If Willa needs something, she'll ask. You and Robby have
been good role models when it comes to all of this. But it's not
about you now. It's about them."

5.

The spell would eventually claim Willa Lang that winter, though first, late that fall, she was obviously under a very different spell, and so was Eli Heller, who had stopped talking to Robby about books. Instead, now, Eli only wanted to talk to Willa. In the beginning, when the two of them were alone, he kept returning to one particular topic. "Is there any way you would ever consider taking your shirt off for me?" he asked her. "Any way I could see you like that?"

"You are getting repetitive," she would say, but she didn't mind. No one had ever spoken this way to her in her life; no one. "Don't you have any other interests at all?" she asked. "Maybe a team sport?"

"No," Eli said, smiling. "Absolutely none."

Early on, the two of them would occasionally go somewhere and toss the topic around like two philosophers discussing the nature of being. They both considered themselves sexually delayed, at least by the standards of most people around them. Both of them were innocent, their mouths having not yet opened onto the hot surprise of any other mouths, their bodies still unfolded and unrevealed. One day, after they had had several conventional conversations about school, and their parents, and the music they each liked (The Lungs, The Simultaneous Urges), he lightly and teasingly began the first conversation about shirt removal, which had made Willa Lang swallow in shock, then quickly recover. After that, the conversation picked up ad hoc whenever it could. Eli spoke plaintively of his desire to see her with her shirt off, "as a start."

"I just think it would be amazing," he said as they sat on a closed dumpster behind the school one windless, early November afternoon. "A rare occurrence. Like seeing an eclipse."

"Yes, it would be amazing for *you*," she said.

"Maybe there would be something in it for you as well." They were sitting side by side on the rough metal surface; they didn't know it yet, but both of them would be marked by where they sat, the asses of their jeans rust- and dust-covered. Both of their mothers, doing laundry in a day or two, would say, "Wait, what's this?" slapping at the denim with a hard hand and seeing orange clouds fly off. Their mothers would have no idea whatsoever. Later on they would—after the fire drill, everyone knew—but not yet. This was still early days, when everything remained for the time being delectable and hidden.

Willa sat with him and tried to figure out how she was supposed to be, how she was meant to talk, and whether she was supposed to laugh a lot, or just listen with a grave expression when he spoke. She knew nothing about what you were meant to do with a boy. Marissa Clayborn, of course, knew everything; Marissa was experienced, having lost her virginity at age fifteen to a boy named Ralph Devereux, the son of family friends from another town. Though quite a few girls in the tenth grade at Elro were no longer virgins either—soccer-playing girls; girls who hung around the art room; members of the pep squad—Marissa was the only one among their circle of girls who had really had significant experience. Both Lucys and Carrie Petito had all "done things," as they put it, but the things they had done had involved hands roaming among body parts, even southern body parts, though it had gone no further than that. Mouths did not come into the picture, except to kiss and be kissed; condoms were not required. Marissa had been so calm and sophisticated about her significant sexual experiences: catlike, sphinxlike, impressively mature. Willa knew that she herself would never be able to simply accept sex as her birthright the way Marissa had done. For a long time Willa Lang hadn't even been able to imagine wanting to sleep with someone someday— but now, since she had met Eli, she imagined it all the time.

He wasn't good-looking, but she still often pictured his hand accidentally bumping against the side of her breast. "Whoops," he'd say, pulling away, but the hand would leave a thousand reverberations. Once, thinking about it in her bedroom, Willa Lang let out an actual, tiny scream. She wanted to text her friends to say: "guess what? i understand finally." Willa was a slow study, but she was, apparently, a study. The fact that Eli, too, had had no experience was part of his appeal.

"I never had a girlfriend," he said now as they sat together. "Back at Cobalt, anyone who wasn't a jock might as well commit *seppuku.* The girls were jocks too. Soccer was the big thing. I just kept to myself a lot, and I assumed I'd keep doing that when we moved here too, but as you can see, it hasn't turned out that way."

Did this mean he thought *she* was his girlfriend? Willa really couldn't say.

"It's sort of interesting, the way you get to know someone," Eli went on. "The way, at first, you think they're one thing, but they turn out to be another. Want to know when you started to change, in my mind?"

"Okay," Willa said, and she waited.

"It was when you put on The Lungs that night in your room, and we sat there." She recalled sitting with him, the aching music between them. He'd closed his eyes when he listened, and she'd noticed the length of his eyelashes, and briefly imagined taking a tape measure to them. The song had gone on and on, while distantly, from downstairs, came the sound of their three parents, laughing. "And then I wondered about you," Eli said. "And later on, your dad said I could come over and talk about books. And whenever I came to your house to see him, there you would be. Just walking around in your flip-flops. I'd hear this *thup-thup-thup* in the background. Your dad's great, by the way. Everyone at school says so."

"Thanks. He *is* a good guy," Willa agreed. They sat in quiet celebration of her father and his decency.

"And your mom too," he added.

"And yours," she said politely.

"Oh, my mom's sort of tough," Eli said. "But she's passionate about things. She loses it sometimes, but my dad is always amused by her. It's pretty funny to see them in action."

"Is it weird not living with him?"

"I'll live with him in Michigan this summer. I always do." Eli shrugged. "It's the peculiar Heller way of doing things, I guess. I got used to it a long time ago."

The day was mild, the parking lot at the school had emptied, and Willa's parents and Eli's mother had all gone home. They watched as some stragglers left, including Paige Straub and Dylan Maleska, the inseparable jockish couple. Paige and Dylan marched together away from the school with matching backpacks on their backs. They stopped at the curb and made out for a few seconds, then continued to walk home. Willa needed Eli to kiss her right then, so she could know what it meant to be kissed by someone very nice with soft lips and a moving tongue, so she could have that knowledge and then have more. She'd spent her whole life without the kiss of any boy, and she'd never really minded, even as her friends were introduced, one by one, to some of the rituals.

Since Willa had started to know Eli, she realized that until this moment she had always been a little bit bored. Stellar Plains was supposed to be such a great place, but Willa knew otherwise. Where were you supposed to go in this town, exactly? On Friday nights Elro put together an event they called "Just Chillin'." People sat around in the cafeteria; a couple of boys stood by the panini-maker and played "Freebird" on their electric guitars. A girl no one liked wore mime makeup and juggled oranges while reciting the opening lines of the Declaration of Independence. A few teachers, on chaperone duty, stood at the side of the room and looked around at the whole, dismal scene. "Sad, sad, sad," Mr. Boyd was overheard whispering to Mr. di Canzio.

Equally sad was Greens and Grains, Willa thought, which,

when it opened a year earlier, all the moms raved about as if it were an amusement park or a sex club that had set up shop in town. The leafy, rooty vegetables you could buy there all tasted the same when brought home and steamed. As the leaves wilted inside the microwave, the smell released was like a rotting forest that Willa would never want to visit. She imagined this forest as being far different from the green and layered world of Farrest, which she and Eli traveled to sometimes at night from their separate laptops in their separate houses.

Meeting up on Farrest, they'd already touched lightly a few times, his handsome centaur head bumping against the neck of her shrouded ninja. His skin looked furred, both in Farrest and in life, she saw now in the school parking lot when he turned his head a little. Men had *fur.* She saw Eli each day in the hallway between classes, and he was always by himself. She, of course, was generally with Marissa or Carrie or one of the two Lucys, and she supposed she could have drawn him into their group; but then her friends would have gotten to know him too, and instinctively she didn't want this to happen.

Willa was afraid, at first, that they would think he was weird. But then, even worse, she was afraid that they wouldn't; that Marissa would remark, "Oh no, Eli isn't weird at all. In fact, I would have to say that he's pretty fascinating." And that then Marissa would turn her gaze to Eli, who would see that she had so much more to offer him—emotionally, sexually, intellectually, you name it—than Willa did.

As they sat together on the dumpster, the light of the sky began to deepen and Willa said something about having to leave soon in order to be home for dinner. "Ah yes, the family dinner," said Eli. "That sacred event. Everyone idealizes the family dinner, even my mom. She wants us to *sit there* together. It's like some study was done, and they found out that people who eat dinner with their family don't do drugs, or something like that."

"People who eat dinner with their family become angels in heaven when they die," said Willa. "Or even before they die."

"People who eat dinner with their family have the power of *invisibility*," he said. "Or they wish they did, so they wouldn't have to sit there at that table."

"My parents make it into such a big ritualized event," Willa said. Suddenly family dinner felt like the biggest injustice. "It's like a goddamn Japanese tea ceremony or something," she said. "I mean," she added nervily, working herself up, "who are they to think it's the most important thing in the world. To think that I have nothing better to do than sit there with them." She pictured her father's long and handsome but slightly faded face, and her mother's pretty, rabbity features, and then she thought of all they had done for her, and she felt guilty. But not too guilty.

They walked in silence back to Tam o' Shanter, entered their separate homes, said cursory hellos to parents—"Hey," Willa said, uninflected, not waiting for them to reply—then she and Eli met up again on Farrest. Though other creatures were in their midst, it seemed as if nobody paid Eli and Willa much attention, and so they were able to be alone together. A hawk flew overhead; this was Marissa Clayborn. She often took the form of this graceful, commanding flying animal, and Willa looked up and watched her circle and dip. Luckily, Marissa didn't seem to want to come in for a landing.

As the days passed and Eli and Willa grew closer, he continued to repeat the remark about wanting to see her with her shirt off. Would she, Willa Lang, a very undaring sophomore who behaved more like a seventh-grader in certain respects, actually take her shirt off for the new boy? Finally, as though an elaborate deal had been brokered between their representatives, it was established that, yes, she would.

One afternoon, when his mother would be staying late after school for some planning meeting about the play, Willa and Eli went to his house. It was there, they both understood, that the removal of the shirt would take place, for a start—the unveiling, the grand moment, the beginning. The living room of the Hellers' house was fairly conventional, Willa was relieved to see when they went inside. The furniture was puffy and swollen and modern, and there were art prints on the walls, and an unflattering childhood photo of Eli in a shirt with a huge, winged collar. On the far wall of the living room hung the masks of tragedy and comedy, one red and one blue, both of them kiln-glazed and shining. "Those are neat," Willa said, feeling so strongly that they were actually ugly and almost grotesque that she had automatically thought to say the opposite of what she felt.

"They sort of creep me out a little," said Eli. "They were given to my mom by the theater department in Cobalt when she left." He grabbed a gallon of milk and two glasses and a couple of packaged doughnuts. "Come on," he instructed, and she followed him up the stairs. Only when they were inside the cool blue of his bedroom— a blue version of Farrest, she thought—did Willa Lang feel relief. They sat on his bed, which he had carefully made that morning. Eli was a neat boy, and a pair of pajamas lay folded on his pillow. In the blue light Eli and Willa faced each other, and he poured her a glass of milk and held it out. "My special concoction," he said. "It's called Shirt-Be-Gone."

She drank, then bit into a doughnut, and he did the same, after which they put glasses and plates aside. Willa reached up with a tentative hand and unbuttoned the top button of her pale yellow blouse. She kept unbuttoning until she was done, and then she swiftly opened her bra, which was one of those front-clasp kinds. The two pieces of it just fell away; she had planned this, of course, had wanted the bra to break apart like the sections of an orange, and so it did.

Eli took in a hard breath. "You are so beautiful," he said in a low, new voice; then, of course, he couldn't help but kiss her and touch her shoulders, and finally, of course, one of her breasts, which all at once changed texture, and so did the other one. It was as though they were corresponding with each other in some secret, unknowable way, like quarks, and then, to her shock, her vagina became part of it all; yes, "vagina" was the only word for it at this moment, for you couldn't say "down there" anymore, which was too dumb and vague. Specificity was required now; *precision*.

She felt as if she were unfolding, unclasping, being saturated, falling to bits, intensely whirled around like someone blindfolded and about to smack a piñata. Truthfully? It was exceptionally great, though there wasn't a free moment in which you could even reflect upon the greatness, for you were too busy. Your body just kept experiencing. It was no wonder that people not only liked to do sexual things, but also made entire multimedia presentations of themselves doing them. It was all fun in the way she used to think a water park was fun, or cawing with laughter with her friends at a joke that would have been hilarious to no one else.

Willa was a shy girl, easily startled, and now she saw that apparently she was easily excited as well, given the right circumstances. Eli was more than the intense new boy, the drama teacher's son, her father's favorite student, a boy who loved books. He also apparently loved breasts, or anyway, he loved hers. He had called them—her—beautiful. "This feels really good," she said.

"Intensely good," he whispered into her neck, beneath the ledge of her hair, and she noticed that he smelled of doughnut and milk, which was exactly the way she smelled too. Willa lay back against his narrow bed and felt the lump of folded pajamas beneath her head as Eli loomed over her. Pleasure and dread fought for primacy inside her crowded, pickled brain, but then dread lost out to pleasure—dread just became inert, and disappeared, and then Willa was oddly fearless, wanting to know what would happen next. Eli took off his shirt, too, lying beside her so they faced each other. His chest was broad and pale with a light scatter of freckles and, again, some fur. She knew that soon they would be making all kinds of leaps: they had already gone from no kissing to kissing; soon they would go from kissing to touching, then one day in the near future from touching to "going the distance," as Marissa Clayborn had referred to her own involvement with two different boys. "Going the distance" seemed a good way to think of what it would be like. *It*—sex, actual sex—created a distance between you and everyone except the other person. You were in a hot-air balloon, and you waved goodbye to your sweet but clueless mother and father, and even your dazed and innocent old dog. *Goodbye, goodbye,* you called as you went the distance.

For now, though, there was only kissing. Eli cupped and held her small breasts, and put his mouth on each of them too, and Willa knew that there was no one in the world she could tell about this, no one at all. It seemed inappropriate to tell Marissa, and definitely inappropriate to tell her mother. But then she thought: I can tell *him*. I can talk to *him*! Somehow, she had forgotten.

6.

M s. Heller told her drama class the name of this year's play, and then Marissa told me what it is, but it went out of my head," Willa said to her parents after school one extremely cold day. She'd wandered home late, as she often did since she'd been seeing Eli. *Seeing.* Dory Lang disliked that word, though it was accurate. Willa and Eli did in fact *see* each other, and they saw almost no one and nothing else. Willa often looked past Robby and Dory at home; she seemed impatient with their slowness, their literalness, their demands on her time. So now, whenever Willa was willing to initiate a conversation with them, to engage fully, Dory was overly happy.

"You don't have any idea what it is?" she asked Willa.

"It's definitely something Greek."

"Well, that narrows it," Robby said.

The play, they learned after Willa texted Marissa to find out, was *Lysistrata*, the Aristophanes comedy, first performed in

411 B.C., about a woman who leads the women of Greece in a sex strike in order to put an end to the drawn-out Peloponnesian War. Dory had seen a version of the play performed back when she and Robby lived in Brooklyn, and she remembered it not only as an antiwar piece, but also an outright sex comedy—a sometimes supremely dirty work in which the women were urged by their leader, Lysistrata, to abstain from having sex with men until all fighting ceased.

"Remember, in the version we saw, that one position they were told to stop doing? I can almost think of the name. . . . Wait, yes, I actually remember. It was called 'The Lioness on the Cheese Grater,'" Dory said. "Whatever that possibly was."

"It sounds painful," Robby said, and Dory agreed, and Willa just looked embarrassed by the whole conversation. The play itself would likely be embarrassing, Dory feared. Men walked around with gigantic erections onstage ("Also painful," Robby remarked later), and there were many explicit sexual references and a wink-wink quality that made it a surprising choice for a high school play.

"What's Fran thinking?" Dory asked. "A play about women turning down men sexually? Parents will complain, even in our town."

"That would have been a good choice," he said.

"What?"

"Our Town," said Robby. "But I think this'll be fine too." He was certain that, in Fran Heller's version of Lysistrata, "sex" would somehow be reframed as "embracing." There would be no lioness, and no cheese grater for the lioness to lie upon, grating, gyrating, humping, shredding, doing whatever was meant to be done in that unlikely sounding position. Or, if the lioness and the cheese grater were allowed to remain, they would be benign and whimsical.

The play would be a cheerful parable about political activism and men and women and love and war, and the principal would send a reassuring e-mail to all parents, letting them know this in advance of auditions. "I applaud our new drama teacher for making such a great and innovative choice," Gavin McCleary would probably write. He wouldn't know, or be able to warn them, that the spell would imminently arrive, and that unhappiness would descend upon them.

"As I think about it more," said Robby, "I suspect the play itself will be pretty easy to do. All you need are a bunch of Styrofoam columns and a frieze and a cornice for a decent-looking Acropolis, which I seem to remember that the Chorus of Women are supposed to *storm,* because the treasury is kept there or something. The stage lighting can be just a series of simple blue and white spots. At the end, there won't be a lot of set to strike. You can clean up and go home. And wait, just watch," he added. "Many parents are actually going to like the choice."

"Why do you think that?" Dory asked.

"Because there are a lot of female parts in the play."

"Indeed there *are,*" she said. They often made jokes like this, back and forth; having lived together so long, they found that their humor was interchangeable. Like most couples, they were funny mostly to themselves and each other.

He was right about the play; there were plenty of roles in which girls could be cast. At a school like Elro, regardless of your talent or lack of it, if you simply showed up to audition you would be put to some sort of use. In addition to the individual speaking parts, there were two choruses in *Lysistrata,* male and female. Casually, Willa told her parents that despite what she'd said at an earlier point, she had decided to try out for the play after all, though she didn't hold out much hope of actually getting a speaking part. Because of her relationship with Eli, she knew it would be nepotism if Fran cast her in a real role. Her parents certainly understood that a starring role would never go to the recessive Willa Lang. It would go, as usual, to Marissa Clayborn, who deserved it.

Two days later, after one intense afternoon of auditions, the cast list was posted. Dory had tried to stay uninvolved, but she couldn't do that. She was pretty sure that Willa would get some sort of nominal part, even though Willa wasn't an actor and likely had no natural ability. Over the years, when Dory had come to watch Willa perform in small classroom presentations, she had worn a mother's bright, excited expression as she observed her daughter's stiffness and listened to her muted speech, whether Willa was a Navajo woman, or Turkey-Lurkey, or, once, a hydrogen atom. Now, Dory just wanted to see Willa's name printed on the cast list. It seemed important that Willa's name *be* there, and even though Dory felt it would, she still worried in a slightly sickened way that somehow it would not.

Carrying her coffee down the hall toward the teachers' room that morning, walking past the glass showcase and the exit sign, she heard shouts up ahead. Girls and a few boys were collected by the bulletin board outside the auditorium, and Willa was somewhere in that cluster. "Oh my God," one girl said to another. "I knew you'd get it." Dory walked over, and the girls parted so that the teacher could get a glimpse too. At the top of the sheet, she saw:

LYSISTRATA . . . . . . Marissa Clayborn

Marissa, coolheaded and straight-backed, was allowing herself to be hugged by her friends. Of course she was Lysistrata; it was a good fit. Fran Heller had explained that there wouldn't be any understudies. She'd never needed them in her entire career in high school theater; probably, Dory thought, this was because the actors would be too daunted at the idea of telling Ms. Heller they were sick and couldn't make a performance. It would be easier to perform with a fever, delirious. Well below Marissa's name, somewhere near the bottom in a heap of the willing, were the names of the others—kids who just wanted to be in a play, any play, and didn't need the glory of a big part:

CHORUS OF WOMEN . . . . . . Lucy Stupak
Lucy Neels
Carrie Petito
Julie Zorn
Jade Stills
Willa Lang

Willa. Yes! thought her mother. Willa had made it. It wasn't much, but she was in, and that was enough. Rehearsals would start that afternoon. It had been snowing all day, and when the bell rang, Dory found herself in coat and scarf, returning to the hallway by the auditorium. She stood beside the showcase, which held old framed photos of previous theatrical productions and a big silver loving cup that had been given by a long-gone graduating class to the cast and crew of *You Can't Take It with You*. The inscription read, "With our heartfelt thanks, from the class of 1969." The silver was tarnished, but the words were still legible. Dory sometimes saw that loving cup behind the glass and thought of all the kids who had been in the plays here at the school, then left, getting older and older. A high school play was a time of high emotion and meaning; if you were in a play, you felt as if the play *mattered*. The success or failure of any production seemed like a real reflection on you personally. Dory had wanted Willa to be part of such an experience, and now it looked as if she would.

Dory walked toward the auditorium, and when she got close, one of the doors was suddenly pushed open from inside, and all at once Dory was like one of the students who were always dying to get a look into the teachers' room. She stopped right where she was and swung her head to see inside, though from here all she could see was dimness, with shapes moving distantly. There came the sound of girls laughing; was that Willa in there already? Even though Dory's coat was on and Robby expected to meet her at the exit near the parking lot so they could drive home together, she very much wanted to go in. If she was really late, he would assume that something had come up, and he'd just go home on his own; this was how it worked between them. So now she grabbed the door before it shut again, and she slipped inside.

Fran Heller stood onstage in front of the cast, which was made up mostly of girls, and a handful of boys, all of them sitting in the first few rows. Many of them didn't yet know Fran Heller well, but the students in her classes thought she was an exciting teacher, if a bit of a loose cannon. They already called her "Ms. H." Apparently, she might say anything, kids warned one another. She might lose her temper in front of her class, but it was only because she was excited about theater, and wanted everyone to do their best. Some of the students knew that they would probably have to be publicly humiliated by Ms. Heller once in a while in order to reap the benefits of being in her class, or in her play, but they didn't seem to mind. Dory Lang, watching Fran conduct the first rehearsal, felt irritated, even a little jealous.

"Welcome, everyone, to the first day of hell," said Fran. "No, seriously, I am definitely going to work you hard, but I expect that we'll all have a great time along the way. The performance—and it's going to be one performance only, opening night and closing night, because that's the way I like to do things—will be on the first Friday in February, which gives us over two months to get it right. I like to take a leisurely time with my rehearsals. We'll work during vacation, so nobody plan to fly somewhere to visit Grandma and Grandpa for Christmas, okay?" There was silence. "Okay?" she asked again, and they understood that the question wasn't rhetorical, and around the room the kids raggedly replied, "Okay."

"Do you know what the name 'Lysistrata' means?" Ms. Heller asked. There were murmurs again, but no one gave an actual answer. It was as if she knew this would be their response, and she looked out at them with her hand shielding her eyes as she articulated, " 'She Who Disbands Armies.' " She gazed directly at Marissa Clayborn, then said, "And throughout the rehearsals, Lysistrata, that will be your job. To disband armies. I'm sure you've had plenty of practice." The room was puzzled. "A *joke*," added the drama teacher, and some of the kids laughed politely. "Okay, let me give you all my sense of the play." Fran lowered herself to sit on the edge of the stage.

"At the time that Aristophanes wrote it, the Peloponnesian War was in its twentieth year," she said. "Maybe you can relate to the frustration and desperation that the characters feel. I mean, here they are, in the middle of a long war—in their case, a civil war—with no end in sight. And such a war, to these women, seems like a no-win situation, not to mention a really depressing one. Imagine if there was a new war right now, and your fathers and your boyfriends were all sent away. Suddenly we'd all have to get along without them. Some of them, many of them, would be killed. Men in their prime—dead. And if the war seemed to go on and on, and the reasons behind it didn't even make sense to you, then what would you do? Really, tell me. What if the government declared war with . . . Canada?" she asked. "Known forever as the Maple Leaf War. Or even Maple Leaf War One, not to be confused with the later Maple Leaf War Two. And the men said, 'Well, we're men, and it's our responsibility to go and fight.' Would you just accept their decision, and say, 'Goodbye and good luck'?" She looked around the room, trawling for an answer.

"I guess I'd have to, but first I'd try to convince them not to go," said Laura Lonergan from the second row.

"And how would you do that, Laura?" Fran asked. "What do you think you could say to convince them? What do you think *you*, a mere high school student, a taker of SATs, a minor, someone who can't even vote or drink and maybe can't even drive, could do?"

"We could beg them," someone said. "We could plead our case. Be extremely insistent."

"We could march on Washington," said someone else.

To which Jeremy Stegner said, "My parents and I marched on Washington against the war in Iraq. Which did *nothing*. They just went ahead with that war, and now we're still stuck with it."

"Why do they always say 'march *on* Washington'?" someone else asked, but no one knew the answer.

"Come on, let's keep thinking about this topic, everybody," Fran said. "Let's try to come up with some viable ideas." Around the room, the kids rustled and stirred. "How else could women in particular stop a war? How could they change the world?" she pushed. They shrugged and looked at one another in mild embarrassment; they knew what she was getting at, but none of them had the nerve to make this vaguely political and dull conversation directly sexual, at least not yet. Jen Heplauer suggested a telethon.

Fran said, "Maybe you would have to try something ingenious that would really make a statement. Something that would deprive the males of what's most important to them. And I know you all know what that would be. Because, look, although this is an ancient Greek play, it's also a strong and hard-hitting and comedic but *dead serious* piece of art. Some people think of Lysistrata as an important feminist text; other people think it basically mocks women and doesn't take them seriously at all as potential agents of change. Whatever *you* happen to think, you'll find that its themes are still sadly relevant today, what with our lousy wars, and that's why I chose it. My point is: men still fight wars. They still fuck up the world—excuse me, I mean screw up the world. Oh, please don't tell mom and dad that I said that; they're still recovering from my choice of play. They probably would have preferred *Arsenic and Old Lace*. And men *still,* above and beyond anything else, want sex from women. Yes, it makes them weak in the knees. You may find it hard to believe, but even I, your forty-two-year-old drama teacher, have a husband whose knees I have weakened every now and then. He'll probably need arthroscopic surgery one of these days." There was blinking, confused silence. "A *joke*," Fran said again.

Here, a few of the kids around the auditorium laughed uncomfortably, and Lucy Neels put two fingers in her mouth and whistled.

"But the women of Greece said, 'No, we're not going to take it anymore,'" Fran Heller continued. "They said, 'We're certainly not going to take it lying down.' They used their cunning and their allure and the fact that they had one thing that their men could not bear to live without. And they agreed to withhold it until the war ended. So that's the central premise here, and I wanted you all to understand the sensibility behind it. Marissa, why don't you and the others from the opening come up onstage with your scripts and take a shot?"

"Maybe that's not the best idea," came Marissa's voice. "I'm not prepared. I've only seen the script during the audition."

"It's okay not to be prepared," said Fran. "Getting prepared is what we do in the theater. Do you know the book *An Actor Prepares*? No? Not to worry. Come on up. We have to start somewhere."

Marissa Clayborn reluctantly rose; she was as tall as a Greek column. God, Dory thought, all the girls had secretly sprung up in height, even as the teachers and mothers had gotten squashed and lost height and calcium, their bones ground down with an invisible pestle. Why hadn't Dory drunk *milk* when she was young and still had a chance to save herself in the future? She instantly knew the answer to this: because when you're young, you don't really believe you'll ever be anything other than young.

Dory sat in the back row of the auditorium in her swollen-looking down coat and a scarf made of rust-brown and mustard-yellow wool. She remembered being drawn to this scarf when she'd seen it at the Saturday flea market in the parking lot behind Chapter and Verse, but lately she'd come to feel that it was the textile equivalent of lentils in a stew: good for you in some way, but never completely lovable. Though the girls liked her pointed, caramel-colored boots, most of them would never have worn an earthy, no-nonsense scarf that hid the wonder of their bodies.

Marissa Clayborn leaped onto the stage, kicking up a little dust with her long legs under the dim lights. Behind her came her obedient followers. They stood in a line, all different sizes and shapes and weights. Some had a beauty that could make the men of Athens or Sparta or the greater New Jersey area lay down their swords; others were less showy; some appeared slumped and afraid.

Fran indicated a particular point in the script, and the girls began to read aloud. Dory tried to watch, but it had been a really long day, and soon she nodded off, as perhaps the audience would do when it came time for the performance. Who could listen to classical language for very long these days, when the world had become peppered with shorthand, and everything was completely fast-moving and ADD? Who could bear to be thrust back into an ancient, snoozy era, unless it was to be involved in some virtual-reality civilization game, where you had to fight to stay alive, and where every move could put you face-to-face with a three-headed dog, or an entire sandaled and raging army?

Dory Lang felt herself fall asleep in the soft seat. This became one of those intense little afternoon naps, and suddenly Dory's eyes opened and she grunted like a sow, and was brought roughly into the present moment, in which the girls onstage were in the middle of their scene. They had begun to *act*, as opposed to just reading lines. Their voices lifted in indignation, or at least enunciation:

> LYSISTRATA: Then I will out with it at last, my mighty secret! Oh! sister women, if we would compel our husbands to make peace, we must refrain . . .
> MYRRHINÉ: Refrain from what? Tell us, tell us!
> LYSISTRATA: But will you do it?
> MYRRHINÉ: We will, we will, though we should die of it.
> LYSISTRATA: We must refrain from the male altogether. . . .

Dory was fully awake. Marissa Clayborn continued to speak in a stirring, almost British stage actor's voice, and Dory leaned forward in her chair to listen:

> Nay, why do you turn your backs on me? Where are you going? So, you bite your lips, and shake your heads, eh? Why these pale, sad looks? Why these tears? Come, will you do it—yes or no? Do you hesitate?
> MYRRHINÉ: No, I will not do it; let the War go on.
> LYSISTRATA: And you, my pretty flat-fish, who declared just now they might split you in two?
> CALONICÉ: Anything, anything but that! Bid me go through the fire, if you will; but to rob us of the sweetest thing in all the world, my dear, dear Lysistrata!

"Thanks, girls," Fran Heller said, raising a hand. "You can stop there. And now would the rest of the cast please come up onstage so we can see how you all look when you're together? Chorus of Old Men, please stand to the left, and Chorus of Women, please stand to the right."

So all the girls and the scatter of boys stood together nervously and artlessly. Quite a few of the boys looked short, Dory noticed, like vulnerable humans among a superior species. There, now, was Willa in the middle of the Chorus of Women. Her red hair glittered in discrete threads. Dory watched as Willa stood, her body outlined under the row of unsubtle lights.

That night was the night the spell took Dory Lang. Before dinner, Robby had gone out to shovel snow, a task he generally took on without being asked, and so over time, tacitly, it became his task. It was December, and the weather was already messy. He scraped piles of snow around the small white house so that he'd created a narrow, curving path from sidewalk to door, while Willa and Dory watched from the kitchen window. Robby hadn't worn a hat; the tips of his ears seemed lit like little flares.

"It's so cold out there," Dory said. "Your dad looks miserable. Do you want to go bring him in?"

Willa, who clearly did not want to do this, went to the side door and waved to him. "Dad!" she called flatly. "Enough!" Robby looked up at her after a long moment, as if he'd been in a shoveling reverie, lost in the crunch and release. Then he shrugged, planting the shovel straight into the deep snow on the lawn, and walked toward the house, his face at that juncture of pink and blue, streaming with cold-weather tears. The family sat down to dinner, and Hazel wandered the floor below the table, trawling and licking.

At first Willa was very quiet at the meal, but at some point she seemed to open up, as if the warm and delicious food had loosened her from her teenaged moorings and reminded her that her family wasn't so bad. Recently she'd been very private and closed; tonight signaled a subtle change, and Dory was pleased. It was as if, in the middle of the meal, Willa had made a conscious decision to be a little more generous with her parents.

"Marissa," Willa suddenly announced, "not only has the lead in the play, but she was also asked to be in *Who's Who of Today's American High School Students*."

"Well, don't be too impressed," said Robby. "That's kind of a scam. They get you to buy the book, and of course it's really expensive. It's probably made of embossed leather or something. From special free-range cows."

"I doubt it, Dad. Oh, and also, Lucy Neels met a boy on a teen tour over the summer," Willa went on. "And now he's texting her all the time. It's like a constant onslaught."

It was as though one of them had asked her, "Tell us, does Lucy Neels receive many text messages?" There seemed to be no segues in conversations with adolescents; they talked about whatever was on their minds at the moment without making some kind of logical leap from the last thing. "He texts her basically every two seconds," Willa went on, "and he lurks around, bothering her on Farrest—his avatar is this emo gremlin—and they barely know each other. He lives in New York City. They met at the Louvre, actually standing in front of the *Mona Lisa*."

"That seems a little stalkerish to me," said Dory. "I don't like the sound of it."

But Willa switched topics again and was now saying that Carrie Petito had gotten her navel pierced, and it had grown infected. "The irony here," Willa said to her parents, "is that things got really critical only because her parents had forbidden her to get any part of her anatomy pierced other than her earlobes. So she had to hide it from them, and basically not take care of it the way she was supposed to, and that's how it got infected. In fact," Willa added, "I bet she wouldn't have even wanted to get anything pierced if they hadn't made such a big thing about it in the first place."

"I'm sure you're right," Dory said.

"Never make your children crave the mundane," Robby quietly pronounced.

"So the infection grew worse and worse," Willa said. "What's the word, 'suppurating'? And then the other day we were all standing around in the locker room before folk dance started, and Carrie pulled up her blouse and showed it to us. It was like a horror movie." Willa described the way she and her friends had stood staring and shaking their heads, saying, "I'm obviously not a doctor, Carrie, but that looks pretty bad to me," and, "Carrie, you have to do something about that, ASAP." Then they were called into the gym, where the nice gym teacher Ms. Winik turned on the recording of sprightly klezmer music, and all the girls linked arms.

That seemed to be the end of the conversation, but after a moment longer at the table Willa added quietly, "We were getting kind of hysterical there. We thought that maybe Carrie would die or something."

"Oh no, that wouldn't have happened," Dory said. "Definitely not."

When Carrie Petito had showed her friends the small, blackened crater of pus beneath her blouse, the girls had contracted in terror, probably reminded of their own mortality. So a few of them had apparently staged an "infected navel intervention," Willa explained. Then she relayed the rest of the story, which had a happy ending involving IV amoxicillin and two loving, attentive parents who had reminded their daughter that she should never be afraid to come tell them whatever was bothering her. "Anything," they said sternly. But Dory thought the Petitos probably suspected, with sorrow, that their daughter would no longer tell them much of anything at all, and had not actually been telling them much of anything for years.

Robby and Dory listened to Willa, and they reiterated their own views; she could tell them not only anything, but everything. Though some information might shock them, they would rather be shocked than ignorant, and no matter what they found out, they would always love her. Maybe, finally, Dory thought, Willa would take this conversation as an invitation to be more open about Eli. Maybe Willa would let her mother in once in a while.

The Langs were done with their sudden speech, and Dory patted her mouth with her napkin. Then Robby said he had to get down to his student papers. "*The Odyssey* awaits," he said. After the conversation about Carrie Petito and Lucy Neels and Marissa Clayborn and the high school play—after a batch of *Odyssey* papers were graded, and a rusted nugget of steel wool was taken to a pan, and the dog was let out into the yard—Robby and Dory Lang got into bed.

They were entirely ignorant of what was about to happen to them, or, rather, what was about to happen to Dory. At first she yawned; she reached out in bed and touched her toes, which seemed very far away.

"When I was shoveling snow before, you know what I thought about?" Robby said. "All the middle-aged men who drop dead of heart attacks doing that. This simple activity, and their life just ends. I thought of how it could be me."

"It wouldn't be you." This was unbearable; she didn't want to have to think about it now.

"It could be. And I wouldn't get to hear about girls with infected navels. Willa seemed like she was going to burst into tears, didn't she?"

"Yeah, she did," said Dory.

"She's so sensitive to everything. Just a bunch of unprotected nerve endings. No myelin sheath. If I died while I was shoveling snow, what would happen to her? And you? Not to mention me?"

"It hasn't happened," Dory said. "You're healthy. You're not going anywhere for a really long time."

Robby slid closer, and it was then that he began to turn her toward him, and then that the wind that had secretly shoved its way inside the house found Dory Lang, and the spell struck her. Robby tried to kiss and touch her face and her mouth and her neck and her pale, pretty breasts, but she felt much too cold for that, and her teeth chattered once, after which she was fully, thoroughly enchanted, and as a result she would have nothing to do with this tonight, and she stopped him then and there.

That was how it happened. Dory Lang kept stopping her

beloved husband night after night, until finally he no longer asked, and until what they'd had together and what they'd done all these years became something from the past, a lost piece of their joined life, a delicious meal they'd once eaten, and were possibly about to forget.

Part | Two

7.

All over town, the spell did its work. No one knew, of course; how could they possibly have known? Even in the absence of a spell, no one ever really knew what went on in anyone else's bed. No one ever really knew what went on in anyone else's kitchen, or bathroom, or upstairs hallway. What actually happened there, and what got said. Couples might put on clown wigs and prance around. Entire families might kneel and chant and eat root soup. Who really knew anything about how other people lived? You might tell a friend some details, but of course you would always carefully choose which ones to reveal, and you would tweak them in some vain or self-protective way. *I watch him sleep sometimes,* you might say. *His mouth is open.* Or, *We have this song we sing.*

For a long time, before the spell came over her and changed her too, Leanne Bannerjee, Ph.D., the school psychologist, led a social life that rivaled that of her students. They would have been impressed, had they known its complexity. They would have been awed by the fact that young Dr. Bannerjee was not monogamous, and had no desire to be. She who spoke so frankly to them about "staying safe" and "thinking with your head, not with some other anatomical feature," was easiest to imagine with a handsome and trim Indian boyfriend—someone who looked like a male version of her, and to whom she'd soon be engaged.

Leanne's friends took pleasure in hearing bulletins from the world of the single and multiply sexually active. The people she'd kept in touch with from graduate school were either in long relationships or completely unattached. "Married to my cable box," a rueful psychologist friend had e-mailed her recently. "We are renewing our vows on a monthly basis." But all of Leanne's friends here in Stellar Plains were paired off and set for life. Everyone she knew from the high school went home at night to a husband or wife, or, in a couple of instances, a same-sex partner. It was highly unusual in this suburb for a woman to be involved with a few different men at one time, but this was the way Leanne chose to live. Dory Lang, not one to judge—except when it came to her own newly sexually active teenaged daughter, about whom she was prurient and, basically, deranged—had instructed Leanne, "Your role is to sleep with various men for those of us who don't."

By virtue of being beautiful and tiny, Leanne Bannerjee had rarely been alone in her life. She had a budlike delicacy that made men often gasp in delight and strain to speak in couplets. How small and perfect they thought she was, and how ethnically exciting. In bed once, a man had cried out, "Oh, Leanne—oh, fuck—you are . . . *vindaloo!*" Back in college she had been pursued continually by unusual-looking men. One of her boyfriends was so blond he had practically been albino, and with her black sheen of hair and maple-brown skin, they were a startling couple. People told them, "You guys should make babies someday, just so we can see what they'd look like."

Leanne liked the broad backs of men, their surprisingly deep voices. She liked how the biggest, strongest man in the world could become passive and awed in bed, or the way someone inarticulate and mute could become operatic. Different men offered different pleasures, and as long as she was physically up to the task—and, actually, didn't see it as a task—then Leanne could enjoy a variety that most people lacked as they grew older. It would be sad to give up variety, and instead to say, well, I need just one thing. Just one good old thing.

When she'd first moved to New Jersey to take the job at Elro two years earlier, various men had suddenly sprung up from the earth as if through spontaneous generation. No one had ever seen these men before, and Leanne knew that after she left Stellar Plains, which she would probably do in a couple of years, no one was likely ever to see them again. In recent months, a few different men had been in and out of her one-bedroom singles condominium, that place with the harvest-hued carpeting and sliding glass doors and the low-slung futon. There was, among them, a long-faced, mournful man named Malcolm Bean who sold foreign cars. In this slow economy he had time on his hands, and he often called Leanne at night and asked if he could come see her.

They'd smoke a joint together in her condo, which still smelled of paint, and maybe for some reason always would. As she lay with Malcolm in a thinning nest of smoke, she imagined the students seeing her and saying, "No offense, Dr. Bannerjee, but you're a hypocrite." It was true that she always counseled them not to smoke weed—"It makes you stupid and boring"—and always, if they insisted on having sex, which she also did not advise, to use condoms. With the joint at her lips, and Malcolm Bean with his sardonic, curly mouth on first one breast and then the other, Leanne found herself in an unambiguous state of ecstasy. He was a good lover, a good fuck, lightly seedy in the way she had always thought of salesmen, maybe unfairly. Like some salesmen, he hustled you and yet gave the illusion that you could take all the time you needed to make up your mind or have an orgasm or whatever was the relevant goal. He spent *forever* on her, but she was eager to get there, to push ahead, even though no one said she had to. Twice, she was ashamed to admit, she had hurried Malcolm along even though the condom remained vacuum-sealed in its wrapper, in the top drawer of her jewelry box all the way across the room. And if he had any condoms stowed somewhere on his person, he certainly wasn't running to put one on. She was idiotic in this way, and in other ways too, just like the kids at school whose lives were in her hands.

Also, as of recently, she had begun seeing Carlos Miranda, a part-time bartender at Peppercorns. Once, when Leanne had gone there after work with her friends Dory and Bev, the young man lingered near them, drying a glass for an excessive amount of time. "Someone likes you," Bev had said, lifting a frozen drink to her lips. Women always needed this kind of drink; maybe life thrust them down so far, Leanne thought, that they needed something bright and sweet in order to lift them back up. This seemed a parallel to how women always needed to sit together in restaurants, pulling apart white-meat chicken and leafy greens like raptors.

"Someone does not like me," Leanne had said.

Except that wasn't true; Bev was sharp-eyed about the attractions people had for other people. The next night, Leanne went back to Peppercorns alone, ordering another drink at the bar. Carlos, narrow-hipped, twenty-five, with a fluffy soul patch on his chin, asked her if she wanted to meet when he got off work at one, and she had said yes she did. She went home for a while and yawned a good deal and glanced at some files—almost every student who was tested seemed to have some degree of attention deficit—and then she went back to Peppercorns, where she waited for this man to emerge. He was a virtual stranger and she was probably about to sleep with him. The idea agitated her as she sat in her car with the heater on; it caused a twitch to pop up in one eye. She saw in him a future of easy, beautiful sex—sensation without other ambitions lurking around the border. He would only want to lie with her, and play with her hair after a good, bracing round of lovemaking. She was right. Carlos was a young man and he wasn't troubled by the anxieties of men the age of Malcolm Bean. Being a bartender wasn't his whole identity. Carlos was sleepy and affectionate, casual but always courteous. Once, while she slept, he washed the dishes in her sink, even though they were not dishes he had eaten from.

Leanne only found that unalloyed sweetness in Carlos, and not in either of the others. The idea of choosing one person, wearing his ring, putting his art on her walls, owing him the courtesy of telling him her whereabouts, was endlessly depressing. Her parents still held hopes that she would enter into an arranged marriage; they knew of a young man named Robert Gopal who taught at a dental school, and who would jump at the chance to meet her. If only Leanne would allow them to set up a date! But she never would.

Tonight she climbed the front steps to Dory and Robby's house for the faculty potluck, her covered dish in her arms. Though it was a Saturday night and she had come alone, that would change soon, at least in a private and compelling way, for Gavin McCleary was also coming. The principal hadn't missed a single potluck in all the years he'd been at the school. Dory Lang was the only one who knew about Leanne and him; Leanne had decided to trust her with this information, because once the affair had started the previous spring, how could she not tell anyone? Sex always needed to be spoken about, though it could never adequately be conveyed. Dory was trustworthy; solid and well married and without jealousy or unhappiness. When Leanne told her, Dory had been surprised and concerned but also, significantly, loving. She hadn't condemned her, or said in a low, superior voice, "But he's *married*, Leanne."

The front door flung open now and Robby Lang appeared, the warm yellow light of the house behind him and around him. "Leanne, great, you made it," he said, as if she had traveled far, on snowshoes.

"I come bearing hummus," was all she could think to say.

"Excellent," said Robby. He was the kind of man who always made you feel that the thing you'd just said was perfect. He found a way to make the kids feel that they had given an interesting answer in class, even when their answers were off by a century or a hemisphere. He made you understand why other women wanted to have husbands, even though Leanne did not.

She stamped her feet on the mat, then kissed Robby on both cheeks, the way everyone had started doing some years ago. These people, her colleagues, whom she saw every day at school; because it was the evening, she now had to kiss them. It made no sense, but these were the rules. Leanne carried her dish down the hallway;

during the ride here, the dish had sat beside her on the empty passenger seat. Every once in a while, as she'd driven through the frozen streets, she'd reached beside her to make sure it wasn't about to go sliding off the seat and onto the floor. When you were on your own in life, even a short car trip with a dish beside you became a concern. If you had a steady boyfriend beside you, how-ever, you just handed him the dish and said "Here," and he sat with it on his big lap, or else you sat with it on *your* lap while he drove you to your shared destination.

McCleary would not be bringing anything with him; Dory would have told him that there was no need to. His wife, Wendy, who had chronic fatigue syndrome, was too ill to go to parties, and McCleary was much too busy to stand in their kitchen making something to bring to a faculty potluck. "Just come, Gavin," Dory would have told him. "We've got more than enough."

He wasn't here yet; Leanne knew this as soon as she walked into the house. She would have felt him already, would have picked up his scent or the invisible feelers he threw out toward her from a great distance. More than that, she would have seen his car out on the street, even though it was small and ordinary and probably speckled with snow. What kind was it again, a Stanza, a Triad, a Dasher, a *Prancer*? It was some mediocre car that Malcolm the car connoisseur would have mocked. But her eye would have gone to it because it was his. She both wanted the principal here and did not. He was one of the three men who had some claim over her right now; if she knew that either Malcolm or Carlos was going to come here this evening, she would have felt the same kind of mixed anticipation.

Now, in the Langs' house, stepping under the archway that led to the living room, Leanne Bannerjee looked around at all the faces out of their school context. One by one she took note of them: the two different math teachers; the nurse; the self-confident if grating new drama teacher; the biology teacher and his longtime boyfriend. They were all here, but she already understood that McCleary was not. Not yet.

"Leanne!" Bev called from the couch, where she sat sunken beside her husband Ed, a guarded, bald, thin man in an expensive sport jacket. "We're like ying and yang," Leanne had once heard Bev say, and Dory had quietly corrected her: "*Yin* and yang." "That's what I said," Bev had said.

Together, though, the Cutlers were really most like the Sprats from the nursery rhyme—one who could eat no fat, the other who could eat no lean—and everyone certainly thought this, but no one would ever say it aloud because they wouldn't have wanted to be offensive in any way. Bev Cutler had improbably become a good friend of Leanne's. She was twenty-three years older and so unhappy in the thick swaddling of her own body; it wasn't Bev's fault that she had slowly gained so much weight and was now bumblebee-shaped at age fifty-two. The other women secretly vowed never to let this happen to themselves.

Coming in from the kitchen was Ruth Winik, here without her sculptor husband, Henry Spangold. The strong, buoyant gym teacher had three young children at home, twins and a baby, and she and her husband split shifts and tag-teamed each other in order to have something resembling a social life on weekends. "Henry couldn't come. He's home nursing," Ruth repeated cheerfully tonight whenever someone asked after him. They were kind of an odd couple, Leanne had always thought. Ruth had a rawboned

Nordic look, and emitted an androgynous lesbian vibe. By all accounts she was wild about her equally strapping husband, who used a blowtorch to make metal environmental sculptures, and was always applying for grants from the State of New Jersey, begging for funds to support his copper and his tin and his constantly rusting, crusting iron ore. Like Dory and Robby, the Winik-Spangolds seemed to be a happy couple, though the happiness of others was still a mystery to Leanne, who was made happy by excitement and friction much more than by ease.

The principal had made her uneasy from the start, if only because he himself was an uneasy person. Unlike most of the men she'd been attracted to, Gavin McCleary did not seem aware of himself as a body in space, nor had he seemed aware of her. So of course she had wanted to make him aware. He was handsome in a regulation way: solid, well formed, with a boyish, flattish face and a bristle-headed haircut that gave his pale hair almost a see-through look, like the cross-hatching of a window screen. He was a former high school wrestler, filling all his suit jackets, always tugging at his cuffs before he got up to speak at an assembly. He was far straighter than the men she usually liked, but what could she say? She liked him.

The school psychologist and the school principal had become involved shortly after a meeting last spring about a troubled, silent boy named Howie Cox, who had now moved away from the district, thank God. Howie had been found writing notes to himself during math class. When Abby Means loomed over him and demanded to see what he had written, he'd handed her a piece of graph paper on which were the words *"There will be retribution."* Abby Means had freaked out—all teachers feared the worst these days—and the boy had been sent down to Leanne's little chlorinated office, where they talked for a while, and he explained that he was merely writing lyrics to a song he'd been composing, and so she nervously released him.

When she went to see McCleary to discuss the episode, the principal, in his starchy shirt and striped tie, sat across from her and played with a few whimsical items on his desk: a stapler in the shape of a pig, a set of wind-up dentures. He saw her looking at his hand moving the objects, and he said, embarrassed, "When you're principal, they give you the pigs. And the wind-up dentures."

"And you have to act like you think they're funny."

"Exactly."

One day when she went into her office she saw that his little pig stapler now sat on her desk. He had been down here to see her, and had left this as a calling card. She immediately went upstairs to return it to him. Gavin McCleary stood up from his desk and walked around to where she stood. The blinds were half-closed, the slats down-tilted, and the room had a sleepy, private-eye's office kind of light.

He reached out to push the door shut. "I may be really misreading this," he said quietly, and he put out both his hands and held Leanne's face, which immediately heated up, and he kissed her on the mouth. She was shocked at how warm and appealing his mouth was, how unbureaucratic.

"Oh, oh, oh," she heard herself say after they'd both pulled back. She rubbed his head, which felt like velour. Soon she would begin calling him "velour head," and he would call her "my dove." He was solid, and he made Malcolm Bean seem like liquid, and made Carlos Miranda seem like some hovering, floating cloud of gas. Gavin was as solid as a slab, a chopping block, and this quality too could excite her. Her tastes were diverse and multiple; she was quietly proud that she hadn't become only one way, interested only in one thing. She sighed as the big block of principal gathered her against him, and she heard him gasp a little, as if he couldn't believe his own good luck, as if he'd tricked someone like her into being attracted to someone like him.

Now Bev Cutler, unambiguously fat in a green Chinese silk jacket, came over in the Langs' living room and whispered to Leanne, "I'm sure you have somewhere better to be on a Saturday night. What time does that nice bartender get off?"

"I have no other plans," said Leanne. "I'm glad to be here." But later, actually, she was supposed to see Carlos. They had agreed that she would call him after the potluck was over.

Bev said, "I tell you, I wish I had somewhere else to be." She motioned toward Ed, who, bored, was playing with his glass of ice. He sucked some of it up into his mouth, then let it fall back into the glass. This happened a few times, like someone rinsing and spitting. Ed Cutler managed a small hedge fund, and though he had been damaged considerably by the downturn, he and Bev were still very rich. They lived in a house far bigger than any other in Stellar Plains, with much more glass, on a road that did not have a sign.

Dory came over and took the hummus from Leanne, stripping it of its foil, then placed it on the dining room table beside an elaborate bouquet of crudités. Purple and cadmium-yellow cauliflower and pale green, pyramidical broccoflower blossomed out like the results of an experiment with irradiated vegetable seeds. All the food that had been brought to the house tonight was gaudy and enticing, except for Leanne's dumped-from-a-supermarket-tub hummus, which seemed to say: *The person who brought me is the young, sexual one who is involved with three different men. She has no time to spend on potluck. Please excuse her.*

Dory said, "You have to try this excellent wine. We just got a few cases."

"Thanks," Leanne said, taking a glass. Idly, drifting around the small room with the warmth and cloud of drink in her head, the evening passed, and when she noticed that no one was eating her hummus, she felt strangely protective of it, as if it were her child, and he or she was being ignored on the playground.

"I think it's going to be a winter of big drinking, at least for me," Dory said, coming back over.

"Why? Because of Willa and Eli and that whole thing between them? Because you're worried about her?"

"No, no. Not that." Dory looked around to see if anyone was listening. "I can't explain it," she said. "But things haven't been great."

"Talk to me," said Leanne.

"Just for a sec," Dory said. The two women went to the window seat and perched there. Leanne looked at Dory expectantly, and her friend's dependable, maternal face seemed about to fall into unhappiness. Dory began, "You know that Robby and I, we have a great marriage."

"Of course," said Leanne, and then she waited. Sometimes, you just had to wait and wait until the other person was ready to speak. It could take a while; it could take forever. Dory had never, in the two years that they had known each other, told Leanne anything particularly dire. Recently, when Willa had started seeing Eli Heller, Dory had had a strange hysterical fit, as if her daughter were twelve years old and sexually active; but beyond that, Dory had always been even-keeled, reliable, constant, content.

"It's like something came over me," Dory said with difficulty. "One night, all of a sudden, I just couldn't do it. And I still can't, Leanne. It felt so familiar to me. So depressing! And I felt the need to sort of destroy it all."

" '*There will be retribution,*' " murmured Leanne.

"What?"

"Just a phrase I heard."

"I don't want retribution, that's the thing. I was happy. And now I've just said, okay, goodbye to all that, no more of it. And there's nothing now, not even as a release. You'd think I'd want that, wouldn't you? Even just to get rid of tension? I feel twinges still, but I swear it's only like . . . what do they call that? Phantom limb pain? Why would I act this way?"

"Act what way, exactly? I don't understand." Leanne reflexively tilted her head like a bird on a branch, the way she did when someone came into her office to talk.

At that moment Abby Means approached, wearing a cherry-bright skirt with squirrel trim, and she said, "Look what I just discovered I can do," and then she bent her thumb backward so that it touched her wrist. Leanne and Dory just looked at her. Dory, who'd been about to express some specific and real unhappiness to Leanne, forced her face into improvised amusement.

"How did you *just* discover you can do that?" asked Dory. "That's the kind of thing you discover when you're nine."

"I guess I just never tried it before," said Abby with a little laugh, and Leanne realized that Abby Means was sort of drunk, and that most of the other teachers in the room probably were as well. Maybe Dory was drunk too, and that's why she seemed so miserable; maybe she had been having a sad-drunk moment, the kind that Carlos told Leanne he witnessed all the time at work, and which had very little significance. People became expressive and full of regret, but as soon as they sobered up, they returned to their inexpressive, regret-making ways.

Drink was in the air now, falling hard upon this party. Usually the high school faculty barely drank, but tonight, because of work, or the snow, or the darkness that had begun to descend each day before the afternoon was technically over, the crowd from Elro guzzled down bottle after bottle of the Langs' pleasingly decent wine, both red and white. Robby, Leanne saw, kept going over to a carton and pulling out more bottles.

"Screw tops," she heard him say to Mandelbaum.

"Ah," said the Spanish teacher. "That sounds dirty."

"Dirty would be nice," said Robby.

"Where's McCleary?" Dave Boyd asked the room. "He get here yet?" Leanne whipped her head around so sharply that something in her neck cracked like a gunshot.

At sometime past nine, Leanne went over to the table and had a look at her hummus, which, still untouched, had formed a pitted, lunar surface. Robby Lang tapped on a glass then and said, "Everyone, listen up." He liked to make announcements and small speeches, Leanne knew.

"People!" called Dave Boyd, and the other teachers laughed.

"Yes, *people*!" said Robby. "We have something really special for you tonight, *people*."

"A quiz," said Dory.

"Actually, a little musical interlude," Robby said. "It turns out that Fran Heller basically knows every show tune ever written. So please come to the piano, if you're so inclined."

The Langs had a small upright, which sat flush against one wall in their living room. It was made of blond wood, roughly the same color as their yellow Lab and their floors and their sofa. A few teachers headed to the piano and consulted seriously with Fran about what they might all sing. Someone begged her to play Sondheim—anything by him at all.

"That might be out of my league," Fran said. "Robby's definitely oversold me." She tried to sound modest, but it was easy to tell that she wasn't really modest at all.

Soon, with their wineglasses on all surfaces, the assembled faculty of Eleanor Roosevelt High School began to sing. They sang songs from *Guys and Dolls* and *My Fair Lady*, and even the shyest among them could be heard. Abby Means became less detestable when it was revealed how terrible her voice was. She had been going through life wearing garish vintage skirts and singing and speaking thoughtlessly, and as a result being thought badly of, but she really had no idea of her effect on people. Maybe, it occurred to Leanne, she had Asperger's syndrome. *Yes,* maybe that was it, and it explained so much—the moment in the teachers' room with Fran Heller and the Diet Splurge, and many, many others. Leanne suddenly felt tender toward Abby Means, and slightly irritable toward Fran Heller. *Go back to where you came from,* Leanne would have liked to whisper to the drama teacher. But the aggressiveness of this thought made her understand that she herself must be as drunk as everyone else.

Outside, snow fell heavily, and in here, the teachers sang and sang. Leanne Bannerjee leaned against the piano and heard her own voice threading through the others. During a pause, when everyone was trying to come up with another song for Fran to play, Mandelbaum said, "It's too bad that *Lysistrata* isn't a Broadway musical."

A few people laughed, and Dave Boyd, in his beautiful gray Shetland sweater, said, "Come on, sing it, Fran. Sing something from your own musical version of *Lysistrata*."

"What am I supposed to sing, exactly?" Fran asked.

"Oh, extemporize," said Dave. "Make something up."

The drama teacher, lively, zealous, and given a chance to show off, ran her hands up and down the keys, stalling for time. "They never asked me to do this at the faculty potlucks in Cobalt," she said, and then she paused, closed her eyes, and began to play the galloping opening strains of "Oklahoma!"

When she started to sing, her voice was pure and piercing. She had changed the lyrics on the spot, and now she squeezed syllables to fit properly, and she sang, *"Lysssssssss-istrata, where the women go turning down the men . . ."*

The laughter was immediate, and everyone insisted she keep going. *"Till the war is stopped,"* she went on, *"there'll be no cherries popped . . ."*

Here, everyone laughed again and clapped, and Fran finished off the line, shrugging, singing, *"And . . . da-da-da-da-da-da-da-daaa . . ."*

Then she segued into a standard doo-wop chord progression and began to sing:

> *"Here's my story, sad but true . . .*
> *About a girl that I once knew . . .*
> *She took her love and withheld it from me . . .*
> *She stopped a war through . . . chas-ti-ty . . ."*

The teachers helped her along, and they all offered giddy new lyrics, some of which made no sense at all. Abby Means sang a line about Lysistrata wearing "a feathery hat and lookin' mighty proud." Fran Heller, poised on the piano bench, seemed composed, almost rhapsodic in the middle of this attentive crowd. She had an interesting marriage, Leanne knew from Dory. Fran almost never saw her husband, who lived in Michigan. You didn't need an on-site husband to be happy, Fran Heller seemed to suggest, and of course Leanne agreed with this. You could be a feisty little drama teacher and move to a suburb in New Jersey where you knew absolutely no one, and you could swoop down upon everyone there, and soon you would be directing the school play and gathering the theater crowd of the school around you. They would admire and worship you, and maybe fear your wrath, and then you would have a similar effect on the faculty, and you would sit around a piano entertaining them on a Saturday night. Some of them would be helpless before you.

Leanne began drinking more red wine now, and through the big bulb of the glass she saw Gavin McCleary appear in the hallway, snow in his hair and on the shoulders of his overcoat. He was a strangely commanding figure, like the captain of a seafaring vessel whom you would trust even as the vessel ran aground.

Leanne reflexively put her glass down, as though she could rush over to him, but of course she knew she probably shouldn't even go near him. She watched as he turned to look behind him, so she looked there as well, and then a woman stepped into view. For a moment Leanne let herself think this was a teacher she somehow didn't recognize; Elro was a big place, and this could be someone from the art department, or even a computer-science person.

"Gavin. Wendy," said Robby. "Both of you!"

Dory looked right at Leanne; the expression was what Leanne, still not comprehending, noticed, for it was searching, sympathetic. McCleary, Leanne finally understood with a slow awareness, had brought his wife, she who was supposedly too ill to show up anywhere. She who didn't even really *exist,* except of course she did, and now here she was. Gavin and Wendy, together at last. Didn't Gavin think Leanne would be thrown by this? Wendy stood in front of her husband in the hallway, waiting for him to remove her coat.

Behind her glass of wine again, unwilling to lower it, Leanne watched. All around her, everyone continued to drink and to gobble bits of food. Abby Means said to Bev Cutler, "I see that Wendy McCleary is here. That's nice. She's had such a hard time."

"I was just reading about chronic fatigue syndrome," said Bev. "They say it's one of those silent epidemics, like lupus. And it affects a lot of women."

"We have reason to be chronically fatigued," said Abby Means.

Leanne drank and drank. She was surprised at her own anxiety right now; it wasn't as if she was in love with Gavin, and it wasn't even as if he was the only man she was seeing. She reminded herself that it was interesting to be able to get a look at Wendy McCleary from across a room. It was like watching wildlife from a distance, and there was no need to leave. Leanne could stay; though if she stayed, at least she would keep drinking.

Gavin had described his wife accurately, Leanne thought as she poured another glass. Wendy McCleary was a *shrimp*; she even resembled one. Her sweater was coral colored; she seemed strange, not quite ready for human company. Now Dory stepped forward to greet the principal and his wife. "Hi, Gavin. I'm glad you came. And Wendy, this is great," she said evenly. "We've got lots to eat and drink. Fran Heller is playing the piano, and she's cracking everyone up." After Dory spoke, she turned to Leanne, making sure Leanne knew she was *just saying this*, and that if it were up to her, she would never have said two words tonight to Lady Lazarus-McCleary.

Leanne watched as Gavin and his wife made the rounds; soon they had entered the living room and pierced the circle of teachers. The principal looked over his shoulder and nodded blankly to Leanne. He ate some food and drank some of the Langs' wine, while his wife stood shrimpily nearby, talking to a few of the other women, who made a fuss over her. Only Dory hung back, and when she went past Leanne on her way into the kitchen, she made sure to brush her hand against Leanne's shoulder.

"It's a Chinese herbal remedy," Wendy McCleary was telling the teachers. "I think it's made from the ground root of the autumn lotus plant."

"Where did you get it?" Ruth Winik asked. "The Internet, I assume?"

"That's where I found a *Diff'rent Strokes* lunchbox," Abby Means said pointlessly.

"No, you know that place right next door to Peppercorns?" said the principal's wife. "That store with no windows, and with the sign out front that says 'DVDs and Chinese Specialty Items'?"

"Oh, the scary store," said Dave's partner Gordon, and everyone agreed that, yes, yes, it *was* scary, what the hell *was* that place?

Chinese mafia? An opium den? They'd all seen it, but none of them had ever gone in over all the years they'd lived in this town. "I'm afraid of it. I always think they shoot snuff films in there," said Gordon. "They have no windows. Why would they choose not to have windows?"

"Don't you think this is a little xenophobic of us?" Dory said. "Because it's a foreign place, it freaks us out."

"Doesn't it disturb you too?" Gordon asked.

"A little," she admitted. "But I'm not proud of it."

"Well, I actually went inside," said Wendy. "By myself. It's two stores, really. Up front they rent DVDs and it's entirely Caucasian, but I swear it's a front for something else. I told them what I wanted, and they pointed toward the Chinese part of the store," she said. "It was a separate room. Smaller. There were a few shelves that were mostly empty, except for a couple of old jars of hoisin sauce and some Pond's cold cream. Then, in the very back, there was a plywood door. And I knocked on it, and a voice said, 'Come in.' So I walked in, and inside a tiny room there was a really old woman. She had all these containers of herbs around her, and ginseng floating in bottles of liquid, and things bubbling on a hot plate. It reminded me of a meth lab."

"That's because it probably *is* a meth lab," said Dave and Gordon at the same time, and then they smiled at each other, pleased.

"No, no," said Wendy McCleary. "It's a legitimate non-Western pharmacy. I told the old pharmacist what was wrong with me, and she looked into my throat and my eyes, and tested my reflexes, and then she gave me some powder in capsule form, and told me to take it every morning. So that's what I've been doing."

"I cannot believe you just took it like that," Bev said.

"Who knows what they gave you," said Ed Cutler. "It could contain lead."

"I was desperate," said Wendy McCleary simply. "I had no life. But now I do."

Leanne wasn't proprietary about Gavin, but this was too uncomfortable for her. She went upstairs, ostensibly to go to the bathroom, but the first door she opened turned out to be Willa's bedroom. "Ooh, sorry," Leanne called out, but no one was in there. Willa was almost certainly out with Eli.

Leanne slipped into the room and first sat, then lay, on the pink bed in the darkness. She could smell some honeydew perfume that had saturated the coverlet. Through the floor, she heard her colleagues talking, and singing, and then a few *plinks* of glass. Someone finally knocked on the bedroom door, and Leanne assumed it was Dory, making sure she was okay. But then the door opened, and framed in the bright hallway was the principal. He ducked into the dark room and sat down beside her, and Leanne sat up.

"I want you to know that I was as surprised as you," he whispered. "She hasn't been to one of these faculty things in *years*. I didn't have time to warn you. I'm so sorry."

The music kept coming up through the floor, and it seemed to get louder. Fran Heller was once again making up lyrics about Lysistrata and her sex strike; it was unusual to have such a funny, ballsy woman at one of these potlucks, or even on the faculty at all. Gavin bent his head down and began to kiss Leanne's neck and collarbone, and she took his head and pulled it away from her, then kissed him hard, feeling how easy it was to respond to him, just the way she'd done when she'd come into his office in the spring.

She heard the start of a creaking moan in her own throat,

but as it came forward the room seemed chilly, and she wondered if Willa had left her window open. Leanne opened her eyes and looked to the side, trying to see the window, but the room was too dim. Was there an actual breeze flowing through here? No, of course not. But there was. A wind practically lifted Leanne Banner-jee's hair from her neck; the spell it carried encircled her efficiently, freezing her, changing her, making her realize that one day, not terribly long from now, she would be older, and she would be considered someone a little wild and embarrassing. A cougar, perhaps. "A *Bengali* cougar," another teacher would titter meanly behind her hand in the teachers' room.

Men could get away with sleeping with various women, but not the other way around. *Get out now,* she thought, or at any rate the spell seemed to tell her this. *Get away from the men you've been seeing. All of them.* She closed her eyes against the cold and felt her teeth snap together once, decisively, as though she were biting down on a rag during electroshock, and then Leanne Bannerjee gave in to the spell without even knowing.

Gavin McCleary's mouth on hers now felt overeager and brash. A funny song about Lysistrata wafted upward, and Leanne was impatient, and had lost all excitement.

She pulled away. "God, Gavin, enough," she said.

"What?"

She looked at him and shook her head, knowing what she had to say. She was done with men for a long, long time, perhaps forever. "I know that this is apparently the only way I can do it— seeing a few different men—but one of these days it's going to look bad," she said. "And I'll seem like this predatory person. And that will be terrible and humiliating."

"What are you saying?" he said. "We enjoy each other."

"We did."

"You're ending it?" he said, and she nodded. "But why?" he asked, shocked.

"I told you why."

"Is it because Wendy showed up tonight?"

"No," Leanne said. "Yes. I don't know. Everyone becomes part of a couple. Everyone. And if I don't want that—and if I stay one of those women who never marries, how will that look? What will it say?"

"It will say that that's your choice. Leanne, if you break this off," he said, "I'm telling you, I'll lose it, I swear I will."

But no matter what he said, he could not sway her. The spell had taken her, and she was already under a snow dome of enchantment, lost to him. Gavin McCleary slumped back onto the bed and closed his eyes. If someone were to come into the room now and find them, there would be no explaining what the principal and the school psychologist were doing together on a teenaged girl's bed in the darkness. But no one came in, and the sloshing, lurching, sing-along party continued downstairs, with the teachers drinking and eating and dropping little pieces of broken chips all around the Langs' living room; and with witty, improvised songs played harder and harder on the upright piano. In various musical idioms, Lysistrata rallied the women of Greece against the men in order to end a war, and they did what she commanded.

Leanne Bannerjee stood up, her heart fast, and left Gavin McCleary on the bed. She hurried down the stairs, almost stumbling over the Langs' dog, who lay at the bottom. The dog picked her head up and gazed at Leanne, then returned to her licking; the sounds of wetness were always being emitted from her like a white-noise machine, or a wet-noise machine. Leanne stepped over her and kept walking. Down the hall, she went past the kitchen, where Dory stood sticking toothpicks into small baked and caramelized things.

"Where were you?" Dory asked Leanne, looking up.

"I'm going home."

"Is that a good idea?" Dory asked. "Maple double-smoked bacon," she added in apology, as she continued spearing. "You're upset."

"I've got to go," Leanne said. Then, casually, "I broke it off."

"You did? Just now?"

"I am so done with all this," Leanne said, and she slipped her cell phone from her pocket. "I'm calling Carlos as soon as I get outside. And Malcolm. With his *cars*," she added snidely, she who had never once minded the cars before.

"Now why don't you just take a minute—"

"I've got to get out of here, Dory. I'm sorry."

Leanne found the pile of coats on the bed in the guest room. Near the top was Gavin's overcoat, and below it, intermingled with it, was a coat that could have belonged to a child. She kept digging, and somewhere near the bottom, among the many drifting, floating coats, was her leather jacket, once owned by a man she had liked in graduate school, and she put it on. The entire pile slid to the floor, an avalanche of teachers' coats, all of them falling, falling. Leanne left them there and walked down the hall. Soon she would be on the phone, telling the two other men what she had decided. "No, I can't meet you tonight," she would say to Carlos when she got out onto the street, but he would barely be able to hear her over the sounds of the bar. "*I cannot see you again,*" she would have to shout. Soon she would hear the men's voices, so small through the phone, and startled.

The principal had come downstairs now, and she saw him walk to the table, standing for a moment in front of her untouched hummus. He knew she had brought it, and so he had gone right over to it, in front of everyone, even in front of his wife, who stood eating nothing. He pushed a baby carrot through the hummus, then put it into his mouth.

As Leanne opened the door to leave, she heard Abby Means ask, "Gavin, are you okay? You're *trembling*."

8.

Like the women of ancient Greece, Dory Lang refrained from the male altogether. One night in bed, when yet another awkward confrontation with Robby took place, she recalled that line from the play. "*We must refrain from the male altogether,*" she thought, and she turned away from him again, unaware of the spell, knowing only that she was different. Robby, at first, was simply confused by Dory's behavior, and seemed to be making an effort not to be too upset or magnify what was happening. Maybe this was a phase, he probably thought. All marriages had them. He remained reasonably good-natured when, in anticipation of what he was about to ask her, or try to do, she would grow tense all over again and quickly say to him, "I'm just so beat," or else, reflexively, vaguely, a couple of times, "I've got that thing."

"What thing is it now?" he asked one night, very late, and for the first time he sounded irritated. It was Friday, the start of a weekend, and there was certainly nothing in the morning that

Dory had to go to. They could both sleep in. Willa could take Hazel out, and the Langs could lie twined and twinned after a night of reunion sex—the resolution to the brief and baffling pause that Dory had insisted upon. The *phase.* "Why do you keep saying this?" he asked her. "Why don't you ever want to touch me or have me touch you anymore?"

"I don't know," she said. "I'm sorry." She couldn't tell him about wanting to shake everything up, or about what she now knew, which was that once you realize you are different from the way you used to be, then you can never be that earlier way again. Awareness changes you forever, and instead of being spontaneous during sex, you will forever be a little self-congratulatory.

Look at me; look at us, you think; it hasn't died yet. It's still here. We still have it—that exquisite and sometimes excruciating excitement that is so precious. Dory put an arm around Robby, and he accepted it, because what was he going to do, shrug her off, go sit somewhere and stew? They lay together for a long time in a kind of open wistfulness, until one of them, then the other, fell asleep.

The next time she refused him, Robby became sarcastic. "Should I find the public access channel with those ads for escorts?" he asked.

"Stop," she said.

"Maybe one of them could be dressed up to resemble you. She could carry a curriculum handbook."

"Come on, please stop."

"Or else," he said, "I could go have a lap dance. There are plenty of places in New Jersey where a man can get a lap dance. At least," he added, "there must be."

She didn't worry that he wanted an escort or a lap dance. She had never once worried that he would ever be unfaithful to her, or she to him. They had made a deal and kept it over all these years. They had long ago acknowledged that they were *alike*, pitched toward each other, neither one in need of outside love or attention, but both of them in need of these elements from the other person. What a coup, they'd always felt.

"I'm not doing this on purpose," Dory said.

"You're not doing it by accident."

This was true too. Her lack of desire seemed neither on purpose nor by accident. The word "lack" was too passive for what was happening; something compelled her, though she was ignorant of what it was. *Not* wanting to sleep with him was a reverse drive, and he seemed to recognize this, and was hurt and angry. "So, are you part of some kind of organized sex strike?" he asked. His quiet sarcasm extended to much of their conversation. He had also been sarcastic to Willa over the past few days, and when she used the sentence "The two Lucys are going to go to the movies with Eli and I," Robby said, "Great. And you have English teachers for parents."

"What?" said Willa.

"Robby," Dory said. "Don't do that."

"Do what?" Willa said. But Robby could not be even slightly unpleasant to his daughter for more than a moment. Toward Dory, though, he could stay cold, if only because she had been cold first.

"Nothing," Robby told Willa. "Absolutely nothing."

Dory quietly endured his sullen remarks. Robby was low-level mean and low-level indifferent. "My *lover*," he remarked to Dory in passing, more than once, as he carried a thick Brazilian novel from kitchen to bathroom to bed. Sexlessness had awakened some churlishness in him. Was this all it took in order to find a bad side of a man? Was it like depriving him of an essential nutrient?

Dory had always taken note when a man in power—a president, member of Congress, even a town councilman—got caught in a scandal involving a woman. It was as if such men needed sex to get them through the long slog of leading a country or passing legislation or writing bylaws. They needed constant female stimulation in order to stay interested, and maybe this was true of Robby too, powerful only in the duchy of his classroom, for now he was as fractious as a baby. He was frustrated; also, he was furious.

And then, after a week of this behavior, he calmed down. First Dory thought that he had accepted the new state between them, but one afternoon when they came home from school, a package awaited them on the front porch, addressed to him. Christmas had come and gone in glum detachment this year; this wasn't a late gift. Robby rarely bought himself anything. "If I think of something, I'll tell you," he always said around the time of his birthday, when pressed. Invariably Dory bought him a gift certificate for dinner someplace new and ethnic in a nearby shopping center. If he didn't redeem it quickly, he might miss out. Recently in the kitchen drawer, between a jumbo pack of AA batteries and the manual to the mini-vac, she'd come across his years-old, crisping, thirty-eighth-birthday gift certificate for dinner at the now-defunct Ethiopian restaurant—a place that had been called, simply, The Ethiopian Restaurant. Subsequently it had become a shoe store, then a nail salon. The Ethiopian owners had gone away, but no one knew where. Robby didn't need most things, and he barely understood that other people did.

On this cold day, she bent down to pick up the package that had been tossed onto the porch. It was big and light, lacking a return address. Inside the house, as Dory took off her coat and went through the uninteresting mail, Robby opened it, revealing a board game that looked off-brand. The typography was poorly done; the silver letters were difficult to read stenciled against the yellow background of the cardboard cover. She came closer and read aloud, "'The Game of Want.'"

"Yes," Robby said, smiling, as though she was supposed to understand what this meant.

"I don't know this game," she tried, and then she understood. It was a sex game for couples who were so far gone that they needed to be rescued. The Adult Entertainment Board Games Commission had given The Game of Want four stars. "I hardly know what to say," Dory said. But she was in no position to make fun of anything that Robby tried to do, or felt, or said. If a board game was introduced into their marriage, she would have to play it.

Willa would be at rehearsal for at least another hour, so the Langs sat on the rug in the den with the box open between them and the dog circling, her tail doing a tentative wag. Robby had taken the notepad that usually sat beside the phone covered with orthodontia appointment times or notes about Odysseus. He was now writing their initials on it in order to keep score. The game involved two players spinning dice and moving their little male- or female-shaped pawns around a ring of squares, all the while answering deeply personal questions and performing deeply personal tasks that were printed on cheap cards in an ink that already seemed a little faded.

"'What is your favorite part of my body?'" Robby read aloud.

The question seemed too bold, as though the asker was fishing for compliments. What if the answer was: *Nothing.* No part. What if the asker had become *completely uninteresting* to the other person, and when this was asked, the question was met with silence, and both players realized the truth. Lives would be ruined in one moment. The game would be a disaster, even though the Adult Entertainment Board Games Commission had approved of it. Luckily, this wasn't the case with the Langs.

"Your hands," she answered, which was true. "You have the longest, most beautiful hands," she went on. "They're like the hands of a Madonna."

"You think I'm effeminate?" Robby asked.

"God, of course not." She had never thought this, never once in her life. He was as male as she had ever wanted him to be, a male who liked the outdoors, and liked hiking and rafting and putting together a tent with swift, masterful motions. But he was also a nice man, a kind and thoughtful, bookish man, and when she was left to speak without considering her words, Dory Lang had compared his hands to those of a Madonna.

"*Your* hands, now that I think of it," said Robby suddenly, "are sort of like a man's."

"What?"

"Well," he said, "I'm not trying to be defensive or anything, but they're kind of big, actually, and they get red and chapped," he said. "Like a pioneer's hands."

They sat staring at each other; there was no going back now. Love was somewhere far away; it was a land that this pioneer woman had left behind when she climbed into her wagon. Dory spun the dice and moved her little womanly game piece. Then she drew a card on which was written an action she was meant to carry out. She read it aloud:

"'Wearing a bandana tied around your neck, square-dance with your partner, without music, and without clothes.'"

The stupidity of the command distracted them both from the mild hostility over the matter of their hands. Neither of them would possibly do the naked square dance, and they both knew it. Dory kept going through the deck, reading aloud to him, and then he to her, their voices arch and condescending toward the creators of these questions. Some cards seemed to have been planted in the middle of the deck as if the writer knew that no one would ever read them, just the way that someone supposedly had once planted money in the middle of various bookstore copies of Stephen Hawking's *A Brief History of Time,* then waited. Because no one announced that they had found any money, obviously no one—so the theory went—actually read the book.

The writer of these cards thought that surely all couples would give up before getting through the deck, and would therefore never even see the card that instructed, *"Two people. One can of chocolate frosting. One birthday candle. The possibilities are infinite. Discover them all."*

"But you just said they were infinite!" cried Robby. "How can we discover them *all?*"

"Jerks!" said Dory.

They were done with the game now for good, and what a relief. It could have been worse, Dory thought; Robby could have bought them a sex toy, a marital aid, something with smooth rubberized surfaces, or even something edible, resembling the Fruit Roll-Ups she used to buy Willa, but with holes for legs to go through. All of it would have been horrifying, she knew, because you could dress love up, but always you would have to confront desire—its absence or presence. Love could wear just a bandana. Love could be frosted. But if it didn't include pleasure, then it was sadder with a bandana, and sadder frosted.

Her remark about Robby's hands, and then his counterpunch, had hurt them both. Wasn't it enough that the Langs had been so much like each other over time? Did they have to be wildly different, each one an exaggeration of his or her gender? Was this why the sex part had finally fallen apart? Dory didn't believe it. The way they lived, the way they spent their time, was the way they liked it. You were entitled to like anything at all. The only requirement was that you had to like it together, or else you would grow apart.

Sometimes, since the spell had stolen over her and she'd started refusing him in bed, when Robby was alone in a room and the door was shut, she became sure that if she opened that door she would find him masturbating to generic, universal porn. So she fiddled loudly with the doorknob, or even sometimes called to him before she entered a room. "Hello!" Dory sang out one afternoon as she came in. He was sitting on the bed grading papers and eating chips, his hand buried deep in the bag. He looked up at her, his mouth full of bad food, his bagged hand unmoving.

Did she actually want to catch him? She didn't even understand the door-flinging farce she was privately enacting. She had no right to see what he was doing; she had to get used to the closed door, the husband with his hand in a bag of chips, the man who might think of someone who is not you. And, for that matter, did she want him to catch *her*? Though she no longer felt attracted to him, once in a while she would have a stray fantasy about a man whose face she couldn't even picture. The spell seemed to allow for the flotsam of sexual feeling, the blips that very occasionally ran across her screen.

One Saturday morning, Dory looked out the window after it had been snowing all night, and saw that while the neighbors' houses all had shoveled walks and navigable driveways, the Langs' front walk and driveway were still covered in snow. Robby, who was not in the bed, hadn't gone out and shoveled as he usually did.

"I don't really feel up to it," he said when she asked him about it a little later.

"Fair enough."

Dory roused Willa from her bed. "I need you," she said. Willa was annoyed at being awakened, but Dory suddenly felt as if the walk and the driveway needed to be cleared right this minute; she couldn't tolerate them left snow-covered like this, as if Robby was saying, *Nothing is going to get done around here anymore.* She would answer the rebuke with a shovel. Two shovels. She and her daughter, wrapped up against the cold, Willa muttering, pitched the silver metal curves of their shovels into the fresh snow and worked until a path could be followed back to the house.

From then on, shoveling became their job, and this was fine with Dory; shoveling wasn't just for men. But Robby removed himself in many other small ways too. He didn't do the dishes with his wife and daughter after dinner. He was separating himself from the house, the home. This was another phase, she was certain, just as the sexlessness she'd introduced was surely a phase too, and so she said nothing.

But then, between third and fourth periods at school one Monday, Dory walked into the teachers' room and found Abby Means sitting on a folding chair in the middle of the room with Robby standing above her, kneading her shoulders. Robby was smiling, his eyes half-closed. While he seemed to be in a light trance, Abby remained open-eyed, composed, like someone receiving physical therapy or getting a haircut. Her body was as slender as a dancer's, her hair was in a braid that bisected the planes of her back, and her orange skirt fanned out around her.

"Is this the place?" Robby asked her, working his hands a little deeper.

"You got it," she said. "Bingo." Then, glancing up, Abby said, "Oh, hi, Dory. Look what Robby's doing. Can I borrow him once in a while?"

Robby opened his eyes, and without moving his head he looked toward the doorway. "Hello," he said. It was hard to tell whether he was surprised to see Dory there, or whether he'd been waiting for her.

"Don't let me interrupt," Dory said, which was like something one of the high school kids might have said, thinking it was a witty parry.

"You're not interrupting," Abby said. "I can talk and get a neck rub at the same time. Even by someone as good as Robby."

Dory realized that Abby Means didn't know better than to talk suggestively about someone else's husband, or ask him for a neck rub in the middle of the teachers' room, or cause him to fall into a state that seemed somewhat erotic in nature. Maybe, Dory even thought, Robby had asked Abby if he could rub her neck. *You look tense*, he might have said. Men often seemed to want to rub the necks and shoulders of women, and everyone knew that this was all a little mating dance, but here it was now, in daylight—at least a one-way version of it—in the teachers' room, with the sun spilling everywhere and Ron di Canzio calmly eating a microwave burrito, and Dory Lang standing in the doorway, watching the show. Maybe Robby was daring Dory to say something, but she had nothing legitimate to say, so she just went to the refrigerator and peered inside, her head lingering in front of the cold and the light.

Robby Lang was a good person, not a cruel one, and he could not keep flirting with another woman in the presence of his wife. After work that day, he came to Dory in the den at home and said, "About us." She looked at him, waiting. "I was thinking, maybe a bath together. Isn't that what they write about in those women's magazines you sometimes bring into the house?"

Surreptitiously Dory had been reading a couple of magazines for guidance. Lately at Cue Foods all the magazines seemed to feature something on the cover about the topic that was now relevant to her. "Midlife Marriage Blues," they announced. "Perk Up the Marital Bed." Or, "Why Can't I Sleep with My Husband? One Woman's All-Too-Common Story."

She had dropped them onto the moving belt at checkout, but it wasn't as if the articles ever had much that was new to say. There was no such thing as female Viagra, at least not yet. One drug had seemed very promising, but finally it was found to cause crushing headaches and gastric explosions. Everyone knew that with men, the foul-up often seemed to exist in the mechanics; with women, it more often lay in desire, that inscrutable thing. Sexual studies had been done recently, one magazine said, which revealed that men and women were "different." Men, according to this magazine, could masturbate forever to an ancient swimsuit picture of the now-dead Farrah Fawcett; but women needed something more. If

Farrah Fawcett were a dark-eyed, well-built man, and he reached out from that picture and said, "I would like to spend a lazy, committed day with you, just the two of us," then women could masturbate to it forever too.

Oh, but wait! Another article insisted this wasn't true at all. Women didn't only want commitment, didn't only want *relationships*. Apparently, data had been collected that showed the plasticity of women's sexual desire. Female subjects had been hooked up with electrodes and tiny cameras on their vaginal walls (They would *have* to be tiny, Dory thought—yet the articles always mentioned their tininess) and shown footage of bears humping each other, and cowgirl lesbians making out, and an old man eating chocolate fondue. And in each instance, arousal took place. It made no sense; there was no way to explain it all.

The magazine articles generally ended with the same nebulous kind of line about how a desire-enhancing drug for women without serious side effects was still in the "development stages." Brain scientists and therapists had to act as though they knew how to treat or think about women who had suddenly risen up from long, happy relationships and inexplicably said no. Women who suddenly felt their disappointment, or their rage, or their ambivalence, or their passivity, or their age, or just the withdrawal from love that biology and evolution and chemicals and male inadequacy and female criticism had yet to explain. No one ever speculated that perhaps at least some of them were under some kind of spell.

A few of the articles, adopting a hopeful tone even after a depressing array of statistics, suggested that women and their partners might take a bath together. So the night after Robby mentioned it, Dory hesitantly ran a bath and poured in a long squeeze of vanilla-verbena-scented oil, holding the bottle upside down for a protracted moment like syrup over pancakes. She and Robby stepped into the water together, but they were like two big dogs in the tub, and the silky, glistening water rose up quickly, and when they lowered themselves they had to be careful. Their knees banged together; Dory could barely get traction, and her body made a terrible flatulence sound along the bottom of the tub. She grabbed Robby's leg to steady herself.

"*Oof,*" Dory said, her hand paddling water. They laughed at how awkward this was, how ludicrous. Not as ludicrous as The Game of Want, but ludicrous enough. Finally they found a way to lie still, and all was calm, with steam rising up around them, and they both appreciated the comical, tender attempt.

The water was losing its heat; when the Langs finally stood up, their bodies got chilly fast, and they shivered and tossed each other big towels, and Dory ended up going downstairs in a robe, wet-headed, then microwaving some canned tomato soup, which they ate while watching an episode of that British TV show, *The Chief-Inspector Garrick Mysteries*, in bed with trays in front of them like invalids. They put the trays aside, the soup cooling in the bowl the way the water had cooled rapidly in the bath. They shut off the light and he kissed her; he smelled of verbena, and his mouth tasted like tomato and tin. They smelled and tasted exactly the same.

Dory wanted to see if she had lost everything she'd ever felt for him. She thought of Leanne suddenly needing to break off her relationship with all three of those men, *chop chop chop,* and though of course Leanne had been in a very different situation from Dory, maybe there was a similarity. Both women, in different ways, had just *had enough*. Damp-headed, soup-flavored, trying hard, Dory opened her husband's robe.

"Whoa," he said. "What's this?"

Dory touched his penis lightly, like someone tapping a microphone; his *"penus,"* as the spam-senders would have spelled it. She was jabbering away inside her head. Did sex need to take place in the absence of thought? Was that the way it had always been for her? Dory tried to remember all those times when they had simply leaped on each other like pixies, like animals in a nature documentary, like lovers. They had just *done* it. Their minds had needed to be neither full nor empty.

She had been too ambitious tonight. Nothing was going to happen between them because she still didn't want it to. She let go of him, and eventually they moved away from each other, silent, grim. In the evenings from then on, Robby sat sadly in his chair in the den and read for marathon stretches; he wrote more comments than usual on his students' papers. ("Mr. L left me a *manifesto*," one boy remarked to a friend in the school corridor, looking at the sheaf of handwritten notes on his paper called *"The Great Gatsby*: Good and Evil in F. Scott Fitzgerald's Famous Fiction Novel.") He sat curved before his laptop for longer periods of time, and when she called to him, he often didn't seem to hear. Robby was grieving, but Dory wouldn't come around.

Then one day she noticed that he just couldn't seem to sustain this level of unhappiness. He wasn't like Gavin McCleary, who, ever since the night of the potluck, had become a little unhinged. More than once McCleary stood up before an assembly and started to speak, then appeared to lose his way. "I can't remember where I was going with this," he explained to the students. "It doesn't matter. You can all leave early." Something was not right with the principal, people said, but almost no one knew what it was. One day, side by side at the urinals in the faculty men's room, the principal said to Dave Boyd, "I'm not going to last the year, Dave." He refused to elaborate. He haunted the hall outside Leanne's basement office, leaving her pleading notes under the door.

Robby wasn't like that, and he also wasn't like Malcolm Bean, the foreign-car dealer, who pointedly roared in his sports car around the perimeter of Leanne Bannerjee's condo, making his unhappy presence known. Carlos Miranda, the bartender, had seemed to take the loss of Leanne in stride; women were always flirting with Carlos, and besides, he was young. The principal was a wreck, and the car dealer was persistent. Robby was certainly suffering, but Dory hadn't ended the whole relationship, just the physical aspect. Finally he started to accept the way their marriage was now. The Langs got into bed each night and lay side by side, not talking about whether or not Dory would sleep with him tonight or on any night in the near future, but instead talking about their days in the same old way that they used to. "What did you do and who did you see?" she asked him, and he told her about his classes, his best students, his worst ones. Eli Heller fired up the whole classroom, Robby said. "He's got life in him. Curiosity."

"Curiosity about Willa," Dory said. "Which is evidently being satisfied."

"You sound a little something about that. Ambivalent."

"I'm not. I think they're good for each other, I do. Since they've been seeing each other, don't you think she's more . . . I don't know how to say this."

"Yes, you do. Interesting."

"Interesting, yeah," Dory said. Sex, or love, or a combination of the two, had brought their daughter into herself. Willa had been tentative before, drifting. But now she was in love with a boy; she was in the school play; she was rising.

"Now you tell me some things," Robby said, arranging his pillows and leaning back, and she talked to him gently about the continuing saga of Booxmartz-plagiarizing Jen Heplauer and her mother. Dory talked and talked, trying to make up for what she had taken away from them, and her voice was like a lullaby.

The Langs were alone together more than ever lately, for on week ends Willa spent all her time with Eli, and on weekdays after school she went to rehearsals for *Lysistrata*. The house was theirs now. One afternoon in the middle of winter, Robby and Dory drove home together as they usually did. Snow had fallen while they'd been inside the building, and the best of the snowfall, the clean part, the majesty, had come and gone quickly. Salt trucks must have appeared on Tam o' Shanter at some point, depositing their load of broken crystal, turning the snow and gravel and dirt into a pinky-beige meal that was flattened and churned by rollers by the time the Langs were through for the day. It was four P.M. and the day looked unbeautiful, but they didn't mind, because all they wanted now was to be home.

On their doorstep lay a package, medium-sized and plain. Dory looked at it as she stamped on the mat. Ice and salt flew off her shoes like dull sparks. "Another board game," she said.

"No."

Inside the house, Robby stood at the kitchen table and opened the package. Soon a folded piece of cloth was revealed, the yellow of a child's raincoat. "What are you doing?" she asked as the enormous bolt of cloth filled the kitchen. Robby placed a corner of it over her head and pulled; she popped through a slit in the fabric, then he worked his own head through a second slit. Together they stood in the kitchen with a field-sized garment all around them, and Dory looked at the packing label, which read "The Cumfy." She recalled that they'd recently seen an ad for this on television. They had been watching the ArtFlick channel, which was showing a wrenching Italian film that took place in the aftermath of World War II. Townspeople scavenged through a broken landscape; a man quietly called out, "Giovanna, Giovanna . . ."

Then the commercial had come on, and, without context or any attempt at appropriateness, there was the Cumfy—part comforter, part two-person bathrobe—the whole item postmodern in that it had been designed to be worn by couples as *they* watched television. The actors in the commercial looked old, having been chosen for their oldness—or anyway, the first couple did. They were retirees; dry climates beckoned out their window. The second couple appeared to be around the Langs' age—forty or so—an age at which you are still questing and improving, still forward-looking, but even so, an age when one thing might happen, or another. You might laugh at the Cumfy, or you might wear it.

"I know it's ugly," Robby said in the kitchen, "but no one else will see us."

He had bought it because of Dory and what she had done to them. He was trying to adapt to this new state that neither of them really understood. He'd given up trying to persuade her back to him; no matter what he'd done, he'd failed. So maybe he wouldn't try anything anymore. But maybe, too, he now thought he had permission to go farther without her. Maybe he would quietly become attached to another woman, someone much more appropriate than Abby Means. A learning specialist, say, who came into the district a few times a week. She and Robby would fall in love, and when Dory wept in protest, he would remind her that he had tried everything.

Still she would say, "There must be something else," for how terrible it was to give up a good and loving marriage because of sex. Because of *no sex*. Many people stayed married forever in low-sex or no-sex marriages. Look around Eleanor Roosevelt High School, Dory thought, and you could find teachers who had let sex disintegrate long ago, and who thought: *good riddance*. Just look at Eleanor Roosevelt herself. Dory had once read a biography of that First Lady (people often gave you such a book if you happened to teach at Elro, and they thought they were the only person ever to do so). Eleanor and Franklin had had six children together, but apparently Eleanor had once described sex with her husband as "an ordeal to be borne."

But the Langs had always been well matched, and suddenly, after the spell came and enchanted her, they weren't. He was entitled to have a physical, sexual life. He deserved it, and Dory knew he would want it, and that he would seek it out and find it fairly easily, too, even though he loved her and had never had any plans for that to change. Humans were adaptive. They sought out what they needed. She was certain of all of this, and now she knew they were in danger, and she wanted to cry.

In English class the Langs both made the kids look everywhere for symbols. They battered them with imagery, metaphor, insistence that they scour a text for something sweeping and big rather than literal and small. Robby Lang didn't really see the Cumfy as a metaphor for what they'd become. To him, this item was simply what it had been advertised as: a blanket and a robe all in one. He had bought it because they were now in a period of life in which they could use it. They were seeking warmth from someplace other than each other.

Robby and Dory turned on the TV and got themselves under the thing.

9.

"You've really let yourself go, haven't you?"

As soon as Ed Cutler spoke these words to his wife, she knew he could never unspeak them. They were like the comments that kids wrote on walls and boards over the Internet: all the graphic sentiments they threw at one another, not really understanding or caring that college admissions officers and future employers would always be able to call them up and read them. Their words were like skywriting that never fully faded.

Ed had said the words to Bev one night the previous spring, long before the spell struck her. They were getting dressed to go out to the senior class banquet and awards dinner, held at the Rock Garden Country Club, a large structure that looked liked Monticello except with a sign looming beside it that read CARPET BAZAAR. They had been getting dressed together in the master bedroom suite of their house; Bev was at the dresser and Ed was behind her, toying at length with his cuff links. She looked up and saw both their reflections in the mirror. Her husband was slender, trim, hairless, patrician, and though his hedge fund had tanked along with everything else in the economy, still he kept his head up, and still they personally stayed rich. Ed Cutler had been part of the ruin of the country in recent years, but Bev had never spoken aloud the disturbing thought she had, which was: *Look what you did. You and all the others.*

She wouldn't have been cruel to him the way he was cruel to her. She was a thoughtful, soft-spoken guidance counselor at school and, to a certain extent, a counselor at home. Ed went on each day as though the markets hadn't crashed, the financial sphere hadn't been proven to be an improvised concoction of smoke and mirrors and shit. At fifty-eight, he was getting up there in years, and younger men kept coming through, pushing on in, so Ed Cutler needed to keep his ego and sense of self, and his wife Bev didn't want to intrude on it or hurt him. They lived in a gigantic, polished house that had been purchased and maintained by hedge-fund money, so she really had no business saying a word.

None of the other members of the Elro faculty lived the way she and Ed lived, not even close. When the Cutlers went to the faculty potlucks in those modest, tidy homes, she was reminded of all she had, and how rare it was. Though at times Bev referred to the house as "the monstrosity," she privately loved its proximity to nature, and felt pride at owning something so big and glorious. She could have been a guidance counselor for a hundred years, and still she would have been unable to purchase such a place herself. Ed's hedge fund had bought the weathered redwood and slate floors and skylights; the fieldstone kitchen with its hanging copper vessels. His hedge fund, even diminished, paid for their kids' college education and post-collegiate loafing. Their daughter Julia was a freshman at Buckland, leaning toward majoring in Queer Studies, though she was not "queer" herself but simply open-minded, she said. And the Cutlers' bass-player son Jeremy, one year out of college, shared an apartment with a few other musicians in Red Hook, Brooklyn, getting gigs whenever they could, but mostly walking around in their underwear in their fully carpeted pad upon awakening each afternoon, eating bowls of milk with little bits of sugary cereal floating in them.

Ed had been in a dark, fixed mood for a long time now, angry about the markets but acting as if the crash was something that had been done to him, and not, certainly, something in which he had been complicit. He referred to the men in charge as "they" and "them." When he and Bev were getting dressed to go out to the senior banquet on that long-ago spring night, and he was in his tuxedo shirt, which plants a man somewhere between murmuring, butter-bearing waiter and captain of the Queen's Navy, he kept trying to do up his own cuff links, but his thick fingers were baffled, and he muttered to himself.

Bev was still in her bra and pantyhose; they found each other in the mirror, and he looked so impressive and she looked bloated, the pantyhose catching her flesh, her breasts barely contained in their nude-colored catchall. If you squinted, you would not have even *seen* any undergarments, but just a vague, blurry, nude-colored woman in her fifties who felt sad about how she looked, but who was still required to stand in front of mirrors once in a while, like everyone.

"You've really let yourself go, haven't you?" Ed said to her then. For a second they continued to look at themselves in the mirror; it occurred to Bev that he hadn't even meant to say this aloud. This was what he really, really thought, in the deepest and most uncensored part of himself. She disgusted him. She was disgusting. Bev stood, and then dashed to the bathroom in tears.

"What?" he called, but he probably knew he had gone too far. "Would you come out here, Bev?"

Finally, after several minutes, Bev came out of the bathroom and silently stepped into her dress. Ed returned to the pursuit of his cuff links, and then, after trying for a while longer, he asked her, flatly but perhaps sheepishly, "Can you help me?"

She went to him and pushed the little silver T-bar through the ungenerous slit in the hard white cotton. She remembered the night of a previous senior banquet, two years earlier, before she had entirely "let herself go." On that particular night, the Cutlers had also looked at themselves in the mirror, but they had still found enough to be pleased with. Bev made that sucked-in face that women make in mirrors, and Ed, who didn't even know about that face, observed their reflections, and they both thought: *we'll do.* Then, somehow, they were in bed, his tuxedo shirt off, her pantyhose scrolled down. Their chairs at the table in the banquet room remained empty that night; the leaves of their salad, hosed down with raspberry vinaigrette, remained uneaten. Abby Means, who chaired the event every year, had probably primly and piously regarded her watch, wondering where the Cutlers were. She hoped they hadn't been killed in a car accident. She hoped they weren't dead, though she was mad at them for being late. They'd *better* be dead.

But they weren't dead, not at all. They were conscious, eyes wide, breathing each other's best, sweet scent. A cuff link might have rolled away into the carpet, lost like a ball in long grass at twilight.

Back in the early 1980s, when Ed and Bev had first started dating in Philadelphia, he had just been coming into his own. He was one of those Wharton School grads who wore suspenders with his white shirts—a brief and unfortunate trend. That era now seemed to Bev as quaint as anything, entirely gone, trampled over. If she was ever in danger of forgetting about that time in their lives, she still kept a photograph in a drawer to remind her. In the picture she showed no hint of the weight to come as she sat on Ed's lap. She was slender and limber, and Ed had hair, and they shared a cigarette.

Bev remembered that they'd been to bed shortly before the photograph was taken; they'd joked in the past about the fact that his fly was actually *still open*. "Open for business," Ed had remarked once with a little laugh. They were at some yuppie finance guy's party in the picture; they had shown up late, and there was a strong bowl of blue punch that everyone called "antifreeze." This much Bev knew, and she had the picture to prove it. She had sat in her husband's lap, and she wasn't too heavy for him yet, and she wouldn't have broken his femur or sterilized him or disgusted him, and she had fit there perfectly.

Originally, he had pursued her the way he pursued everything, and at night in bed he spoke to her about his ambitions for himself, then later on his ambitions for *them*. She had never known someone who cared so much about doing well in life, mastering everything he tried. She'd always known she would work in a school, and she liked the environment, and the energy of teenagers; she liked helping them along, shuttling them gently from this part of their lives into the next. It was a good job, and she was lucky. But Ed was anxious and wound-up and crazy about work, and she was the only one able to soothe him. In those early days she enjoyed being the person he could talk to, and the one who said, "You're really hyper," and "*Shhh.*" She enjoyed the way lovemaking could be both an antianxiety agent and an antidepressant at the same time. Her small, nimble body pulsed and chimed.

But later on, less small, it pulsed and chimed more slowly; after giving birth she tried to fight the change the same way that everyone did, but soon it was too demanding, and she didn't know how to do it, and she couldn't bear to talk about it to anyone. During sex her body began to feel cumbersome; she closed her eyes so she would not have to see parts of herself suddenly rising up—thighs that were too wide and white, breasts that seemed like *flan*, belonging to someone she didn't know. She wanted sex to take place under a blanket, and then she wanted it to take place in darkness. They still made love, but less frequently. It was difficult for her, and she didn't know what it was like for him.

Over time Bev Cutler had let herself go. Ed had expressed his disgust at her physical self in one single, eviscerating line, and he could never take it back, no matter what. Their sex life had shut down as soon as he said it that night the previous spring, and it hadn't revived itself since then; it had just never been discussed again. Privately, secretly, shortly after that evening took place, Bev enrolled in an expensive program called Susie Sanders' Wait-Enders, whose name didn't even really make sense, if you thought about it. What "wait" were you supposed to want to end? The wait between fatness and thinness? The wait between now and dinner? On the program, you were sent diet supplements in the mail and frozen meals that arrived in hampers of ice. But the supplements made her heart race, and the meals were as desiccated as astronaut food, as if Susie Sanders herself—if she was even a real person instead of a taunting, perfect idea of a person—didn't really want those women to lose weight. After one month, Bev canceled her subscription. It wasn't only that she hated the program; she also didn't like seeming so reactive to Ed's unfeeling words.

So her weight did not *end*; it kept going up and up until she hardly resembled herself at all. Ed had made his remark, and their sex life ended with a shudder.

Bev was positive she was not alone in this. Surely there were other women in Stellar Plains who had given up what they'd had with their husbands. Not her friends, though; her friends were really happy. Dory and Robby were just so fantastic together; you could picture them delightedly stripping for each other and having sex, and then reciting to each other from, oh God, *Mrs. Dalloway*. And the gym teacher Ruth Winik had that big, messy sculptor husband Henry, and all those children as proof of their robust bedroom activity. And Leanne, well, she had broken up with a car dealer and a bartender, but it was hard to feel sorry for her because she could have everyone she wanted. Even Fran Heller the extroverted drama teacher had a long-distance husband whom she loved—as well as, for all anyone knew, a secret giant vibrator in a drawer at home, designed to look like a warrior's jumbo phallus from the Peloponnesian War.

Everyone Bev Cutler knew was probably having tons of sex. But there had to be other women nearby who had "let themselves go," and whose love lives had become unhinged. Some women became Manchurian Candidates of midlife married abstinence, barely remembering much of what they were missing. But Bev remembered. And though she had been the one to "let herself go," Ed was the one who had said those words to her that you should never say to a person you love. Oh, the words tore at her; they ripped her up. They made it so that *he* was the one who had set the gears of abstinence in motion. Before he'd said it, she'd obviously known that her weight was out of control, and she didn't like it either. But the comment about how she had let herself go was unforgivable. In saying it, Ed had taken control of their marriage and their bed.

Months had passed, and Bev seethed. At dinner they talked about their grown children, and sometimes about the economy. Once in a while, if it wasn't too boring for him, she talked about school. She'd said to him, recently, "That boy Eli, the drama teacher's son—you know, the son of Fran, the one who sang those funny songs about *Lysistrata* when we were at Dory and Robby's for faculty potluck?"

"I remember."

"Well, he took a few SAT IIs, and his scores were perfect. He's going to go really far. And I'm going to call him into my office and tell him. I'm certain he could go to Harvard or Yale. His teachers love him too; he'll get great recommendations from everyone. They'll all go to bat for him."

"Nice."

"I'm going to enjoy helping him with colleges. I bet he could get a big scholarship. I doubt that the Hellers have a lot of money."

"Good for him."

"Also, I told Fran I'd lend her some bedsheets for the play. Well, not lend, *give*. The parents who are volunteering to help out are going to cut them up and make them into Greek costumes. Chitons. Fran probably figured we have lots of spare sheets in this house, what with the kids gone, and how big the place is."

"Sure, go for it," Ed said.

After dinner, Ed did what he always did: took the day's papers, the regular ones and the financial ones with their fruity, edible-looking colors, and sat in the living room with all of them spread out on the coffee table. The newspapers covered the table's surface, draped over the sides, and he sat in his shirtsleeves with a glass of bourbon, peacefully reading.

Bev Cutler went upstairs and entered the walk-in linen closet to get the sheets that Fran Heller had requested. Being in this room, with its smells of laundry in the air, pushed Bev back into an earlier time, when her family was in one piece, everyone still living in the house. Suddenly unusually nostalgic, she sat down on a stepstool and put her head in her hands, and soon she found herself crying a little.

Bev recalled giving her son Jeremy some sheets to take to his spoiled-boy's zoo of an apartment in Red Hook. She couldn't imagine him buying sheets for himself, or even knowing what size his bed was. He was helpless that way, just like his father. Julia, up in college, needed extra-longs to fit on her bed, as Bev had once needed them too. Buckland was the same small, progressive liberal arts school that three generations of her family had attended. The school now boasted a coed touch-football team, a lute band, and a transgender dorm. Julia had said—and Bev didn't know whether she was just teasing her—that she was considering taking a seminar next semester called "Dogs and Film."

When Bev was a student there in the late 1970s, back when she was called Bev Bracken and was skinny and tart and open to everything that the world displayed, poetry was forever being set to music in the concert hall. A soprano would stand alone onstage and sing, "*So much de-PENNNNNDS upon a RED wheel-BAR-rowww . . .*" her voice shooting up and down in erratic calliope fashion. The library at Buckland was modest and understocked, and the endowment laughably tiny, but still the college stayed proudly alive.

Every winter afternoon these days, the sky at Buckland took on a blue-bottle complexion, and the students walked in packs like reindeer, inseparable. On weekends they sometimes went night sledding, drunk, down a perilous hill. The students were eighteen to twenty-two years old, beautiful or homely, with faces painted or studded, or open and full like unplowed fields; but most of them, male or female, felt equality pulsing through themselves. To them, neither men nor women ruled the world. Julia did not understand that her own father treated her mother with contempt.

Or if she did understand it—if, when she had still lived at home last spring, she'd seen the shift in her mother after her father had said, "You've really let yourself go, haven't you?" she didn't let on. Children were narcissistic to their core, and Bev's children had been spared knowing the pain of their parents' marriage. Julia, in her e-mails from college that were often sent in the middle of the night, wrote to her mother, "I can't believe the conversations we have in class, or even at night, hanging out at The Kiln. And the classes are so much better than at Elro, no offense."

Only a freshman, or a "year one'r," as they called them at
Buckland in all seriousness, Julia was moments away from officially
declaring herself a Queer Studies major, also in all seriousness.
Julia had hinted that in her bed, upon the extra-long sheets her
mother had given her, she was sleeping with a boy named Holden
who lived in the transgender dorm. It was difficult for Bev, from
this e-mail, to tell if the boy was really a boy, or else if he was a girl,
formerly named, say, Hannah. (Idly, Bev wondered why so many
transgender people elected to keep the first letter of their names
when they made the switch. It wasn't as if they already had a lot
of monogrammed items at home.) Bev couldn't ask her daughter
about the original gender of this boy, and God knows she couldn't
discuss it with Ed, who had wanted Julia to go to Penn; specifically,
to Wharton. Julia was free-thinking, completely independent. She
had a good mind and a solid, chunky body that she apparently
enjoyed fully. Ed didn't approve of her interests, but he was proud
of her, and not in the least disgusted by her.

To have a husband who was disgusted by you was unbearable.
All around Stellar Plains you could see men who were unabashedly
in love with women, and boys who were wild about girls. Tenderness and love flowed everywhere between them, but it did not flow
here. Men worshipped women, were made humble by them. Once,
Bev, Leanne, and Dory were out at a kebab house for an early dinner, and a waiter had come over and placed a sizzling metal plate
in front of Leanne. "Lady, this lamb platter is from the owner,"
he said quietly. "He would like you to enjoy it, for you are a very
beautiful lady."

Lamb for Leanne, but none for Bev or Dory. "When I'm

actually the only one of us who would really enjoy it," Bev had said. They'd all laughed, and then they'd dug into the charred and spitting meat meant for the very beautiful lady, but Bev understood not only that Leanne was desirable to many men, but also that they treated her in a way that Ed no longer treated his own wife.

Bev Cutler had gained sixty-five pounds between the day she and Ed got married in Philadelphia and the evening he said, "You've really let yourself go, haven't you?" The weight gain had been slow and sneaky; she'd held on to some of the weight she'd gained when she was pregnant both times, and as the years passed she'd continually added to it. She'd let herself be humiliated by what he'd said, and they'd turned away from each other in bed every night since then.

Bev had been crying hard in the linen closet and her face and neck were now wet. She stood up and took an armful of sheets from the shelf, using them like a bloom of tissues that a lonely giant might use, blotting all her tears. She took another load from the shelf above it; she was piling her arms high with sheets for *Lysistrata*. She would give them all to Fran Heller in the morning. Marissa Clayborn, naturally, would play the leader of the women who went on a sex strike against the men. Marissa's mother would cut armholes in Bev's sheets, and that charismatic girl would slip her arms inside and stand tall on the shining stage.

Bev grabbed yet another sheet, and that was when the cold air almost knocked her back. She staggered under the pile, aware that she was freezing, dizzy, shivering; then Bev straightened up and held herself in defense against the windless wind that seemed to have entered the small space through some unknown source. She was so cold, she was being surrounded by cold. The spell spent quite a while enveloping her. In the closet, the wind was so strong that the sheets and towels lying folded on their shelves actually lifted slightly at the edges. A washcloth flapped a few times, as if waving for help. Bev Cutler felt the strange and shocking cold air rush up through the bottom of her elastic-waisted pants, flying up her body close to her skin, freezing every part of her as it went. Now a thigh, now the place where leg met crotch, now the field of her stomach, now the cresting swell of her bosom. She was frozen; she was dumbfounded; she was thoroughly enchanted. She hugged the sheets tighter against herself, and they were very cold now too, like a new bed she was about to climb into.

She thought: *I weigh a lot more than I used to, but so what? So fucking what?* He'd had no right to speak to her this way. The spell had taken her over, and she was done with him, done.

Bev Cutler carried the stack of sheets back downstairs and went into the living room, where Ed was still reading the papers. Newspapers were going the way of everything else from the cast-off twentieth century. Why not give him this moment of pleasure, he with his dying papers spread out and draped over the table like sheets themselves. But she couldn't do that. "Ed," she said. He didn't respond. "Ed," she said again, and he looked up. "I have to tell you something. Our sex life is over."

"What's that?"

"Our sex life. It's over."

He softly closed his newspaper. "I know that, Bev," he said. "It's been true for quite a while."

"Yes. It's been true ever since that terrible thing you said."

"What thing did I say?" he asked, but she ignored this.

"It's been true ever since then," she went on, "but I am not letting you have the last word. I am not letting you be the one to have done this to us." His face flushed; his entire bald head flushed. "This time, I am the one doing it, not you," she said. "So I am telling you: starting now, our sex life is over, really over. And I am the one who has ended it."

10.

The entire Chorus of Women had been a real disappointment, Ms. Heller told them, and they all deserved to be replaced. "February is much sooner than you think, people, and just look at you," the drama teacher said in a frantic pitch as she paced back and forth before the stage. The girls stood in a row, slouching and yawning from general exhaustion and being yelled at. They didn't want to displease their drama teacher, who could be very difficult, but whose opinion mattered to them. Willa Lang, second from the right, had given up on getting Eli's mother to really like her. Ms. Heller was not particularly nice to Willa, and various cast members had noticed this and mentioned it to her. She had made her peace with it, though, for what mattered to her was only that Eli still liked her. She thought about him all the time; it was debilitating to think about someone so much.

Even now, at rehearsal, it was as if they were together the entire time, for while Willa stood onstage under the hard white lights, he was there in her brain, observing her onstage, taking in the full length of her. Willa was among the girls who were "a real disappointment." Though she had been to every rehearsal, her attention was only intermittently in ancient Athens; more to the point, it was here in Stellar Plains, on the old sofa in the furnished basement of the Hellers' house, with Eli.

Thinking about him onstage, she half-smiled serenely to herself.

"Willa, what's funny?" Fran Heller asked, positioning herself right below Willa Lang and peering upward.

"Nothing. Sorry."

Later, on Farrest together, with Willa as the ninja and Eli as the centaur, she wrote him about how his mother seemed so critical of her lately.

"obviously she doesnt like me," she said.

"i cant imagine why not. u r exceedingly likeable," he wrote.

They were about to say goodbye and log out for the night, when he casually told her that Ms. Cutler had called him into her office and said that she was paying special attention to him; that he could probably go to Harvard or Yale on a scholarship, and that all he had to do was keep his eye on the prize, whatever that meant. Willa didn't know how she was supposed to respond, so she didn't say anything. A little later, she went downstairs to get ice cream, and there were her parents sitting on the couch in the den under that awful yellow piece of cloth, already eating ice cream themselves. Some British mystery show was on TV. "Come join us!" called Willa's mother.

"Can't," Willa said. She left her parents there, their disembodied heads eating ice cream and watching TV, and she barely noticed anything about them. They were her parents; that was all she knew, and all she needed to know. She loved them, but she didn't think about them as much as she used to, or even very much at all. Willa climbed the stairs. The spell was days away from striking her; she sat in bed and ate her own ice cream, and closed her eyes, and thought of Eli.

On Saturday night, Willa Lang walked along the street to the Hellers' house, her backpack on her back. Since she and Eli had started going out, they had reserved Saturday nights for each other. "Go on in, Willa; you know where he is," Ms. Heller said without much inflection at the front door, which was painted turquoise, while the rest of the house was that cantaloupe color, meant to resemble baked clay. Right now, at night, under the porch light, the colors seemed a little sad to Willa. She wondered if Eli wished his house were more ordinary, and his parents too; though when your house and your parents were ordinary—as hers were—that in itself could be sad.

Ms. Heller wore a big old *Guys and Dolls* T-shirt and her head was cradling a cordless phone; she was obviously in for the evening, which was disappointing to Willa, who preferred it when she and Eli were alone in the house, even though Ms. Heller would never dare come downstairs when the couple was there together. Not to mention that there was a lock on the door of the furnished room in the basement. Willa smiled tensely, mumbled something to Ms. Heller, then walked past the kitchen, where the convex curves and edges of cups and plates could be seen in the sink like the glinting hints of a shipwreck. Beyond the kitchen, on the living room wall, hung the masks of tragedy and comedy. Willa walked past them into the back hallway, opening the basement door.

"I have arrived," she said into the darkness, and down she went.

They sat together on the brown ultrasuede sofa with the ping-pong table hulking uselessly nearby, and a dehumidifier sucking and sporing the air. His feet were in her lap. "I brought something for you," she told him.

"Do I deserve it?"

"Yes."

She unzipped her backpack and took out her flute case; then she assembled the pieces, played a few scales, and was ready. Facing him and taking a hard breath, Willa Lang played the flute version of The Lungs' song "When You Have Me," the same song that they had sat listening to in her bedroom that first night when the Hellers came to dinner at the Langs'. She'd worked hard on the flute arrangement for him, writing out the individual notes in her music notebook, and though her tone was tentative and imperfect and she'd added a few too many grace notes, he was awed.

"You did that for me," he said when she was done. "I loved it. Come here." Willa put the flute aside and went close, curling against him. All the lights were off except for the single overhead bulb. It was probably living a little dangerously to do what they sometimes did down here even with his mother in the house, but for an extremely busy person, Ms. Heller was often around, and they did not want to be denied.

As they kissed now, Willa could hear every tick as lip separated from lip. Eli rubbed his hand against her pants, which brought on a wave of insanity, and then he unbuttoned her button and slipped his hand inside, just playing, just fiddling, as he had once called it, but this excited her so much, so quickly, that she was forced to grab hold of his wrist. You didn't have to know much of anything in life, and still you knew what you liked. You could be the shyest person in the world, just a member of the Chorus of Women, standing meekly in a crowd, and still you were an expert in letting a boy touch you. Willa and Eli cried out, they held each other's wrists and begged for what they wanted. They both knew how to do this. He pulled off his skinny jeans, yanking them from the jutting bones of his ankles, and then she handed him a condom from the bottom of the old cardboard ping-pong ball box, where they kept them. He unwrapped it in the dark, and the sound it made was like a candy wrapper being opened in a movie theater.

"Hurry up," Willa commanded in a stern voice. How strange that she spoke this way, and that she *wanted* this; no one could ever explain why. She'd tried to discuss the topic with Marissa Clayborn recently, for Marissa would surely have some wise observations. Willa had begun the conversation by saying to her, "I completely agree with the general idea that sex is this great thing, but what I don't understand is *why* it's great. I don't even have any idea, Marissa, do you? I know in health class they gave us all kinds of biological explanations, but having had a little personal experience myself this year, I don't agree that we're basically a collection of cells and hormones. We also have feelings, obviously, and for some reason my feelings tell me: *I like that. I like that and I really want it.* Which is the freakiest thing I know. Not to mention the fact that don't you think a penis looks anatomically absurd? And it looks more absurd than usual when it's stuffed into a condom. It's not even objectively attractive. It's *ugly*. So what I want to know is whether we are actually attracted to it. It looks to me like one of those pastry tubes they use on the Food Network. And I am definitely not attracted to pastry tubes."

When she was done with her chattery, naïve soliloquy, Marissa Clayborn made an expression of contempt; her mouth became uncharitable, and Willa was embarrassed. Marissa, always willing to help explain a particularly difficult passage in their French homework, seemed to be a snob when it came to discussing sex. Apparently there was a club of girls and women in the world who understood the astral secrets of Fucking and Why We Want It. Marissa was probably the leader of that club; she probably got up at their annual meeting and performed a brilliant and moving monologue.

If Marissa would not explain why Willa longed to sleep with Eli again and again, then Willa would simply have to keep wanting it without understanding it. She would remain rapt by Eli and his beautiful eyes and his name written in bubble letters in her notebook, and his inflamed skin, and his shining center-parted hair, and his heavy, thick penis, and his seemingly unwavering affection for her. She had every expectation of doing this, but suddenly now, through the low, pipe-crossed ceiling of the Hellers' basement, Eli's mother's voice could be heard. Ms. Heller was obviously situated near some duct that led directly down here. Her voice was so clear all at once that it seemed to be coming in through a sophisticated amplification system.

"I think we're coming along just fine," Willa heard Ms. Heller say. "My lead is fantastic, babe. And, interestingly, black, which gives it an extra dimension, I think. Anyway, she's wonderful." Willa shifted against Eli, hardly breathing, listening closely. "Some of the others," Mrs. Heller went on, "are less wonderful. They stand there grinning at rehearsals, as if they think they're in a production of *The Happy Happy Play*. No, I just made that up, you nut. What did you think it was, Samuel Beckett? Ha ha, right, a recently unearthed, never-performed work. Listen, did you get an estimate on that weatherproofing? Good. You are the best. What, *I* am? No, no, you are. I insist that you are, my darling. All right, *I'm* the best. Case closed."

The conversation poured into the basement, and all sexual activity had now stopped. Willa thought of herself among the girls onstage, awkward and grinning, and she was immediately embarrassed. "You *don't* stand there grinning," Eli whispered. "You look amazing onstage," he added seriously. "I've looked in during rehearsals."

"Thank you," Willa said. "I assume that's your dad on the phone?"

"Yeah."

He began to kiss her neck again, and as she mewed involuntarily and turned her head to allow him better access, the spell came without warning. It seemed to have to work harder than usual to get her, its cold wind sneaking up around her and being entirely ignored at first, so transfixed was she by this boy, and by the sensations he elicited. But still she was human, and female, and vulnerable. Its cold wind slapped her in the face, then roared downward, filling up the tiny spaces where her body and Eli's weren't perfectly aligned. Air-blasted, with her eyes shut and her jaw set, and with her first boyfriend kissing her neck, the suddenly spellbound Willa Lang moved slightly away from him, thinking: *This is never going to last. Oh, what is the point?*

She and Eli would go to different colleges and meet other people. He would meet some girl at Harvard or Yale, according to Ms. Cutler, schools that Willa would never go to, for her grades weren't nearly good enough. And they would talk about the books they loved, and they would make sly, private jokes, and then off they would go into the rest of their lives. Why hadn't this ever occurred to her before? Even if Willa and Eli did find a way to stay together long-distance after high school, they might end up like her parents, sitting together watching TV under a *Cumfy*, of all things, trapped forever like two figures in a his-and-hers sarcophagus. But the chances were that she and Eli wouldn't last that long; almost no high school couples lasted.

Now that she thought of it, there had been several bad breakups already this winter. Chloe Vincent and Max Holleran had recently announced that they were no longer "an entity." No further explanations were given, but just the other day, Max and two friends were suspended for spray-painting the words "CV is a Bitch" on the overpass near the school. And Paige Straub and Dylan Maleska, who both possessed muscled legs and a confident, symmetrical shallowness, had also abruptly ended their relationship recently; or rather, Paige had ended it, saying that Dylan was boring and that she wanted more from a boyfriend, and he couldn't give it to her. He had called in sick frequently since then. High school love felt so important at the moment it was gearing up and happening, Willa thought, but it really wasn't important at all. It was completely meaningless. It was as temporary as anything. It was *pathetic*.

"Where'd you go?" Eli asked her. "You got all distant."

"It's going to end," Willa said.

"What is?"

"Us."

"Our lives?" he said with a small smile. "Existentialism comes to Willa Lang."

"No. This. *This.*" She gestured around her to indicate their half-dressed bodies in the murky basement, their clothes on the ping-pong table, and all else that was associated with this night and these sensations.

"It doesn't have to," Eli said, suddenly a little panicky now, but clearly trying to keep his voice calm. "It can just go on and on. It can even mysteriously accelerate," he tried.

"But it won't," said Willa. "That's the point; don't you get what I'm saying?" She was choking up, even gagging a little. "There have been a lot of breakups lately. People realizing that if they really face the facts, they probably have no future together. And you know it too, Eli. You're going to go somewhere without me eventually; it's just inevitable. And I'm going to go somewhere without you."

"No, that's not true," he said. "I mean, you were just playing me a song on your *flute*. And it killed me, how amazing it was. You were just lying here with me, about to let me go *inside* you. What was *that* about? Doesn't it count for anything?"

"Of course."

"Then what, Willa? I mean, *Jesus*."

"What I said. We can't see each other anymore."

"Oh, come on," Eli said. "Please don't do this to me."

She almost let him call her back, but the new spell had over-taken the one that had first wrapped them in each other that fall. So she said no to him now. The spell had frozen her up and grabbed her by all the parts of her body that had been touching all the parts of his.

He pulled away from her and then stood up, looking down to where she still half-sat, undressed, on the couch. "Get out of here," he said.

"What?"

"Leave my house," said Eli, and he took her bra from the ping-pong table and threw it at her—that little scrunched-up piece of aqua sea foam that barely seemed capable of holding anything, let alone her breasts, which Eli had loved. Frantically Willa tried to put the bra back on, scooping each breast into a cup; but now Eli was tossing her blouse at her too, and she had to let go of the bra and catch the blouse. Her arms were full of her own clothes, and he kept telling her to get out, to leave, and he was crying already, his voice mucousy and heavy and unfamiliar.

"Please, wait," Willa said, but he wouldn't. He wanted her to leave, *now*. He hustled her up the narrow basement steps as she struggled back into the bra, and then half-back into the blouse, but there wasn't enough time to get fully dressed. At the top of the stairs he pushed open the door for her and she ducked out of the darkness and into the light.

His mother was standing in the hallway, leaning against a wall still cradling her phone, when Willa Lang tripped out from the doorway. It was Fran Heller's right to stand anywhere she wanted in her own house, but it couldn't help but seem as if she had been lis-tening to the breakup. Willa stood facing her with her hair slashed across her face and one breast completely out of its cup beneath the thin cotton of the blouse, which, she could now see, was on both inside out and backward. It was like a bib, with the label showing, providing proof that Willa was a baby who didn't deserve a boyfriend anyway. Eli's behavior had only proven the same thing; he wasn't ready for a girlfriend either. They were two babies and it had all been a mistake, and thank God it was over now.

She walked quickly back through the hall, and when she got out the front door, Willa Lang broke into a run. She wanted her mother, but she also didn't want her; her mother would be *so concerned* when she heard they'd broken up. She'd be all over Willa, and she'd want to know everything that had happened. Willa was already exhausted just thinking about her mother's somber, anxious face coming so close to Willa's, asking her if she wanted to talk. *No,* Willa thought, *I do not want to talk.* Not to her mother, and not to her father either, for what could he do to make her feel better? What could anyone do? No one could do anything. Tam o' Shanter Drive was absolutely silent and comatose on this Saturday night as she ran down the middle of the icy street, occasionally skidding, almost falling, but making it home in one piece. As she put her key in the door, she realized that she'd left her flute in the Hellers' basement, and she had to wonder if she'd ever see it again, and even if she did, if she'd ever play it.

The news about the breakup of Willa and Eli would soon hit her circle of friends, and Farrest, and elsewhere. Chloe Vincent, who had never really been a good friend of Willa's, texted her in the middle of the night, saying, "if u want to talk i am around." By Monday, the news would be all over the school. For a few days Willa and Eli's breakup would be a big story, at least among the people they knew, like those other recent breakups had been. But after a while it would die down, and perhaps, by graduation in two years, it would seem as if they had never been involved at all. No one would think about this boy and girl who had been in love. Only the teachers, staying behind in the school and occasionally haunted by the ghosts of students who had walked those halls, might remember.

11.

The gym teacher, entering her house at the end of the day, dropped her key chain into the metal pie tin on the front hall table and waited for them to come. They always came within seconds. That chink of keys against tin was their signal, and no matter how loud the television was, or the *blam blams* or *vroom vrooms* that had been coming from their mouths almost since the second they were born (Ruth Winik swore that, on the ride home from the hospital, one of the twins had cased the interior of the car with lusty vehicular approval), they heard that key chain against pie tin, and they came to her.

Or maybe they heard the door first. Or the car in the driveway. Whatever it was, they *heard* it, and they dropped everything and ran. Ruth had to go to the bathroom badly, but she would wait for them to come first. She couldn't bear not seeing them right away. Distantly now Ruth Winik heard the clatter of indestructible toys being flung to the upstairs floor and bouncing off some hard surface—a head, maybe. The twins both called out, "Mama! Mama!" in near synchrony, and came thudding along the upstairs hallway and then down the carpeted stairs. They appeared before her, showing themselves to her in their glory. Ryan wore plastic knight armor; Brant wore nothing but training pants. One side of his face curiously appeared corrugated, as though he had fallen asleep on an accordion. Both boys thrust their enormous, hard heads against her legs, and Ryan wept, perhaps simply out of relief that his mother had returned, that she was really and truly still *alive*, as though she had been abducted, while Brant stood in easy, patient silence, his embossed face and naked torso and crimped, vulcanized undergarment aligning themselves efficiently against Ruth Winik's legs.

Slowly now, easing down the stairs, came Ruth's husband Henry Spangold, with the infant Kyle slung casually over one shoulder, the way Ruth sometimes carried a mesh bag of volley-balls as she led a group of ninth-grade girls out into the middle of the gym. Henry was sleepy, his black hair chick-headed, and he handed the baby over to her. Perhaps he had been the one to throw a toy to the floor when she came in; he was often as boyish as his boys. The Winik-Spangold household was a world of males, and Ruth lived in it like Snow White among the dwarves, or like Wendy among the Lost Boys. It was easy to feel special in such a situation, and to get credit merely for being a woman, even if you weren't all that womanly to begin with, as Ruth was not. All of them, herself included, she sometimes thought, were like a gang of some kind, or perhaps like a team. A great deal of roughhousing took place in their house.

Henry kissed her hard. *"Mm-hmm!"* he said for emphasis,

and then he said, "Let's have a date tonight, okay?" which was code. He wanted a date probably five times a week, and because of their lack of privacy and time, the date in bed was usually straight-forward and brief. He smelled of apple juice now, as if he'd been swigging it warm from a juice box.

"I have to pee," she said. "Wait, wait." Ruth handed the baby back to him, then walked swiftly to the front hall bathroom, and though Henry respectfully stayed where he was, the twins followed her inside.

As she sat on the toilet, both boys observed her from a critical distance of a few inches. Brant turned to Ryan and said, "Mama sits down when she wees. She *sits down.*"

"Why?" Ryan asked. "Why you sit down, Mama?" He stepped closer and placed an open hand on her bare thigh, peering into the shadowed slice of toilet bowl between her legs.

"Oh," she said, "well, because it's easier for me. You know."

But he didn't know. He knew nothing yet about distinctions in anatomy, or the ways of the world. Its chaos, its sadness. He peered between her legs as though the secrets of the universe were stored in the shallow water. Ruth released an involuntary puff of gas then, and Brant casually said, "Oh, that was gas. Was there beans today, Mama?"

She thought back to lunch, and the salad bar in the school cafeteria: the chickpeas unjacketing in their metal tub of water. She said, "Yes, Brant, there were beans at lunch. You're psychic."

The boys solemnly stood and listened and appraised her wiping style, and looked between her legs like grim nineteenth-century consulting gynecologists. They took her full measure when she stood with her blond pubic hair exposed for a half second. No part of her was more unusual to them than any other part; all were compelling. They owned her, and in the tiny room they flanked her, asserting their ownership. When she left the bathroom they followed hard behind; they gave chase.

Most nights, when the twins were meant to be in their small beds in the room down the hall from the master bedroom, they would inevitably end up in their parents' bed, appearing like apparitions shortly after they had been tucked in. Sometimes Ruth and Henry were stern with them, but it was much easier not to be. A child, or two children, usually slept between the parents or down at the foot of the bed. Once, Ruth had accidentally kicked one of the twins in her sleep and sent him flying to the hard floor. The baby sometimes spent the night in the bed too, though Ruth had read stories of suffocation, a big parent rolling over and crushing a tiny baby. The entire bed felt crowded and unmanageable.

Still, it was easy to let her husband and sons love her, and to love them back, and not feel stiff or embarrassed. How did fussy women manage? How did those society women in their pencil skirts and with their fist-sized handbags and those sticks up their asses manage having little boys who watched them urinate, and listened to them stutter-fart on the toilet, and touched their tended, scented bodies in casual ownership? Maybe those women actually didn't manage, Ruth thought; maybe there was a kind of woman who couldn't manage at all, and who closed the door of the bathroom and double-locked it with deadbolts, keeping those children waiting outside, desperate to come in. But Ruth Winik would always let them come in; how could she keep them out? Why would she?

The boys inspired fierceness in her; their need to be with her and watch her do ordinary but private actions seemed like a literal representation of love. She couldn't imagine what it would be like to be the mother of one of those simpering little girls she sometimes saw around town—pale-skinned, pale-haired, utterly-silent-when-spoken-to creatures who liked having their faces glitter-painted at carnivals, and who often stayed pressed against their mothers, and, like chameleons, eventually disappeared against their mothers' glittering legs. She suspected that she would have been an impatient mother to a femmy girl, and she was grateful that Henry's sperm seemed to contain only Y chromosomes.

Ruth Winik, who taught girls' field sports and indoor sports and sometimes a folk dance elective at Elro, was the mother of twin boys, aged three, and now yet another boy, an infant. She was also the wife of a husband who sprouted facial hair five minutes after shaving. The irony of the manliness of the household wasn't lost on her—she who had been a lesbian during the opening years of her twenties. She'd been in graduate school in physical education at Ohio State, and during that time, while taking classes in soft-ball team management and first aid and even a seminar on steroid use, she'd gotten involved with a few other women getting their degrees in this area. There had been a corn-fed, clean quality to those women. They wore Lacoste shirts with the collars up; their skin was a ruddy tan from the hours they clocked outdoors. They had good, blunt haircuts, and more than one of them was named Chris. They were a hoot in bed, a pleasure.

Ruth Winik laughed her way through Ohio State, and got her degree and her teaching certificate, and when she moved to suburban New Jersey to take the job at Eleanor Roosevelt High School, she was shocked one weekend afternoon to fall immediately in love, at the farmer's market set up in the parking lot behind Chapter and Verse, with a local sculptor named Henry Spangold, who was there searching for parts to use in a new sculpture that was still in the planning stages.

Henry Spangold had nothing female about him, nothing that made him a variation on the theme of lesbianism. He was a sculptor of enormous environmental pieces, who used a blowtorch and often smelled of burned and twisted metal, an aroma that reminded Ruth of "evil s'mores," she told him. He dressed for work in jumpsuits like the kind janitors or gas station attendants wore. He was big, sexy, bearlike, curly-haired, quite loud. He would have done anything for Ruth. He wasn't threatened that she'd been involved with women so extensively and so recently. He felt proud of her for having done exactly what she liked, and then for taking a sharp turn and doing something else, which meant: loving him.

Henry tried to do his artwork in their converted garage a few hours a day, but mostly he did childcare now. The art market had dried up; even corporations weren't buying sculptures for the big open plazas in front of their buildings, or at any rate, they weren't buying his. It was all slowing down, and he was on his way toward being a full-time father, though neither he nor Ruth ever admitted this. As a parent, Henry was more patient than she was, but he had patches of negligence that troubled her. Just yesterday she had come home from school to find Brant contentedly sucking on a kitchen sponge that had once been light blue but was so old and filthy that it was now the color of a bad bruise; all the ancient flavors of soap and chicken and apple juice flowed into his small, supple mouth.

Tonight, at their five-thirty dinner, which was when they always ate these days, Ruth sat at the small, grimy table nursing the baby, and the twins sat in their booster seats, and Henry tended to the microwave, which was lit up like a stage set as a frozen fried chicken Kidz Meal turned slowly and bubbled toward edibility. A second one waited on the counter for its moment in the sun. The whole kitchen of the small starter house smelled fried, and Henry popped opened a beer, which also bubbled and foamed. He leaned against the fridge, sending a few alphabet magnets and preschool-related notices cascading downward.

"Tell me something from the outside world," he said.

"That overrated place," said Ruth. "Okay. The drama teacher asked me to choreograph a dance for the big finale in the school play."

"That's great, Ruth."

"I'm not crazy about her, personally, but I'm glad to be part of it. It's a Greek play. *Lysistrata*. I think it's a comedy. They had actual laugh-out-loud comedies back then, which is so amazing. Do you know what it's about?"

"I know what it's about," said Ryan.

Henry and Ruth smiled over their son's head. "It's the one with the sex strike, right?" Henry said. "To end a war?"

"Right," said Ruth.

"So show us the dance. We all want to see it."

"The dance?"

"Have you started choreographing it yet?"

"I've just started thinking about it a little. It's supposed to be Greek, as I said, but the only Greek music I really know is the song from *Zorba the Greek*, with that instrument, the bouzouki. Remember that song, from a million years ago? My dad used to play the record all the time," she said.

"Yes," said Henry. "I do."

She had gotten an old cassette of the music that day from the school library, which still carried a small and arbitrary assortment located in a drawer in the back marked CASSETTES—which at this point in time might have been marked SCRIMSHAW. Ruth brought an old boom box into the kitchen, then unplugged one of the many appliances that grew from the wall, and turned it on.

Henry held the baby and Ruth stood in the middle of the yellow kitchen, waiting until the music started. She was mostly a standard gym teacher, but she'd always liked teaching the folk-dance elective. She knew what people thought of gym teachers; she knew the jokes they made. Ruth was a tall blond woman with broad shoulders and straight hair and excellent, square teeth. Now she let her arms go up over her head and did a couple of finger-snaps as she moved sidelong across the floor, the least Greek-looking person she knew, and the least dancerly. She wasn't overly graceful, just forceful, but she was never embarrassed in front of these people, her men.

"It'll probably go like this," she explained, and her husband and sons were fascinated. "The dance will come at the very end of the play, and it'll involve the whole cast coming onstage. Some happy thing takes place, and everything is resolved. I suppose the war ends, whatever war it is. I know the play was supposed to be a little risqué, and Fran Heller had to tone it down. But it's definitely upbeat at the end, with celebrating. I'm going to have the actors all join hands and do the *Zorba* dance around the stage, and then everybody's going to go into the aisles, I think. Fran said that audiences love it when you go into the aisles."

"*I* love it," said Henry. "It sounds great. Do you like this music, guys?" he asked the twins, and they both said yes, yes, they did.

As Ruth did her Greek dance around the small kitchen, she became aware that her bare feet were cold. The stick-on honeycomb tiles of the floor actually seemed freezing to her, and her first thought was that she needed socks. But socks wouldn't have helped, for the spell was circling the room, closing in on her in time to the bouzouki music. Its cold air went up her legs and then down along her arms. She hugged herself, chattering, but this seemed to Henry just to be part of the dance, and he smiled at her in enjoyment of her physical freedom and openness. No one else in the kitchen seemed cold, but she became colder and colder, and she moved at an accelerated clip, and as she did, one of the twins began to smack the surface of the table, keeping time with a flat and splayed hand.

Ruth thought: *How did I get here, among all these males? I am overrun by them.* Freezing under the force of the spell, she thought of how, later that night, she would get into bed beside her husband, and he would say, "The date begins!" Then he too would touch her breasts and her face and the rest of her. There would be a few minutes of this, and they always tried to hurry, so that at the very least Henry could have an orgasm. Ruth took longer, and she disliked being rushed, so sometimes she pretended she was done when she wasn't. She didn't even mind pretending, though it wasn't something she wanted to advertise, because Henry would have been so hurt. They were both aware of the narrow slip of time they had before a child would begin to scream, and before another child—or more than one—would appear beside them. A child would observe Henry and Ruth's entanglement, see their mother's head turned at such an odd angle, as though she'd fallen and broken her neck. "*Guernica*," her artist husband had once called the look. Or, if the blanket was pulled up above her feet, the boys might see her toes curled under. They had certainly seen a lot in their short time on earth.

But she couldn't bear the idea of getting into bed with Henry tonight, and of being touched by him, or anyone else. She realized now that she had been *overtouched*; she was like a computer with a thousand fingerprints on the screen. How did anyone tolerate being touched? she wondered. How did her friends stand it? It was terrible, all that touching.

The spell took hold of Ruth Winik, a girls' gym teacher at Elro, and as the frantic music reached its climax, she fell to the floor, no, was *thrown* to the floor, like just another one of her sons' toys, or a ceramic bowl that she'd dared not buy, because this is what would have happened to it. The spell had shattered *her*, made her indifferent. She knew she could no longer take part in those continual dates with Henry, and she felt dreadful about this. The boys seemed to represent the collateral damage of sex. *Look at them,* she thought. *I cannot take them anymore either.*

They all stared down at her in terror. "Oh Mama," moaned one of them. "Mama."

"My God, Ruth," said Henry, kneeling down and taking her cold hand. "Are you okay?"

The music had finished, and the old boom box clicked off.

"I can't," was what she said, looking up at him. Then she added, miserably, "Please don't ever ask me again."

12.

But the spell, though it had been so proficient, was nowhere near being finished. Under the arch of her canopy bed, in a house eight blocks away from Ruth Winik's house, Marissa Clayborn was overcome by it, too. Had she known this was happening to her, she would have been shocked, for she was not the kind of person to be frequently overcome by anything. Common colds had rarely felled Marissa Clayborn; sad movies tended to leave her tearless. Yet when the spell came for her, she was as susceptible as the rest of them.

Marissa had been working all year at Froze, the dessert place in the mall, which she sometimes referred to as "Cottage Cheese for Suckers." The product did have a curdlike, highly textured quality as it slowly emerged from a nozzle. It wasn't cottage cheese, but it wasn't officially yogurt either, or ice cream. No one really knew what it was, but three evenings a week Marissa sold it to customers, almost all women. Customers who admitted that the one thing they looked forward to in the evening was a cup of Froze that they could put a lid on and take home to their house, or else just eat right in the store, blunting the pointed peak with a grateful tongue. So many women who came to the store in the mall said they *craved* Froze; that was the word they used. Just the other evening, Ms. Cutler had been in, and she'd ordered a large cup with jimmies and coconut shreds and cookie crumbs, saying, "Now you know my guilty pleasure." Marissa watched as the guidance counselor went and sat on a stool, hunching over her little dish protectively, as if she were from some primitive culture and thought someone might take away her kill.

Marissa Clayborn was one of those girls who was not interested in sweet desserts, or in food of any kind, really. She'd never had an eating disorder, but had been thin and rangy as long as she could recall. She had been given the female lead in the school play virtually every year; one year, though, when she was thirteen, she'd contracted mono and couldn't even audition. That year, Paige Straub had been cast instead, but everyone quickly realized that it was a mistake, for Paige was like a robot in front of an audience. Marissa was known throughout the school for her talent, her speaking voice, her composure, and the way she looked. If her face wasn't completely beautiful, it was angular in a way that made it appear faceted, and her skin was closer to black than brown. There were twenty black kids in the grade at Elro, and she was friends with a few, though almost none of them had been in middle school with Marissa, when her most intense friendships had begun. She was good friends with a girl named Jade Stills, who was a drummer. ("African drumming?" Carrie's mother had asked with interest when Marissa and Jade went over to the Petitos'. "No, just *regular,*

Mom," Carrie had hurried to say, mortified.) Marissa's friends from middle school had remained her real crowd; they were the ones she truly knew, even if, she sometimes thought, they did not know her that well anymore.

During ninth grade, Marissa had sex with one boy, and then, over the summer before tenth grade, with another. She did not feel strongly about either of them at the time, but when they had showed an interest in her she had been curious to see what would happen. Quite a few other girls at Elro were sexually experienced too. There was Chloe Vincent, obviously, who had been sleeping with Max Holleran since last year, the two of them in love, though since their breakup he now loathed her. And there was sad-sack Becca Nilsson, who drank insanely and slept with anything. And there was talented Eva Scarpin, who'd had apparently enjoyable hookups with a couple of different senior boys and a man in his twenties. Eva wanted to be a designer, and she drew detailed pictures of models in gowns across the covers of her notebooks and even her textbooks. All of the women in the drawings had the same half-smile on their lips that Eva had. It was as if they all *knew* something. Jen Heplauer had had sex too, of course, but certainly no one wanted to follow her example. Laura Lonergan, another non-virgin, was an interesting emo girl who submitted short stories to the literary magazine *The New Deal* about a moody young girl involved with an older guy.

In a high school like Elro, people knew things about you; and by now a certain number of people had heard that Marissa Clayborn had slept with two boys. It had become common and acceptable in recent years to go far with a guy, or with different ones. If someone called you a slut it was probably one of your friends saying it as a joke, and you could justifiably reply, "Thank you." But as the first girl in her immediate group of friends to have hooked up in any capacity—and then as the first one to actually lose her virginity—Marissa had been expected to report back to the others in detail.

Willa Lang had been particularly interested in hearing a step-by-step account back at the end of ninth grade, and she'd asked Marissa a series of exhausting questions: *What was it like? Did it hurt? Did you like it? Did you love it? How would you rate it on a scale of one to ten?* They were up in Lucy Neels' room at the time, all of them piled onto the bed and the rug, the other girls looking worshipfully at Marissa, who had become their de facto spiritual and sexual leader.

She didn't know how to respond, for she didn't like the idea of disappointing them the way she had been disappointed. Ralph Devereux, age seventeen, the son of her parents' good friends, was a senior over in Deer Heights, his skin light brown and touched with old, faint acne scars. He and Marissa had known each other since they were small and their families had frequently gotten together for warm-weather backyard parties. Her mother would light citronella candles and the Clayborns and the Devereux would sit at the picnic table and on lawn chairs until it grew late and Mrs. Devereux reminded her husband that they had a drive ahead of them.

For a long time Ralph had just seemed mildly annoying, teasing Marissa about how thin she was, but once he hit fifteen she noticed that he had begun to lift weights, and his previously soft arms were different. Also, he teased her less, and when he arrived in the backyard with his family, he now hung back, sitting on the redwood glider by himself, watching everyone as if from a great distance. Then, when he was seventeen, he returned to the house without his family, just for the purpose of seeing fifteen-year-old Marissa, which pleased her, not because she particularly liked him, but because the way they might be with each other was potentially private, unrelated to anyone else in either family.

Their first evening together was unremarkable, filled with talk that went nowhere, and occasional jabs at each other about nothing. "So what's your situation?" he asked as he drove her home from a diner in his parents' car. He had eaten a fish fillet sandwich, onion rings, and a large square piece of seven-layer cake. She had had a Sprite.

"What do you mean?"

"In school."

"I'm in honors classes."

"I mean are you in a relationship?"

She almost laughed. She was fifteen, and relationships were what you heard about from other people. But as soon as Ralph said it, she didn't want to tell him anything about herself, to give it all up so quickly. "I might be," she said.

He was going off to Rutgers to study business next fall, and the third time he took Marissa out, he turned to her in the car and said, "I'm going to be working my balls off at my uncle's paint store this summer, and then I'm leaving for college in the fall. So if you want anything from me, you'd better get it now. Kitchen's closing."

"I don't want anything from you," she said.

"Okay, whatever, just letting you know," he said, and then he put an arm around her. Marissa didn't move away, but sat under the weight of it, trying to decide what she thought. It wasn't unpleasant, but it wasn't much of anything either. She would let him keep it there, she decided as he drove them to a defunct overpass and then parked. Ralph looked at her, raising his eyebrows, which was meant to be a question of some sort. She raised her eyebrows back, which, she supposed, was her answer.

He said, "You're cute," and put a finger on the tip of her nose. She didn't move away. Then he said, "Now, we're on the same page here, right?" and she said yes. "Okay," Ralph said. Then he nodded gravely and cast his eyes downward toward his fly, which he unzipped with a loud single syllable, revealing an anatomical part that was pretty much as Marissa expected, since she and her friends had been studying them online since seventh grade.

Marissa was shocked by his action, but abstractly interested. He motioned to her, and for some reason she slid toward him. They sat unmoving, and then he nodded again, encouragingly, and dipped his head in suggestion. She understood, and she followed, tentatively ducking down low and putting her mouth on his penis. But as soon as she did this, he put his hands on the back of her head and steered her as if she were a video game console. Within moments he was moving fast and repeating a word that sounded like *"jeez,"* or *"sheesh,"* or *"cheese,"* and she understood what this was all about; she picked up the nuances of this episode quickly, the same way she always memorized lines from a play or French verbs to conjugate. The end, the little explosion, was not too different from what she'd thought, and anything she could think about the way semen tasted had already been thought by someone else more descriptive, so she did not even try. After he cried an awful strangled cry—*"gaaa"*—he recovered quickly, zipped his pants, and said, "Who would have thought?" and then touched her nose again and drove her home. "I guess the kitchen hasn't officially closed yet," he said.

"Shut up, Ralph."

"Okay," he said cheerfully.

That night, she told a few friends, and they were quietly awed. "It just happened?" Willa said. "I mean, how did you know what he meant when he said that thing about being on the same page?" Marissa couldn't explain how she knew—"I just knew," she said cryptically—but Willa also had other questions for her. She wanted to know if Marissa felt very different, and Marissa realized the answer was no, which she supposed was good, because not feeling different allowed you to view sex as a normal part of life. As a reasonable activity that you could engage in with another person whenever you were both in the mood.

She got together with Ralph on two other evenings, and then he thought it was time to take it to the next step. She knew he thought this, because he said to her in a text, "lets be together longer 2nite."

When it happened, Marissa regarded the experience of going the distance with Ralph Devereux from somewhere high above, like a hawk circling the car. She couldn't decide what she thought about it, beyond the fact that it hurt far too much at first for something that was supposed to be natural. With their pants at their ankles and a condom safely snapped onto him, she felt it was a point of pride not to express pain here. He didn't know whether or not she was a virgin, and she didn't want him ever to know. That was her business. It was entirely possible that he had never done this before either; his style wasn't so suave. Willa, of course, begged to know everything again, which not only included the technical parts but also the feelings, the sensations. She wanted a subjective description of sex and a catalogue; she also wanted something poetic.

Marissa couldn't imagine what she was meant to say, but finally she just coolly said, "That's kind of private."

In the summer, Ralph Devereux started his job at his uncle's store and had no time to come over anymore, which was fine with her. But almost as if she gave off some signal that she was now more available, a boy named Dean Stanley who was a swimming counselor to little kids at the Y, where Marissa had a volunteer job stuffing envelopes, hung around her all the time before and after work, finally asking her to go out with him. "Why would I want to do that?" she asked, which threw him.

"Because you're nice?" he said hesitantly.

Dean, a white, extremely white, 6'5" swimmer with greenish-gold hair from pool water, was forthright in a way that was similar to Ralph; he seemed to enjoy being a young male and all it entailed, and why shouldn't he? Marissa would probably have enjoyed it too. When he kissed her with a muscley tongue at the multiplex, she let him, and when it progressed from there at the studio apartment he had borrowed from an older lifeguard, she didn't try to stop it, even though she didn't feel much of anything beyond the enjoyment once again of having an experience that was hers alone, and that she could master. Marissa knew that most people did not approach sex the way she did. Even Eva Scarpin, who had supposedly been to bed with her father's business partner, a handbag importer of *twenty-seven,* said it was "amazing," though Marissa knew instinctively not to ask Eva the kinds of questions Willa had asked *her,* like, *Did you feel a lot?* and, *Was it wonderful?*—because she was afraid she knew what the answers would be.

Once, years earlier, Marissa Clayborn's toddler brother had had to be rushed to the hospital after eating a dozen aspirins one by one. In the ambulance, their mother had said to him, "Conrad, didn't they taste bad?" And Conrad had said yes, yes, they had tasted horrible. "Then why did you keep eating them, sweetheart?" she asked. "Because," he explained as he cried, "I wanted to find one that tasted *good.*" A rationale that his sister definitely understood.

At age sixteen now, neither of the two boys she had been with so far had tasted good, so to speak. Truthfully, sex bothered her, because it was not nearly as intense as it was reported to be. She liked being in charge of herself, being responsible, being poker-faced and serious and precocious and skillful; she had conducted herself this way in all other areas, to real success, so why not in sex too? But sex didn't fill her with a warmth that she had never previously known. Melissa Clayborn was dexterous in sex, she didn't mind it, and, most of all, it was *hers.* This was how she felt about acting in plays too. Dean Stanley disappeared after the summer, and he occasionally texted her, but they had zero to say.

So there she was, leaning against the counter one winter night at Froze, reading the *Lysistrata* script, her mouth moving silently as she committed her lines to memory, when Jason Manousis walked in with his young son. Jason, of the legendary Jason Manousis and Cami Fennig high school pregnancy scandal of several years earlier. He had gotten Cami pregnant and they had immediately left school. Cami had had the baby, and Jason had wigged out about fatherhood and enlisted in the army and gone to Afghanistan, where he was blinded in one eye, and was sent back home looking like this.

"You're Jason Manousis," she said when he approached the counter. "You graduated from Elro with my sister," she added.

"I didn't graduate," he said.

"Well, I mean, you were in her class. Tara Clayborn."

"Yeah, Tara," he said without recognition. "How's she doing?"

"Good," said Marissa. "She's still out in Palo Alto. I'll tell her I saw you."

He nodded, and they both knew that she would say to her sister, *Remember Jason Manousis, who got that girl pregnant and then went off to Afghanistan? I saw him. God, it's extremely sad.* There was no way around this outcome, and Marissa already felt guilty about it, as if she had betrayed him in advance, though she had never meant to do so.

"Daddy, I want ice cream," his son announced.

"If he really wants ice cream," Marissa said, "I would take him somewhere else. He'll hate this."

"We're fine here," said Jason Manousis, but it was no surprise when, after he ordered a cup of original regular, the boy spit out the first mouthful with a vengeance, shocked.

"They add the tang chemically," Marissa explained to Jason. "I'm not supposed to say this, but the taste is basically fake. You're supposed to think it's got all these healthy live cultures in it, but it's got nothing." She insisted on giving him his money back, and then she sent them on their way, but not before hearing a little bit from him about his time in Afghanistan, where he had taken shrapnel to his eye.

The war was a disgusting waste of energy and time and life, he said to her. "No one can ever win it, and everyone knows that, but there we are, acting like we can," he said. "The war's intractable," he told Marissa. "Intractable," he repeated, as though he'd just discovered the word. "We had no choice at first, but now we do. We shouldn't be adding more troops like this. It's going nowhere. It's a rotten mistake. It all just sucks, it really does."

He spoke in a soft rush, as though they knew each other intimately, or as though the connection with her sister gave them a reason to be talking. Her sister Tara had barely known him; they'd been in the same grade years earlier, but Tara Clayborn had been an academically fast-tracked girl, and Jason Manousis had been a poor student with no interest in anything at the time but smoking weed, and his girlfriend Cami. When Jason got Cami pregnant, the two of them had headed off into life together like two people holding hands and jumping feet-first into a volcano. They soon became a cautionary tale about teenaged sexual activity: Jason and Cami and their mistake of a baby with that mistake of a name, Trivet.

Then Jason had gone to Afghanistan, and now here he was at the mall, no longer a joke, no longer just the duncey young father of a baby he couldn't even name right. He was a veteran of war with a face that could not be loved unless you also loved the person inside it. And who would do that? Jason and Cami were long broken up and now shared custody of their son, though Cami had apparently proved to be a less than ideal mother, going off on drinking benders from which she could not be retrieved for weeks.

Marissa ascertained that Jason Manousis was on disability, and that he hoped to find a job in electronics. "If you know anything . . ." he said, perfunctorily. His life, described by him without self-pity, seemed as unreal to Marissa as the life of a character in a play. It was as though he was speaking lines that weren't really true, except there in front of her was the evidence of his partly ruined face, and she couldn't imagine how to make sense of it. She whose worst problem was not having spending money or free time, for in addition to rehearsals, three evenings a week she had to go to her job. She whose parents were always anxious about money, warning their children that they had to keep their grades up and take part in an inhumane number of extracurricular activities in order to get college scholarships when the time came. There was no wiggle room in the Clayborn family, but of course, with Jason Manousis's life set into relief against her own, she remembered that hers wasn't a tragedy.

So began their friendship. She went to work at Froze, and at some point in the evening he wandered in to see her. Marissa noticed that people looked at Jason's facial disfigurement in a frank and shocked manner, as if when confronted by such a sight they forgot they were adults and reverted to some primitive child-state in which you were *allowed* to stare and make comments to yourself or your friends, which might be overheard by the man with the half-ruined face.

Jason and Triv returned to the store on Saturday night, when the mall was as crowded as it would ever be—not as crowded as it had been in the old days, but not a ghost town either. Kids from the high school roamed listlessly in packs; from behind the stainless-steel counter she saw Danny Fratangelo and Doug Zwern. Danny had once tried to copy from Marissa's history exam, and had been angry when she wouldn't move her hand to give him better access. "Why didn't you let me?" he'd complained after class, following her down the hall. "I would have let *you*," he said, which was an absurd idea. She didn't remember ever having any reason to speak to him after that. Doug Zwern was known at school as a notorious dealer of J Juice, that liquid drug that made people hyper and gave an animated edge to everything they saw. Occasionally people on J Juice lay back happily in bathtubs or pools and drowned; sometimes they didn't sleep for days. Mostly they had a good time. The J Juice trade was apparently lucrative lately; it was said that Doug Zwern was saving up to buy himself a car by the time he got his license. As Danny and Doug passed back and forth in front of Froze a few times, like a repeating loop of scenery out a car window in a low-budget movie, Marissa felt a current of wariness.

Triv said, "Dad, I don't want this."

"You don't have to eat it," his father said. "We are just visiting with our friend Marissa." Jason smiled a little, which pulled at the skin under his bad eye. He was challenging her, seeing whether two people who didn't know each other at all could be friends, could strike up something that had meaning. But *why* would they do that? What was the point? Marissa didn't know, and yet they stood there like friends, talking more about the war, and about Kunar Province, where he'd spent a lot of time, and about the other vets he had become friends with, a few who had been killed, and about fatherhood.

Then, as if the details of her life were remotely close in importance to his, he asked her about school, and being in the play. He emphasized that she should call him if she ever needed anything, and he asked her to enter his number into her own phone, which she did, feeling generous for doing it, for she was as likely to need his help as she was to need an academic boost from Danny

Fratangelo. But while Marissa couldn't imagine needing anything from Jason, she appreciated how kind he was. So much kinder than Ralph Devereux or Dean Stanley. Marissa had her script out because she'd been studying her lines again, and Jason said, "Actually, do you need help with that?"

To be polite, again, she said, "Yeah, I do. There's this one part where Lysistrata says an oath, and another woman has to repeat the lines back to her. You could help me with that. You could be the other woman, Calonicé."

"You don't have a guy's part for me?"

"This is the section I need to learn."

"Okay," he said. "I can deal." She handed him the script, closed her eyes, and back and forth they went. Her voice, as it always was when she had to read aloud, became full-throated and emphatic:

LYSISTRATA: Come, then, Lampito, and all of you, put your hands to the bowl; and do you, Calonicé, repeat in the name of all the solemn terms I am going to recite. Then you must all swear, and pledge yourselves by the same promises: I will have naught to do whether with lover or husband . . .

CALONICÉ: I will have naught to do whether with lover or husband . . .

LYSISTRATA: Albeit he come to me with strength and passion . . .

CALONICÉ: Albeit he come to me with strength and passion . . . Oh! Lysistrata, I cannot bear it!

LYSISTRATA: I will live at home in perfect chastity . . .

CALONICÉ: I will live at home in perfect chastity . . .

Danny Fratangelo and Doug Zwern entered the store as Marissa and Jason rehearsed the scene; they watched them from the doorway, then came up to the counter and stood in elaborate scrutiny of the board and all its choices. Marissa put the script down and turned to them.

"Hey," she said flatly.

"Hey, Marissa Clayborn," said Doug Zwern. "I didn't know you worked here."

"Yeah, I do."

"Do you get free ice cream?"

"It's not ice cream."

"No it's not," said Jason.

"Hey," said Doug Zwern. "You're Jason Manousis." Jason nodded. "You served. We're supposed to thank you, man. So thank you."

Jason paused. "You're welcome," he finally said. His son danced around his father, saying, "Can Marissa come out into the mall?"

Doug and Danny looked at father and son, and then, in curiosity, at Marissa. They clearly couldn't understand this scene—what someone like Marissa would be doing with the physically destroyed Jason Manousis. And they couldn't just leave it a mystery, they couldn't just thank him for his service to their country and go. They finally looked at each other in confusion and irritation, and then something built between them; the two boys twitched at each other, gearing up.

Danny Fratangelo said to Doug Zwern, "The school play is Greek. You ever learn Greek things, Doug? Like, mythology?"

Doug just looked at him. "I don't know where you're going with this, Danny."

"Just answer me."

"*Yes.*"

"Okay, good. Who's your favorite character from Greek mythology?"

"What? How would I know?"

"Pick one."

"Oedipus."

"He's not mythology. You know who mine is? Cyclops. Just saying," Danny added.

There was a long pause, and then Doug said, softly, "Cyclops. You *douche,*" but still he began to laugh, and Danny laughed quietly too. Marissa couldn't even stand to look at Jason during this. Instead she kept looking hard at Doug and Danny, those loser clowns, those *pricks.* Laughing and falling against each other, they left the store before anyone could say another word.

ate that night, after her parents and her siblings were asleep, Marissa Clayborn sat on her canopy bed with her laptop open before her. She went online and searched "Afghanistan" and "intractable," and the results tumbled in. Everyone apparently agreed with Jason Manousis's assessment of the war, or more to the point, he agreed with theirs. Despite the counterinsurgency, the allies, the whole nine yards, Afghanistan was impossible, a failure. She was embarrassed that she had known so little about the war up until now; that she lived in such a liberal, harmonious town but had thought about the subject so infrequently and lazily.

Marissa went onto Farrest to see who was there, for it calmed her down whenever she was agitated, as she was now. She soon became a hawk, flying around the top of the screen, where the green world gave way to who knew what. Below her was Willa Lang, pacing back and forth in a patch of forest.

"r u ok?" she asked Willa, even though she knew that this would only lead to a conversation about the breakup between Willa and Eli, which was all that Willa Lang could think about or talk about or write about.

"not really," Willa wrote, looking up at her with those cartoony ninja eyes. "i cant tell u how hard it is with me and eli. and my mom wont leave me alone, surprise surprise. i mean what does she think, i am going to have a breakdown???"

"well r u?"

"of course not. but its very very hard. i knew we wouldnt last, so I had to end it. but i still feel so much for him. i am sure u know what thats like."

For consistency's sake, and out of pride, Marissa could only tell Willa that yes, she understood. Then Marissa took off again above the trees into the pale green sky, and as she flew, she thought that soon she might have some kind of hookup with Jason Manousis. It was the right thing to do, and he would be grateful. They would go to his apartment where he lived alone, out on the turnpike, past Peppercorns and past the DVDs and Chinese Specialty Items store, and across the way from a shopping center that used to hold that Ethiopian restaurant that she and Jade Stills had been to once, and had gotten such a kick out of because they'd had to eat their meal entirely with their hands. They had tried to go back, but the restaurant had been gone; they hadn't patronized it enough. No one had, and they both felt bad. Marissa knew Jason's building; it had a sagging outdoor wooden stairway like a motel, and she pictured him standing with his key chain, squinting with his good eye and trying to find the key that fit the door. She hated the idea of him out there, struggling, being alone. She would go to bed with him in his apartment; it wouldn't matter that she wouldn't particularly like it. Kissing Jason Manousis would be a serious act of kindness; it would return him to his former self, restoring his eye, and his appearance, and his psyche.

Now, flying around Farrest, she spoke the line from the play: *I will have naught to do whether with lover or husband . . .*

It seemed all at once like the most exquisite and tantalizing line imaginable, and suddenly, as she kept flying, she entered a dense, cold patch of air, as though the atmosphere at the very top of Farrest had changed. Her bird-self and her girl-self were now both freezing. Was it the temperature in the bedroom or in Farrest? For a brief and slightly delirious moment, she could not tell the difference between the two worlds, or her two selves. A cold wind slapped Marissa along her shoulders and arms and face, and also struck the chest feathers of her hawk's body.

The spell grabbed her even as she flew, and she thought: *I don't want to have sex with him or anyone. I have never liked it enough. I have never felt about it the way I want to.* It had all been a cheat, a rip-off, and maybe someday it would start to get better when she found "the right person," as everyone said, but who wanted to stick around that long, doing that kind of thing? *Not* touching Jason, *not* doing anything with him or anyone else, she realized, would be far better. Like Willa, Marissa was suddenly done with that. Boys knew *nothing.* They wanted what they wanted. "Kitchen's closing," Ralph Devereux had said to her in his car, nervily.

The one she cared about—and it wasn't sexual—was Jason

Manousis. He was deformed, according to Danny Fratangelo and Doug Zwern; he was a monster, and he wasn't entitled to get a hot girl to hang around him. Jason had once been handsome, and Cami Fennig had liked him and had had sex with him, but the war in Afghanistan had ruined him.

It was all unspeakable, the war, its mutilation and destruction and death, and Marissa couldn't bear the sadness; she knew it could break her down. Suddenly, on top of not wanting to sleep with anyone, she wanted to do something to protest the war. If she wasn't going to be thought of as coolly sexual anymore, then at least let her be asexual for a *reason*. Just as she'd become sexual overnight—and now, suddenly, *not* sexual—so too would she be political. It was her prerogative. Ms. Heller talked to the cast all the time about the political ramifications of the play, trying to get the actors to think about them when preparing to go onstage. Marissa Clayborn logged out of Farrest now, and quickly went from being a hawk to being a girl. Fully spellbound, she tried to figure out how to bring together her new desire to have nothing to do with sex and her other new desire to protest the war.

She stood and walked to the foot of her bed, grabbing the footboard and yanking hard. The whole bed shifted with surprising ease.

Just before dawn, Jason Manousis's pickup truck pulled up on the street in front of the Clayborn house, and Marissa ducked quickly outside. Her family were all fairly deep sleepers, and she turned the knob of the front door carefully. Jason got out and stood beside his truck; in the streetlamp light his face appeared almost normal, just a little bit ridged and uneven, and he whispered to her, "This was a surprise."

"You said I could call."

"You're not doing this for me, I hope," he said.

"No," she said. "Not for you."

"Okay. Because it sounds pretty fucked up to me."

"Do you want me to explain it more?"

"No," he said. "Please don't. I'll change my mind." He looked toward her house and asked, "So where's this bed?"

She led him inside; he took off his shoes for silence purposes, but his tread was heavy, and every step made the objects in the living room china cabinet tremble and nearly sing. From down the hall, Marissa's little brother Conrad quietly called out, "Mom?" and Marissa poked her head into his bedroom and said, "Go back to sleep, Con."

"Is it morning?"

"No, not yet."

"I'm presenting my findings in Science today."

"That's good. Go back to sleep."

So her brother kept sleeping, and so did her little sister, Vivian, and so did their parents, all of the Clayborns slumbering for another hour, she hoped, at which point they would wake up and find out what she had done, the stand she had taken. Now Marissa and Jason went into her bedroom. She flipped on the light, revealing her white bed in all its cheesy glory. He absorbed the sight of the scrollwork on the curving headboard, the tall, tapering posts, and the white canopy, which hadn't been cleaned in who knew how long. The top of it was probably breaded with dust by now. When Marissa had first picked the bed out as a nine-year-old, her parents had been unhappy with her choice. The canopy was a dust-catcher, her mother had said, and the white posts were as shaky as newly planted baby trees. But Marissa, who was in all other ways no-nonsense, had wanted it, and her parents had relented. She'd loved the bed for a long time, and then of course she'd outgrown it and couldn't believe she'd ever wanted such a bed, but here it was, hers until college, so she thought she might as well finally put it to use.

"It's actually very lightweight," Marissa said, and Jason Manousis walked over and lifted the footboard, dragging the whole thing a couple of feet.

"So it is," he said. He inspected it, gently unscrewing one of the posts from its base. "I don't even need you for this," he said. "You can go do something else. I can take this apart in like five minutes."

Soon they were in his pickup with the disassembled bed in the back, and as they pulled away from the house, she saw the front porch light pop on, and the figure of someone in a bathrobe—her mother, her father; it was hard to tell which one, for they were sometimes interchangeable from a distance—opening the door and looking out in worry and confusion. Something had been different about her parents lately, Marissa had thought, but she didn't know what was the matter, for no one in her family talked about too much except: *Did you hand in your paper yet?* and, *I saw Janine Devereux at the Bakeleys. She said Ralph joined a fraternity at Rutgers.* The figure raised a hand now, saying *Stop,* or *What are you doing?* stunned by the sight of a departing daughter in a stranger's truck.

She had left her parents a note on the floor where her bed no longer was—a note in an envelope on that rectangle of bright, unfaded carpet—telling them in her good handwriting not to worry; she said she had something she needed to do, something political rather than theatrical or academic for a change, and that she would be fine. "You know that I have been the kind of person to make clearheaded decisions my entire life," she wrote. "Please trust me that that hasn't changed, even though I'm sure you'll find this out of character for me." Now the canopy, in the back of the truck, was like a sailboat that they were taking to the water for an early morning launch. The sun rose upon it, and all the ruffles shivered as one.

A while later, the first people to arrive at the school were the old cafeteria lady and her husband the janitor. It was gray outside, but there was no precipitation. The Evanses got out of their car slowly; Marissa watched as they approached her. There she lay in the bed, under the blankets wearing a hat and gloves and a down jacket. She just lay there completely still, patiently waiting for the day to start and the teachers and students to arrive and ask her what the hell was going on.

"This is a prank, I suppose?" said the janitor.

"Why do you think that?" asked his wife. "You always think you *know*."

"Don't start up again."

"It's not a prank," Marissa said. "It's a statement against the war in Afghanistan. I want to encourage women to stop sleeping with men until this war is brought to a close."

"You've got to be kidding," said Mrs. Evans, and she laughed.

"No." Marissa flushed in self-consciousness.

"I'm an old lady who lived in the South during segregation. I have seen political protest, and it doesn't look like this."

"No, it doesn't," said her husband, but his wife just ignored him.

"Well, I appreciate that," said Marissa. "But people have been confused about this war—the news basically tells you nothing, and the president is really vague—and if you think about the Taliban, and al-Qaeda, you get overwhelmed. But it's become a pointless mission, and it's killing soldiers at an alarming rate. I'm asking other women to stop sleeping with men until the war ends. I'm lying alone in my own bed as a symbol of the sex strike."

"And what do you hope to gain, exactly, being out here like this?" Mr. Evans asked.

"Attention," Marissa Clayborn said. Moments after the spell had hit her, she'd come up with the idea for the sex strike. At the very beginning of the play, she'd recalled, Lysistrata says a line about how whenever women were "summoned to meet for a matter of the last importance, they lie abed instead of coming." She thought she could do something with the idea of lying "abed"—turning it into something useful. Marissa had been going to rehearsals day upon day, and though *Lysistrata* was of course just the play she was currently starring in, it had a message that hadn't been lost on her. Men had been fighting wars forever; what was *wrong* with them? Why were they *like* this? It was so horrible, and all you could do was throw up your hands about it and tear out your hair. Unless, of course, you did something public. So she decided to stay in her bed, alone, symbolically boycotting sex.

As Marissa Clayborn cruised around online she'd read that there had been other sex strikes in the world in recent years. In

Kenya, a group of women had organized a sex strike for one week, as a way to call attention to rampant ethnic strife. Even the wife of the Kenyan prime minister had joined in, and though Marissa didn't know whether the attention to strife did anything to calm it, there was something exciting in the fact that it had been reported around the world.

The attention that Marissa's bed-in might receive would probably start small. Local news, a blog or two, but things could take off, and lots of women could join. There was no guarantee that this would get any attention at all, of course. She wasn't a coalition of Kenyan women; she wasn't Lysistrata. But anything was possible, and she had to see. The janitor turned away from the bed to make a phone call, and soon other people were standing around the bed too. The compact cars of teachers began to arrive, and school buses pulled up. Everyone milled around the parking lot as though at an open-air winter concert. "What's it doing there?" they asked each other, and when they found out, one of them said, "Maybe they'll close the school and give us a day off. We deserve it." Another girl exclaimed over how complicated Marissa was. "She is way beyond us in every way." "She is way beyond her time," said another girl, seriously. "I think she just wants attention," said a boy. "*Obviously,*" a girl practically spat at him.

When the principal arrived, the crowds parted to let him through. Solemnly he approached the side of the canopy bed. "Marissa," he said quietly, "it's Principal McCleary," as though she had been struck blind and couldn't tell who he was. "Did some other girls dare you to do this?" he asked.

"Of course not."

"Then is it performance art?"

"No," she said. "I am encouraging women to stop sleeping with men until the war in Afghanistan ends."

"Are you trying to get more people to come to the play next week?" he asked gently. "Did Ms. Heller ask you to do this? It's okay if she did; I'd just like to know."

"What? *No*," Marissa said. "This has nothing to do with Ms. Heller. Yes, the play gave me the idea, of course, Mr. McCleary, but it's more than that." But she wasn't sure how to explain it beyond stating the initial impulse, which had occurred to her all at once, with no preamble and no planning, right after she was hit by the spell.

On the other side of the bed, Dr. Bannerjee appeared; she and Mr. McCleary spoke to each other across Marissa. "Hello, Leanne," said the principal.

"Hello, Gavin."

"Did you get the notes I put under your office door yesterday?"

"Yes. You are prolific."

"You have no idea how prolific."

Marissa watched the scene with curiosity, her head going back and forth. The principal and the school psychologist almost seemed to have forgotten that Marissa was there. They might have continued their strange conversation for quite some time, so Marissa decided to speak.

"I'm not trying to cause problems," she said. For an extra moment, the two adults lingered in their private, encrypted world and then, at last, Dr. Bannerjee saw Marissa's questioning face and smiled.

"We know you're not, Marissa," she said. "I think we all understand that you're passionate about what you believe in. It's a little dramatic," she said. "But I guess so are all passions. Do you want to come on in and we can talk about it in my office?"

"No, thank you," said Marissa.

"How long were you planning on being out here?" Mr. McCleary asked. "Because I have to tell you, I'm pretty sure maintenance is going to cart this whole thing away within the hour. So I would say, you have about an hour left to be passionate and political."

"Oh," said the spellbound girl, who didn't really know what to say, for of course she hadn't planned the sex strike carefully, and hadn't arranged for contingencies, nor figured out a single, lucid sound bite. The strike was becoming real right in front of her; it was real because she'd created it, and now it was hers. The principal was saying something about how, of course, he couldn't prevent her from staying in her bed *at home,* but that she should think seriously about the academic consequences.

"You're an excellent student," he said. "I'd hate to see you miss class and have your grades affected."

Was that a threat? Maybe it was. She would take her chances, Marissa thought. She could do her work from her bed at home, the same way she had done back when she'd had mono. People came and went now, stopping gravely by her bedside like visitors in a hospital. Willa put her arms around Marissa. Jade Stills brought her a Danish and a latte, for Marissa had forgotten all about breakfast. Then Ms. Heller showed up and anxiously asked Marissa her plans for the performance.

"My plans?" said Marissa, who had neglected to think about this at all. How crazy was that? she thought.

"You are Lysistrata," the drama teacher reminded her. "I did not cast you in that part lightly. It's an honor to have that role. You can't let us down; that would be a calamity. Tell me you'll be at the dress rehearsal and the performance." Marissa didn't reply immediately. "*Swear an oath*," Ms. Heller said.

Her voice was a little too urgent, like always, but Marissa reluctantly agreed that she would stay in bed until the dress rehearsal, at which point she would leave it until after the performance, and then she would immediately return to the bed.

"Good," said Ms. Heller. "Thank you."

The drama teacher went back inside the school, and the two Lucys appeared, and so did Julie Zorn and Carrie Petito, everyone showing support even as they looked at her as if she had lost her mind. In the background, Marissa noticed a boy named Alex taking pictures with his cell phone. He was on the staff of the high school paper, *The Campobello Courier.* The paper usually only published sports pictures of athletes with long torsos and arms that reached up toward something just out of frame. Marissa was calmly talking to Willa and Carrie, when suddenly the whole bed was shoved forward as if it had been hit by something, and Marissa felt her head slam against the headboard. She looked up and saw Max Holleran and Dylan Maleska pushing the bed.

"Stop that!" Marissa shouted, but they wouldn't. Because the parking lot was icy, the bed moved in long and short bursts like a sleigh. The boys were laughing, but their faces were unfriendly. That asshole Doug Zwern joined them, all of them trying to push her bed around, making it move a foot or so at a time, stopping and starting.

"Stop!" Marissa heard Willa cry too, and Willa swung an arm

at Dylan and Max and Doug, who just ignored her. They would have overturned this bed if they could, tipping Marissa headfirst onto the parking lot. She wanted to say, *Look at yourselves,* and *Now you see why I have to do this.* Marissa reached backward and grabbed onto the headboard, holding on for dear life.

13.

Dory Lang didn't even notice the commotion when they first arrived at school, because she was still talking to Willa in the mirror over the passenger seat. "So you'll come home right after rehearsal?" she was saying. "And feel free to bring one of your friends to dinner."

"Why would I bring someone home to dinner?" Willa said irritably. "I've got homework and everything. God, Mom, you think I'm so upset that I can't be on my own for two minutes. Don't you remember? *I* broke up with *him*."

"Leave her alone, Dory," Robby murmured from the wheel, but he was an outsider in this drama. In recent days, he'd retreated increasingly into himself, puttering aimlessly and eating more than usual. He had begun to develop a sad middle-aged gut, which he'd never had before in his life. It looked strange on his long, thin body, as if he were smuggling something across a border.

Robby seemed to have very little awareness of Willa's despair over her recent breakup with Eli. He knew that it was over between them, but the specifics of his teenaged daughter's unhappiness were lost on him. Much was lost on Dory as well, despite her efforts to understand. Since Willa had fallen under the spell and told Eli that they were done, she did not want to talk. Not at all. It was worse than when she and Eli were in love. It didn't matter that Willa had been the one to break up with him; teenaged breakups practically killed both parties involved. Dory had only even learned about it when Fran Heller had told her at school on the Monday after it happened. Over that weekend, Willa had merely seemed moodier than usual, but she still hadn't told her mother anything.

"Your daughter's a heartbreaker," Fran had said in the teachers' room with a shake of her head.

"What do you mean?"

"Willa called it off," said Fran. "It's over, just like that. She stormed out of our house on Saturday night. He's pretty crushed, poor kid."

"Are you positive? It doesn't sound like her," Dory said. She knew of parents who suddenly found out that their kids were taking meth, their kids were pregnant, their kids were in trouble, and she'd always thought that she would be the kind of parent who would know what was going on, but she knew now that she would have known nothing; that she did know nothing. Even Carrie Petito's home-pierced navel had festered for a long time before her parents had learned about it. The paradox was that so much information was out there and available to everyone now. You could learn everything about any topic imaginable, and you could stuff a paper for school with all the details that you could find, but you could not learn that Willa Lang had broken up with Eli Heller, until his mother happened to let you know.

The night after she'd heard the news, Dory cornered Willa at home, outside the upstairs bathroom; Willa nodded wearily and said yes, it was true, it was over between them, but she didn't want to discuss it. "Are you sure?" Dory asked. "I just mean, isn't there anything Dad or I can do to help you?" Willa regarded her with an expression of exaggerated incredulity.

They lived in a time in which it was tremendously difficult, as parents, to let children endure any pain. If you sensed their despair, you took it on as if it were your own. You let it ruin you, imagining that they, somehow, would be spared. They would live, and thrive, while you would die of their transferred misery. Lately, more than ever at the high school, Dory received e-mails from mothers when their children were having difficulties. They wrote:

> Dear Ms. Lang,
>
> Hello. I am Kevin Derringer's mom. Though I know in his essay he refers repeatedly to the author of *To Kill a Mockingbird* as "Mr." Lee, Kevin did pay attention in class. Plus, it's worth mentioning that he had blepharitis (an eyelid infection) the night before it was due, and that might have adversely affected his work.
>
> Sincerely,
> Marly Derringer

Parents stepped in whenever they could, because they could not bear to see their children suffer. Dory Lang knew she was no different. But Willa wouldn't let her in; in the hallway of the house, she had walked past Dory to the bathroom, and run the water for a long time, and probably cried, but Dory couldn't do anything. "Would you look at that," Robby said now as their car pulled into the parking lot. Willa and Dory turned away from their mirror stare-off and looked.

A canopy bed was wedged sideways across two spaces. It was a girl's bed, big and white. The canopy was arched and scalloped, and various people stood around it, taking pictures with their cell phones. A van from News 8 was parked near the bed, and a cameraman was trying to find the best angle to shoot from. None of the Langs understood what was happening. Willa's irritated gloom gave way to interest, and she said suddenly, "It's *Marissa*."

"It is?"

"Yes, that's her bed," said Willa, who had lain across the foot of her friend's bed for many hours over the years and knew it well. "I'm positive, Mom. Dad, let me out, let me out," she said, and Robby stopped the car and she unbelted herself and ran. Robby circled the lot, getting as close as he could, and they all saw that yes, it was Marissa Clayborn under the covers of the bed. Teachers and students surrounded her as if they were all at some sort of carnival and she was a centerpiece—say, the woman in a dunking booth.

"What do you think this is?" Robby asked.

They both agreed that they had no idea.

Marissa would not go back to school, she had apparently announced. "I'm going to stay in this bed, even if it's moved from the school grounds, which I have been told it soon will be," she told the reporter from News 8. "I will stay in my bed alone for as long as it takes, day and night. I'd like to be a symbol, and I'd like to encourage all other women to lie alone in their own beds, so to speak—to turn down sex with men until the war in Afghanistan is over. I am well aware that this will be considered a political stunt. But I'll do whatever it takes. No more sex," she said. "No more Lioness on the Cheese Grater."

"What?" said the reporter. "What are you talking about?"

Dory had seen politically active kids before, over her years at the school. They wore armbands whenever it was called for, and once in a while they even lay down on their backs in the road. Some days at the entrance to the school, these same kids sold slices of a damp marble pound cake that a couple of girls had baked; other days they sold T-shirts. She used to give money to the kids who were protesting the war in Iraq; every day they sat there before classes started, and she thought they'd be there as long as the war went on. But one morning the folding table was gone, and a few days after that, the table was back, but with different students behind it. The two girls in the folding chairs wore cheerleading sweaters and skirts; one of the girls was pointy-nosed, haughty. There was a new sign up announcing that tickets were "onsale" for the Booster Gurlz Pep Rally. "Please help our cause," the girls called when anyone walked by.

Back inside the school now, the hallways were loud with chatter. Dory Lang swung into the teachers' room, Robby right behind her. Several teachers were already in there discussing Marissa and her bed. "Yeah, I get that she's protesting the war in Afghanistan," Mandelbaum was saying hotly to Abby Means, "and I agree that we should probably pull out all our troops as fast as we can and just focus on eliminating terrorists. But as far as I've heard, she has never once shown a political side. Why now, all of a sudden? It's a legitimate question."

"Very few of them are political," said Bev Cutler.

"That isn't true," Robby put in. "Some are political online. I've got a couple of environmentalists in my class. They don't do it in person in the way we're used to. They have their blogs, and their urgent one-line messages, and they send mass e-mails. They organize."

"I just don't want her to lose her concentration," said Fran Heller, pacing. "I went out there and got her to promise that she will be at the dress rehearsal and the performance; I told her that one of her friends could replace her in the bed when she came to the theater. That some other girl could be a 'bed proxy.' I made it sound like it was a real phrase. Anyway, all that matters is that she agreed she'd be there. The play will go on."

"I heard," said Abby Means, "that the actor who played Sherlock Holmes really began to believe he was Sherlock Holmes. He wore those clothes even off set. They say that he eventually went mad."

There was silence; no one knew quite what to say, as usual, to Abby. Marissa Clayborn was not mentally ill. She was stronger and more clearheaded than almost all of the kids at school. The teachers dispersed; Dory went and stood before her first-period class, looking at their needy faces. Most of them were excited about Marissa and her bed. One girl said that it was clear that Marissa was angering the boys; a few of them had tried to push the bed around, the girl said, until the teachers had broken it up and made them go inside. There was definitely tension between people lately, observed the girl who juggled oranges and recited the Declaration of Independence on Friday nights at Just Chillin'. She added that, at this rate, by the end of the year no one would be involved with anyone. "We're going to be *nuns*," she said. Jen Heplauer, who had been dozing in the back of the room, her chin lowering then snapping up, suddenly awoke and nodded in agreement.

In the middle of class a boy said, *"Look,"* and they watched from the window as four men in maintenance uniforms gently lifted the bed, with Marissa still in it, and began to carry it off school grounds. She would continue her bed strike in her own bedroom; she would tell everyone that it didn't matter where the bed was, just as long as she was in it and other people knew about it. Marissa looked up toward the window as the bed went by, and though it was hard to tell for sure, it seemed to Dory Lang as if she was making eye contact with her alone.

Occasionally, during the remaining hours of the school day, Dory thought about how Marissa Clayborn had looked at her from the moving bed. Marissa knew nothing of the Langs' sexual impasse, of course. But Dory kept thinking about it. Between classes, she texted Leanne and asked her if she wanted to go to Peppercorns at the end of the day. "yes please," Leanne wrote back. So there they were in the darkened interior at three thirty. It was probably too early to drink, but this was the hour of their liberation.

At the booth in the quiet, dead restaurant, the waitress dropped a couple of tabletlike menus. Soon the two women, their faces still cold and slapped-looking, gratefully swiped rounds of bread through the warm glue of a spinach-artichoke dip. "What a strange thing it was today, that bed," said Leanne.

"But I almost understand it," said Dory. "It's dramatic more than political. It shakes everything up. I like that idea."

"Oh, you and destroying things. That's your theme, right?"

"What?"

"You said something about it at the potluck."

"Right," said Dory, "I did say that." She looked down at her hands, her pioneer's hands. "I have the nicest husband in the world," she said, "and I've wrecked things. I've made him unhappy."

"This was what you were talking about?" asked Leanne.

"Yeah. I basically gave up on the whole sleeping-together thing. I just stopped it. It's been a while."

"Oh. I'm sorry," said Leanne. "I wish I'd asked you more about it. I wish I hadn't been so self-absorbed that night. But Gavin showed up with his wife, and since then it's all been so strange. The car dealer keeps driving in circles around my condo. See? I'm still self-absorbed."

"No," said Dory. "You're a good friend. I wasn't ready to say anything at the time, really. I had no idea it was going to become a permanent thing. I didn't know what I was doing."

"Here's my question to you," Leanne said, putting down her water glass. "Is the choice in life to either have some overly intense and basically impractical relationships with men or else to settle down? Are those our only options? And if so, how depressing is that?"

What was there to tell her? Yes, Leanne, you can be either excited or bored. And you can choose excited, but even so, if you decide to settle down with one of the people who excites you, for a while it will be like living inside a magical cupboard together, and then one day you will realize that the excitement you used to feel has diminished. And then, another day, that it is gone, and your heart will break.

"It can be depressing," Dory agreed. "But you—you should do exactly what you want, Leanne. You should sleep with whoever you like."

"One day it'll all look bad, Dory. Me and my different men. People will say things about me."

"Who cares what they say?" said Dory. "Really. You need to just live."

"I guess I can't," Leanne said.

While they'd been talking, a wave of people had arrived at the restaurant: a group of men in jackets and ties beneath opened parkas, fresh from work. The hostess moved the men to a table, and behind them in the doorway Bev Cutler and Ruth Winik were revealed, standing with Abby Means, who held herself slightly apart. She had never come here with any of them before.

Dory didn't want the other women to see her and Leanne; this wasn't meant to be a group conversation, so she tipped her head away even from her good friend Bev. The hostess marched the three women to a table in a different section, but Abby saw Dory and Leanne and spun around and waved, and the three women in their dripping winter coats headed for the booth. Someone said to pull up a chair; it might have been Dory, or it might have been Leanne, and it was spoken in an unconvincing voice. It would have been rude not to invite them. It also seemed as if, given the events of the day, and the quest for midafternoon alcohol, that there was an implied theme to these separate visits to Peppercorns.

"We'll just sit for a second," Bev said. It was decided that the three women would have a drink with the two, and then they would take their own table for dinner.

Everyone, it was quickly determined, could relate in some way to Marissa Clayborn's bed refusal. Bev said that maybe it was only because it was winter, and the days were short and the nights were long, and during this time of year it was easy to take full measure of where your life had brought you at this point in time—but oh, she felt unhappy about what had happened between her and Ed.

"What happened?" Ruth asked. "I don't think I know about this."

So Bev told them what had happened, and she said that Ed had always had a pirate's cruelty in him, and she'd known it was there, but he'd also had other, dear qualities that her friends couldn't see. She'd felt that she could never complain about him, because she had made her bargain. "It was as if, in the early days," she said, "he was doing battle with money, and then he'd come home and we'd both be all hopped up about it. I participated in that. I lived in that house. I still live there. And the money was made the way it was made, and now the world's in trouble, and I suppose my marriage is too."

She told them that for the past six weeks or so, since she'd confronted him, Ed literally no longer spoke to her. They now occupied separate wings of the house. They took meals at different times too. She had no idea what he was thinking, and she told them that she was so lonely that all she could think about was her loneliness, or food. She'd been eating Froze more than usual, driving to the mall sometimes twice a day. Ed didn't say goodbye when he left for the city in the morning, but moved past her showily, in sharp and ungiving profile. "And I keep thinking," Bev said, "how did this happen? For a long time, it wasn't like this."

"You love someone," said Ruth Winik, "but it changes over time. Hormones kick in, or maybe it's that they kick out. We're all held hostage by what's in our bloodstream."

"You think that's what it is?" Dory asked. "Just that?"

"Why, what else?" said Ruth.

"Oh, what isn't it? It's everything," Dory said. "The minute you realize it's no longer exactly the way it used to be, from then on it's even more different." Her voice sounded despairing, and they asked her to tell them what she meant. So she told them about that night in bed in December, when she had felt the need to make up an excuse to Robby about her conference with Jen Heplauer and her mother, and how it had all flowered from there. She described the way celibacy had become a refuge, a revenge, an obscure, perhaps female, necessity.

Around them in the restaurant came laughter and the sounds of dishes and silver. "We should go get our table," Bev said, but she didn't get up to leave, and no one else did either.

"Just the other day," said Leanne, "I heard two women talking in Greens and Grains, and one of them actually said, 'I would pay someone to have sex with my husband.' They were *done* with sex, they told each other, and they laughed a little. They weren't even old at all. But here's the kicker. Another woman was wheeling her cart past at that moment, and she heard them too, and said, 'Amen.'"

"I saw a really old movie on TV once," Bev said, "in which Lionel Barrymore, who plays the grandfather of a little boy, finds a way to trick Death into climbing an apple tree. And as long as Death is up in the tree, then no one in the world can die. Not even a little fly."

"So what happens?" Ruth asked.

"Death is apparently more cunning than humans are. Death does his own trick. The little boy, whose name is Pud—"

"Who would name a little boy Pud?" asked Leanne.

"Who would name a little boy Trivet?" said Ruth.

"—is convinced by Death to climb the apple tree too," Bev said. "And he goes too high, and he falls and breaks his back. He's lying there crying and in pain, and all Lionel Barrymore wants is for Pud to die. But of course he can't, because Death is still up the tree. So Lionel Barrymore has to agree to let Death come down from the tree, and then the little boy dies. So Death takes Lionel Barrymore too, but don't worry, the boy and his grandfather go up to heaven, where the rest of the family   who already died at the beginning of the movie—is waiting for them."

"So you think that'll happen here?" said Dory. "Sex will come down from its tree?"

The gym teacher took a drink. "I don't know how to make it do that for me," she said. "And Henry is really disappointed in me. Not angry, he says, disappointed, but I know he's angry too. He says he wonders if I really am a lesbian after all. If that's still what I want. And yeah, I get attractions, but I am not thinking about women. Seriously, I just want to be alone."

"When you're young," Dory said, "sex is this startling new thing. And it gets easy, and you do it as much as you want. And then if you want to have a family, you don't have to think about birth control, and it's like this big, shared project. I loved that time," she said.

They were all thoughtful and sad. It was decided that Bev, Ruth, and Abby would stay at the table and they'd all order some dinner together. When the waitress reappeared at the booth, inno-cent with her skirt and white blouse and little pad, they rattled off the names of entrées and side dishes, and then she retreated.

"I still have these generic moments of longing occasionally," Bev said. "I don't know if I'm alone in that."

"No, no, you're not. I've lost interest in my boyfriend too," said Abby, "but I look at porn every once in a while these days. Only on my phone, though; not on the computer, because he might see it there." She took out her cell phone, and then they all leaned in around the booth in the darkness, the candle in the middle giving the gallery of images the stuttering quality of a silent movie. They sat in contemplation as Abby Means scrolled through the slide show.

Dory thought of Robby's body when he was young, the first time he'd taken off his clothes for her. She thought of how, one time, they had kissed and kissed in a movie theater in their twen-ties, back when screens were single, not multiple, and were as big and silky and open as beds.

"Perimenopause did me in," Bev said. "I couldn't remember how to fall asleep at night. And during the day I got really hungry. I needed chips, fried things, salt. And milk chocolate, not heart-healthy dark chocolate. My body changed, I just lost control of it, and then Ed turned against me and I was humiliated. I miss what we used to do!" she said with a cry. "I miss it so much. What we did, and who I was. How I felt. I didn't feel that shame. I liked what we did."

"Maybe sex doesn't even belong to us anymore," Dory said. "It belongs mostly to the kids, and we're just hanging around too long." But sex, for the kids, she'd noticed, was different from how it had been for her at their age. For the kids now it was part of the everyday landscape, and they had grown used to it. Sex held great interest for them, but so did everything else fast, transmittable. They needed to see what was happening, to find out what came next, or what came simultaneously. Everyone seemed to have abbreviated focus, and Dory wondered: How could you make love if you couldn't pay attention?

The women all looked again at the tiny screen of Abby's cell phone, where a man's penis had now gotten out of his pants like a tiger escaping a zoo. Their faces adopted studious expressions. They were mesmerized by the ferocity of these random sexual images—a quality that they no longer had in their lives but still longed for—and no one realized that the waitress had returned with two big trays of steaming items.

"Here you go, ladies," she said. "I hope you have an appetite."

They all pulled back quickly, except Abby, who kept looking, not at all self-conscious. Leanne reached over calmly and shut off Abby's phone for her, and the very last image, all muscle and pore and hair and lip and breast and testicle, disappeared into a single point of skin-colored light, and was then snuffed out like a star.

I n the parking lot after dinner, the purplish-white sodium lights snapped and buzzed in the cold air, and everyone said goodnight, see you tomorrow, I am so glad we met up, it turns out I needed this, I think we all did. Dory walked to her cold car and sat for a moment. She looked over toward the turnpike and the raft of stores that lined it, and their lit-up, chaotic signs. Beside Peppercorns was the windowless building with its offering of DVDs and

Chinese Specialty Items. Gavin McCleary's formerly unwell wife, Wendy, had rhapsodically told of going in there and being given a dose of autumn lotus root powder. She was now up and about; she was now a member of the living.

Perhaps it was because Dory had been drinking, though she wasn't at all drunk, just a little loosely strung; or because she was full of food and had talked and talked. Perhaps it was because she was entirely out of ideas, but Dory Lang got out of her car and stood in the parking lot again. The other women's cars were already gone.

It would make an amusing story to tell Leanne tomorrow, she thought as she walked toward the windowless store, but she wasn't going in there for the anecdote. She walked into the store with a galloping step at first, an ironic gait, but soon she slowed. The ominous DVDs and specialty items store did seem to be, as Wendy had said, actually two stores in one; up front was the DVD part, where a young white guy in a feed cap sat behind the counter eating dinner from a Styrofoam box. High on a wall, an action movie played on an old Panasonic. Two men stood flipping through the thin collection of DVDs, but Dory thought they barely seemed to be paying attention. They were waiting for something; and then she realized, oh, maybe they were waiting for her to leave. The man behind the counter inclined his head.

"Help you?" he asked.

"Chinese. Herbs," whispered Dory, awkwardly.

He nodded. "Go on through."

She walked across the room and through another doorway. On one wall was a laminated reflexology chart; on another were views of Asian sunsets. The shelves lining the far wall held bottles of powders and herbs along with some unrelated and unconnected items: an electric shaver in its dusty box, a dusty blender not in its box, and jars of hoisin sauce and cold cream side by side, just as Wendy McCleary had described. Dory felt a need to flee, but still she allowed herself to move deeper into the store. In the back room, by a small space heater that glowed at her feet, the old Chinese woman pharmacist sat at a table with powder and a scoop.

"Hello," Dory said. "A friend came here a while ago? She said you helped her?"

The woman nodded, accepting this assessment.

"I have a different problem from her," Dory said, and she was dying here, dying. She had revealed herself tonight at dinner, and now she was doing it again before a stranger. "I'm just at a point in my life," she said to the old woman, who looked at her impassively, "at which I've lost the ability to be . . ." Her voice faded. "I guess, intimate," she finally said.

"Desire," the pharmacist articulated.

"Right." Then, with the abruptness and intensity of a junkie, she asked, "Do you have something?"

The woman nodded. Probably other women had come in, sad and confused by what had happened to them. Now a powder was weighed and measured; Dory was weighed as well. The bill came to thirty-six dollars for a single pill, and she was shocked by the price but mutely paid. The pharmacist handed her a glassine envelope with one capsule of ash-gray powder inside.

"Is your husband home?" she asked Dory.

"Tonight? Yes."

"Take this now and go there."

"How long will it take?"

"Right away, if it is going to work," said the old woman. "No guarantees. You know," she added, "you need the mind too."

"Pardon?"

"You need to want it."

"Oh. Well, I do," said Dory.

A paper cup of warmish water was produced, and Dory Lang swallowed the pill. She walked back into the DVD room, which was very dim now, almost dark, and where, in a corner, partly blocked by a standing carousel of DVDs, two young women were softly talking with two men. One woman's face was spackled with circusy makeup. Dory realized that Wendy McCleary could be right, and the DVDs were probably just a front, or else a minor business compared with whatever else was going on here. The Chinese pharmacy was legitimate, but this was not. One of the men stood up after the made-up woman motioned that he should follow her through a side door. Dory saw only the back of his head, the baldness with the clipped hair around the edges; and then, for just a moment, she heard his voice, and she thought: God, is that Ed Cutler? Or maybe it was someone else. The man had gone into that room, and she couldn't follow him in and find out. Even if it was Ed, she couldn't hate him. What was he supposed to do? What were any of them supposed to do?

Dory quickly left the store, and the cold air in the parking lot was a relief now. The capsule had begun to make her feel hot-faced, or was that just the mortification and the shock of what she'd just seen, or had thought she'd seen? No, it wasn't Ed, she decided. Yes, it was, she thought a second later. No, it wasn't. It really wasn't; a lot of men looked like that. Dory wondered if she should even be driving now; she got into the car and was immediately nauseated, but still she drove along the turnpike, and then through streets on which slush had collected and been pushed to the sides.

The lights were all on inside the house. She stepped in with wet feet and walked on through, tracking in water, looking for Robby. She wanted to tell him she was so sorry, and to see his solemn face and his brainy-man eyeglasses and his long, slender hands, and remember all over that this was him, someone she had always been attracted to. "Robby?" she called.

He appeared in the doorway of the den, where he'd been napping on the couch. His eyeglasses were atilt. "Hi," he said.

"Hi."

Dory didn't know what the principal's wife had been given when she came into the back of that store, but it had worked for her. Maybe all the women who came in were given the same thing: pencil shavings and breadcrumbs. Dirt from beneath someone's fingernails and mineral powder makeup. Anything that would make a woman feel she'd been given a second chance, whether she had chronic fatigue syndrome or loss of desire or some more obscure condition. The cure had worked for Wendy McCleary, but all Dory felt now was sick—sick and far away from touching and love.

The pharmacist had said that Dory would have to want it to work, but no, apparently she didn't want it to work at all. She still didn't want to lie down with Robby, and she had no idea of what to do next. Maybe Dory would become one of those women who sometimes remembered what had once been, and couldn't care less, and was *fine* with it, or one who kept the pain of it from herself with a joke, with a hand on the hip and a roll of the eye, as if to suggest that all women understood and all women would agree: Sex was a thing of the past, and frankly, good riddance.

"Anything new here?" Dory asked Robby.

"Nah. Willa's working on that history outline. I'm reading."

"Anything good?"

"No, just crap. I don't really have the concentration."

She could have said: Come upstairs. But she didn't say it, and he went back to the den, where he would spend the night. Dory climbed the stairs, going past her daughter's room with its closed door and muted stir of electronic life, and she entered her own bedroom and went straight through into the bathroom and closed the door, then knelt down in front of the toilet. Outside, past the edge of the neighborhood, and out past the turnpike, the state of New Jersey stood tall and short, with all its industrial parks and water towers and tire stores and nail salons and struggling restaurants and homes. In her own home, Dory Lang vomited up the ashy root powder she had recently swallowed. Maybe the powder had actually helped other women, but it couldn't help her. She remained where she was, unmoved. He wasn't there to hold her hair off her face, or to lean against, or to walk her back to bed, where they both belonged.

Part | Three

14.

On the evening of the dress rehearsal of *Lysistrata*, Lucy Stupak ran like a winged messenger down the long, polished corridor of the high school. She passed the empty classrooms, and the showcase with its old photos of theatrical productions, and the loving cup once presented to the cast and crew of a play performed in 1969. Some of those thespians and tech people had probably gone to Vietnam, and maybe a couple of them had been killed. Maybe quite a few were dead by now from other causes. Lucy Stupak, her whole life invested in the world of this school, skidded past the red pool of reflected light from the exit sign and took a hard right, heading toward the vacuum-shut doors of the auditorium, already calling the drama teacher's name, shouting it in a voice both self-important and afraid.

As later described, Lucy pushed through the doors and ran down the sloping aisle, crying, "Ms. Heller, are you here? Somebody find Ms. Heller!" In the distance lay the Acropolis, magnificent under the placid blue and white spots. The drama teacher appeared with hammer in hand; she wore a work shirt and a do-rag. She shielded her eyes so she could see out into the audience, and she said, "Who's that?"

"It's me. Lucy Stupak."

"Yes, Lucy. What's the emergency?"

Ms. Heller walked forward onto the apron of the stage. She seemed to take a long breath and stood up straighter, as if preparing herself for what this girl had to say to her, which was: "Marissa Clayborn said to tell you she can't come."

"What do you mean she can't come?"

"She said she can't."

"Of course she can," said Fran Heller. She squinted at her watch. "Dress rehearsal is in an hour. We got her chiton back from the dry cleaner's. In her bed in the parking lot the other day she promised me she would be here for the dress rehearsal. And then again tomorrow night for the performance."

"I know, Ms. Heller. But she told me just *now* that she changed her mind. See, she's been discussing it online. A few different women posted on Marissa's wall and offered all this encouragement, and told her she should stay in the bed. So Marissa decided that she can't just 'come and go' whenever she pleases. That's not how you do a sex strike."

"Oh it's not?" said Fran Heller. "I'll have to remember that next time. I have never, in all my years of directing high school plays, had a lead actor who missed the dress rehearsal."

Lucy Stupak paused, then she said, "Listen to me, Ms. H. Marissa says she's really, really sorry to let you down—you and everybody else who's been working so hard. The thing is, she's not going to do the play at *all*. She's not going to be Lysistrata. She thinks it's more important that she does it in real life."

The drama teacher dropped her hammer, showily. *Pa-thunk.* Then, saying nothing, she went to get her coat, and left the building, followed by a couple of very faithful members of cast and crew. Four abreast, they marched to the Clayborn house around the corner. Marissa was propped up against some pillows in her canopy bed, eating dinner on a tray and doing her French homework. Her mother had brokered a deal with the school that allowed Marissa to protest the war and still keep up her grades. The administration clearly thought that she would fold pretty soon anyway, but even if she didn't, it behooved the school to accommodate her, as she was one of their strongest students and one of their best candidates for a top college. At first there was some concern that other kids would subsequently insist on skipping school too, in the name of this political cause or even others, but this didn't happen. Everyone was always so worried about their own academic records, and most of them knew that they couldn't possibly keep up the way Marissa could.

The cameras from a couple of local news stations, which had gamely hung around for the first day, had retreated. There was a more pressing story having to do with a potentially toxic landfill over near Morristown. But Alex, the reporter from *The Campobello Courier*, hadn't left. He had been pursuing the story, and Marissa had granted him an interview that had taken place over much of the afternoon today and into the evening. He sat on a chair quietly beside her bed now, blogging for the *Courier*'s website and eating a plate of salmon and couscous that Mrs. Clayborn had kindly put together for him. The drama teacher and the drama henchgirls appeared in the bedroom, and all of them began to implore Marissa to reconsider.

"You swore an *oath*," Ms. Heller reminded her, but Marissa remained resolute in her decision not to leave the bed at all. Her mother showed the theater people to the door.

Back at the school, the girls in the play had set up a large-scale, open dressing room in the cafeteria. Some of their mothers were there tonight to help out, including Dory Lang, who after some wheedling had been allowed by Willa to come. Right now none of the mothers knew quite what to do. Some had pins in their mouths, hemming chitons, but most of them, like Dory, were just waiting for Fran Heller to return so they could find out what was going to happen now. The boys, who had been down the hall in the music room with their fathers, joined the girls in the cafeteria. Everyone stood around, feverishly discussing the Marissa Clayborn problem. Some of them said that it wasn't possible to perform the play without Marissa.

"The whole thing should just be canceled," Jeremy Stegner said to the room, and there were nods and syllables of agreement.

Now the drama teacher entered the cafeteria with a grim expression, and they all knew that she had been unable to lure Marissa Clayborn up from her bed. "Ms. Heller," said Jeremy, stepping forward into the center of the room that still smelled from whatever oil had been used to cook lunch. "We were talking, and we thought that, if Marissa can't do it, then the show should be canceled. People will understand."

"*No*," said Fran Heller. "That is not acceptable." She ran her hands through her hair. "We have a responsibility to this community.

We told them we would put on a play, and that's what we're going to do. The tickets raise funds for the school. And anyway, we're in the middle of a long winter," she went on. "Everyone needs a play now. Plays bring a community together. We are not canceling this."

"But who can be Lysistrata?" said Lucy Stupak. "I mean, in all honesty, Ms. Heller, no one even comes close. Marissa is the greatest actor in this whole school. None of us can do what she can."

"That is not true," Fran Heller said, even though it so obviously was. She seemed determined, almost desperate, to keep the play alive. After all, Dory thought, Fran had been brought here to do this, and this was her culminating moment, the climax of her year. After the play ended she would be involved in small evenings of one-acts with her more advanced students, but nothing nearly as big as the winter play. "We're not quitters," Fran added, as if she'd been listening in on the lingo of the locker room, where Ruth Winik sometimes pumped up her volleyball or basketball players after a bad game. "And we're going to find a way out of this." She looked all around the room, taking the measure of each girl. Everyone was very still, allowing themselves to be assessed.

Fran Heller looked and looked, and though it was true that no one here seemed an obvious choice for Lysistrata—no one had the elegance and vocal command that Marissa did—she paused for a second, then said, "Willa, can I see you?"

Willa Lang was the only Willa in the school, but still she put her hand to her heart and said, "Me?"

Dory, beside her, looked up in concern, so Fran said, "Dory, you can listen too. Come on." The three of them went into a huddle over at the side of the room by the empty steam tables. The drama teacher said to Willa, "I need you to be Lysistrata."

"What?" Willa said dumbly. The play was tomorrow night. Dory felt her heart flutter and bloom. "I can't do that, Ms. Heller," Willa continued.

But the drama teacher was firm. "Don't say 'can't'; hasn't anyone taught you that, Willa? You're my best bet. You've got that glorious red hair, which I've noticed looks good under the lights. Take your shyness and turn it into an intensity. You probably know a lot of the lines just from being at rehearsals, but we'll definitely give you a prompter in the wings. You will have to work very hard between now and then, and you will have to let me help you." Willa didn't say anything. "Of course I can't force you," Fran Heller continued. "But it's a pretty sweet opportunity, and you may look back on it one day and be glad you did it."

There was no way to know, thought Dory. You bumped stupidly ahead through life, and you couldn't know if starring in a play, or sleeping with someone, or marrying someone, or picking a particular college, or even taking a walk down a street, was going to lead to happiness or sorrow. How could you know? A mother couldn't advise her daughter in such matters, except in the most nebulous and anemic way.

"Well," Dory said to Willa. "Ms. Heller's right. You may be glad about it one day. On the other hand," she felt she had to add, "you may not."

Fran Heller put an arm around Willa's shoulders and said look, she was aware that it had been awkward between them, what with her breakup from Eli. But there was no need to feel awkward now. The two mothers had their arms all over this girl, whose freckly, susceptible skin seemed to be percolating with panic.

"Okay?" Ms. Heller said. "What do you think?"

"Okay," said Willa, though no sound came out. Dory was reminded of how Willa's flute had sounded back in fourth grade, when she'd begun to play. She blew and blew, and her face got red, and only the faintest hoot was conveyed, like a damsel calling for help from a tower in a castle. Willa, almost against her will, was saying yes to the persuasive Fran Heller, who turned to Dory and instructed her to go home.

"It'll only make her self-conscious if she knows you're out in the audience tonight. I'll take care of her from here on in. Don't worry."

So Dory gathered her belongings and left. She could not imagine her daughter being able to get up onstage and play the lead—play Lysistrata, she who disbanded whole armies! Willa didn't have the clarity or directness or independence of Marissa Clayborn. She had been chosen for some reason that Dory couldn't understand. Maybe it was out of cruelty, Dory even thought; maybe it was because Fran knew she would fail and wanted to punish this girl: She Who Broke Up with Sons.

Shortly before midnight that night, Eli Heller stood out in the backyard of the Langs' house down Tam o' Shanter, ankle-deep in the snow, beneath Willa's dark second-floor window. He tossed up handfuls of pebbles, an act that accomplished nothing and soon gave way to tossing up handfuls of dirt and snow and ice. Willa was awake, reading the Aristophanes script with a tiny book light, the way she'd read many books in bed: secretly, almost illicitly. She spoke the lines quietly to herself, trying hard to feel their meaning instead of just reciting a collection of linked words.

She imagined the strong-minded Lysistrata as a bit of a loudmouth like Ms. Heller, but also as someone who got things done, like Marissa Clayborn. Willa thought that she herself was a little bit like Lysistrata too, because both of them surely knew the intensity of what could happen between two people in a bed.

In a quiet stage voice, Willa read aloud:

> Ah, ha! so you thought you had only to do with a set of slave-women! you did not know the ardour that fills the bosom of free-born dames.

Then she heard a slap, and then another and another, at her window. At first it seemed branchlike, or even like hail, but then it was too rhythmic for that. Willa went to the window as a big clod of ice and snow and dirt hit the pane and made her jump back. Stepping forward, she looked out and saw Eli standing below, lit up by the outside light over the back door. Looking down at the top of his hair and his unmittened hands, she was reminded again that he would not be hers forever, that he was not hers now, and that her decision had been harsh but correct.

Willa unfastened the window and leaned out. "Eli," she said. "What are you doing? Go home."

"I wanted you to see what's going on with me," he said. "What you *did*. You see me at school since we broke up, and you think I'm doing okay, right? You think I must be *managing* because I'm not lying down dead in the hallway, and I'm not spray-painting things about you on the overpass. Well, I'm not doing okay, for your information." He pulled a whiskey bottle from his pocket, unscrewed the top, and dramatically flipped his head back to drink. When he was done, he said, "I've had a lot to drink tonight, Willa, and that's not all I had."

"What?"

"I had some J Juice," he said in a slightly bragging tone. "I bought it from Doug Zwern."

"Oh, you did not." Eli wasn't the type; only once, the two of them had smoked weed together, and another time they'd shared a bottle of wine stolen from the Langs' basement, where there was a whole case left over from her parents' faculty potluck. In both instances, Eli had said he disliked the feeling of being off-balance. But here he was now, defiantly staring up at her in the middle of the night, and with his other hand he took a tiny bottle from his pocket and held it up as evidence. He was agitated and inebriated and tripping, and also probably freezing. She couldn't leave him there. "I'll come down and walk you home," she said.

"Will you go out with me again?"

"What? *No.*"

"Then don't do me any fucking favors," he said. "I mean, really, Willa. Walking me home like you're the big chaperone. You're not in charge, Willa."

But the one who loved less—or acted as if they did—was always in charge, and that was the way the world went. She was in charge, and he couldn't do anything besides get drunk and take J Juice and have a freak-out in her backyard in the middle of the night.

"I didn't even *like* your flute playing, by the way," he called up to her. "It was mediocre. And what we did together? On the couch in my basement all those times? Totally mediocre too."

"Eli, stop talking," she said, raising her voice. "Just stop already."

"Wow, your voice projects really well. No wonder my mother picked you for the lead."

"Whatever reason she picked me, it was a mistake," Willa said, and then she added, "I thought she hated me."

"No one hates you. I don't even hate you," said Eli, and then he lurched away from the window, collapsing a few yards away in the snow, facedown.

"Oh *shit*," Willa said, and she slammed the window shut and made her way downstairs in the dark. At the back door she slipped into a pair of boots waiting there—her father's enormous boots—and clomped out into the yard. Somehow she got Eli up and he leaned on her and she brought him inside. He smelled ridiculously bad, and he had cut his lip when he fell. She put him in the easy chair in the living room, and almost immediately her mother appeared from upstairs, and then her father appeared from the den; what had he been doing in the den so late at night? Everyone in her family was *off,* Willa thought. Eli belched and closed his eyes now, and said to her parents, "Oh, Mr. and Ms. L, I can't believe you're seeing me like this," and then he belched again and turned his head away, as if by doing this he might become invisible to them.

Willa's mother got on the phone, and within ten minutes the drama teacher was at their door. Her son was sick-drunk and high, but all three parents decided that he didn't seem so far gone that he would need to go to the ER, like those teenagers over in Woodvale. Eli turned to look at Willa as he leaned against his mother on the way out. It was humiliating to have to be taken home by your mother, by your mommy. To have to be seen this way by the girl you loved, who had been your lover. He was a big, broad-shouldered boy, and his mother was small, but she could have held up a building right now. Eli's expression was dog-eyed, full of longing, and on the way out the Langs' front door he said to Willa, "Take me back." She said nothing. It was the night before the play, and yet all of them were wide awake. "You'll do great tomorrow," he added, as his mother led him away.

15

Winter, not enchantment, conjured the wind that swung the heavy blue metal doors back on their hinges during the evening of the performance of *Lysistrata*. Winter, with its strong wind, sent parents, teachers, and children flying inside Elro, grateful to be indoors, though actually, they noticed, it was not very warm in the building either. Still, many of the females who flowed through the doors on that clear, dead-cold February night had already fallen under the enchantment of the spell. The uncoupling had been cumulative over all these many weeks, and impressive in its reach. As the Langs walked in, Dory heard pieces of conversations—beginnings, middles, and ends that highlighted unhappiness and restlessness and unease. She heard, "Fine, I'll sit elsewhere," and, "I said we'll talk about this *later*," and, "Not in front of the kids," and, from a teenaged girl, "Oh, fuck you, Bryce, I mean really, fuck you." Dory heard it and took note of it, but she and Robby walked on in, opening their coats, standing with the others in the well-lit and slightly underheated lobby. The crowd tonight was on edge, though also muted and cautious.

But those involved with the play—despite the personal relationship unhappiness that many of them felt—had fallen into the state of typical, suppressed hysteria often seen right before high school plays. A few girls darted back and forth across the lobby, giving each other urgent messages about blocks of reserved seats ("Señor Mandelbaum is bringing his paraplegic sister; they *must— have—an—aisle!*"), and whether they could find a third parent to help out with Lysistrata's lightning-fast costume change. One boy needed more paper napkins for the red velvet cupcakes that would be sold during intermission.

Backstage, Ms. Heller gathered the cast together and motioned for them to stand in a large circle and hold hands. They did so with extreme self-consciousness; some hands were wet or sticky, others were cold, and still others seemed as if they were burning hot. After a few moments of giggling, or glaring, or extreme discomfort, the cast members calmed down and stood silently in formation in their chitons and sandals, looking for all the world like the participants in the first Olympics.

"Good evening, everyone," Ms. Heller said in the quietest voice they'd ever heard her use. "I am so glad all of you decided to make it." There was light laughter, as they realized this was a jab-bing reference to Marissa's absence. "Tonight is going to be amaz-ing," she said. "I can just feel it. You've worked very hard, and this will be the payoff. And it will be worth it. Now I'd like everyone to close their eyes, and I'm going to start sending an electrical charge around the circle. When you feel it, please send it to the next per-son, and when it's gone all the way around, you may let it go." She squeezed the hand of one of the Chorus of Old Men, her artisanal rings digging into his hand so that he jolted to painful attention and squeezed the hand of the girl beside him, and around went the electrical charge, and everyone felt themselves invigorated, and finally they flung their hands apart in astonishment, asking one another, "Did you feel it? *I* did."

But a little while later, pacing in the cafeteria with the stage makeup thick and orange on her face, her eyes ringed and accentuated, Willa had a failure of nerve, and she said to Carrie Petito and the two Lucys in a low, sick voice, "They should've canceled the play. How can I go out there? I'm a wreck about it. About Eli. About *everything*." Her friends told her that she just had to walk out there and think about whatever it was actors think about when they are trying to give the performance of their lives.

"Here's the thing," said Carrie. "Everyone in that audience is going to know how hard this is, what you're doing; and everyone in the cast and crew is going to be sending you amazing-acting vibes."

"That is totally true," said Lucy Neels.

"No, I am screwed," said Willa. "I should never have said yes."

"Look," said Carrie. "Remember in eighth grade when I had that eating disorder and my parents made me join that support group in the basement of the synagogue? I hated it more than anything; I told them I was going to get nothing out of it. But I went to it, and I did get a lot out of it. It did something to me, and then I didn't need it anymore. And this," she said with authority, "will do something to you."

"It'll kill me."

"No it won't."

Carrie Petito hugged her friend, and then the two Lucys did

too, their narrow bodies pressed into her as hard as girls' bodies could ever press, sending yet more electrical charges of luck
and love.

By ten minutes to seven the auditorium was filled. Dory and
Robby Lang headed down the aisle toward their reserved seats in
the sixth row. Earlier tonight, when they were about to leave the
house, he'd said, "Tonight everyone's going to say how proud we
must be."

"And we will be."

"Of course. But one of the things I always liked about us,"
Robby said, "is that we weren't one of those couples who only think
and talk about their kids. But now maybe we're heading there."

"I'm sorry," she said. She was worn out from her own insistence on busting up what had been good and solid. Tonight would
be about Willa, and that was appropriate. Let it be about Willa so it
did not have to be about them.

Robby led the way to their seats; he slapped hands with a few
boys and shook hands with a few fathers and mothers. Dory was
stopped by students who still got a kick out of seeing their teachers
after hours. She waved to the shy exchange student from Mexico.
There was Marissa Clayborn's family; her father was studying the
stage bill with an intense focus, and he barely looked up. Marissa's
mother, Paula, quietly explained to Dory that even though Marissa
had made "a radical choice," the Clayborns wanted to show their
support of the play, and of Willa.

Around them, other families and kids were waving and wanting to say hello to Mr. and Ms. L. There, Dory saw, was Paige Straub,
of course not sitting with Dylan Maleska. The teenaged part of the
audience appeared partly sex-segregated, Dory noticed. There had

apparently been quite a few breakups, Leanne had told her, and everyone had drawn ranks around their friends. Boys protected wounded boys; girls used other girls for justification of their actions.

The house lights dimmed now, and Dory Lang slipped into her seat beside Robby. Their arms lay side by side on the shared armrest. In a moment, Ms. Heller's distinctive voice warned the audience from somewhere about their cell phones, and dutifully, around the room, came compliant trills and flutters.

Please, Dory thought, *let this go okay.* At last the heavy stage curtains shooshed open upon ancient Greece, with a house and some columns and a gateway leading to the Acropolis. Fran Heller had wanted only one set; she thought the Acropolis was too fragile to be moved, so the whole thing sat there from the start. Dory was paying scrupulous, wild attention; beside her, Robby stared straight ahead, and she wanted to take his hand and hold it, but somehow she worried that the gesture would seem like a consolation prize. They sat waiting and watching as their daughter came onstage. When she appeared at last, she was beautiful.

"Oh," Dory whispered.

That chiton was pitifully thin; it was made from Bev Cutler's children's bedsheets, and it must have made Willa feel so naked up there on that big, wide stage, in front of hundreds of people she'd known all her life. Dory wished she could throw a cardigan over her shoulders. Willa stood center stage, and she looked out over the room. Dory strained to catch her eye, but she knew that Willa couldn't see her, and shouldn't see her anyway.

Willa gazed straight out and began to speak, her voice flat and quavering, and at one point even sounding as though she were suppressing something digestive:

Ah! If only they had been invited to a Bacchic revelling, or a feast of Pan or Aphrodité or Genetyllis! The streets would have been impassable for the thronging tambourines! Now there's never a woman here—ah! Except my neighbour Calonicé, whom I see approaching yonder. . . . Good day, Calonicé.

At this point, the girl known to Dory mostly as Slut I appeared. Playing Calonicé, she began a conversation with Lysistrata about why Lysistrata had arranged for a gathering of the women. Calonicé, Dory realized with a little relief, was not so much better onstage than Willa. It was true that Willa sounded more nervous, but the other girl could barely project. The opening was stiff, certainly, but it was not humiliating, Dory thought; that was much too strong a word.

Then, as the play struggled along, something else began to happen, unknown to Dory and the audience: from an infinitesimal space between the vacuum-closed doors, a curl of cold wind found its way into the auditorium and fanned out through the rows. It was the spell, of course, which now entranced every relevant person whom it had previously missed. Here it was in its final visit, this spell that made women turn away from men, and which only began to appear during the lead-up to a high school production of *Lysistrata*.

As the two months of rehearsal had passed, the spell had spread quietly, changing everyone it touched. The *Lysistrata* spell was a phenomenon that very few people knew about, but it was real, and it was here.

In the twelfth row, on the far side of the auditorium now,

the sixty-nine-year-old school librarian Mrs. Kessler suddenly thought: *If Marcus wants to be with me that way again tonight I will tell him, "Don't even think of it. We are much too old."*

Up in the balcony, Sarah Milkin thought: *I am done with Todd Eberstadt forever.*

In one of the very back seats, the head of the debate team, who just last weekend at a meet had sneaked into the hotel room of the head of the debate team from a school in Maine, thought: *He was clueless about euthanasia. He and I are done.*

All around the auditorium, the spell roared past and among them, beneath their seats, up the aisles, silent and powerful as it made its way. Onstage, after a little while, unaware of this, Lysistrata and Calonicé became slightly more comfortable and began to speak their lines a bit more naturally and with increased volume. Dory felt a vague loosening of her jaw, which she hadn't even realized had been so tight and jutting. Lysistrata started to get to the point:

> Don't you feel sad and sorry because the fathers of your chil-
> dren are far away from you with the army? For I'll under-
> take, there is not one of you whose husband is not abroad
> at this moment.

Dory's daughter seemed to be easing into the part, and the play was becoming more like a breakthrough rehearsal than a performance. It was like one of those rehearsals in which the actor *gets it* for the first time, and you see it happening before you, and as a result the other actors get it too. She flings the excitement and new understanding all around, and the director says, "Yes!" Except tonight the director couldn't say anything, for this was a performance, with an audience; but Willa Lang's mother, her posture now a little more that of a theatergoer than a sprinter about to spring, quietly said *yes* inside her head.

Dory felt herself relax further; she leaned back, and let the velvet curve of the chair receive her. The play began to go more swiftly past, with lines batted back and forth, though Dory could only really concentrate on Willa, who was now speaking some of the lines that Dory had heard Marissa Clayborn read on that very first day of rehearsals. The day of the night that Dory had ended up first refusing Robby in bed.

" 'We must refrain from the male altogether,' " Willa said, and the words were stirring, but more than that, Willa was stirring, and it seemed to Dory as if the rest of the audience felt it too. Willa said:

> Nay, why do you turn your backs on me? Where are you going? So, you bite your lips, and shake your heads, eh? Why these pale, sad looks? Why these tears? Come, will you do it—yes or no? Do you hesitate?

Dory felt sixteen years of shame concentrated into the opening of this play. She thought of how she had underappreciated her daughter, condemning her as average, not a big reader, just a constant user of Farrest, merely a regular girl, not one of the ones who knocked everyone out with their specialness. She had underappreciated not only Willa, but perhaps most of the students she taught. She'd always liked thinking of them as "the kids." The young people were the kids, and the old ones were the adults, but really, she thought now, look at these people onstage; they stirred her and thickened her throat. They were not only emotionally affecting her and the rest of the audience; they were also clearly affecting one another too, and this in turn affected her further. She could see the way they shook a little as they spoke about changing the world through unorthodox means. *People!* teachers called out in the classroom to get their attention, and that word described them best.

Lucky them, those not really kids, who were constantly having experiences and would once in a while actually try to change the world. Lucky them, with their recent-vintage powerhouse bodies and their passions for all things electronic and fast, all things dissonant and inexplicable. Lucky them, for the public square. Dory had maintained that the world was worse now, for a world without intimacy—what kind of a world was that? And a world of glibness and shallow references only to events that had taken place five minutes earlier—what kind of a place was *that*? She felt that these had been inaccurate descriptions, or at least incomplete ones. There was shallowness all around her, certainly, along with exhibitionism and a preoccupation with the transitory and the dumb, but that wasn't the whole tale. And yes, the public square could be treacherous, but so were subways at night, yet teenagers from Elro went into the city and rode them anyway, transporting themselves in clusters, swinging from handrails, calling attention to their ecstatic, suburban selves. But also, lucky them for the future, and the love that lay waiting. They could make whichever analogies they chose: the love that lay waiting like a web page as yet undesigned, or maybe even like a forest as yet unwalked in. A bafflingly simple forest green and virtual, or one wet and dark and real. Lucky them.

She had underestimated them, and now she felt only regret.

Willa, full-throated, standing in what seemed a new posture, was speaking again:

> Oh, wanton, vicious sex! the poets have done well to make tragedies upon us; we are good for nothing then but love and lewdness! But you, my dear, you from hardy Sparta, if *you* join me, all may yet be well; help me, second me, I conjure you.

The girls onstage who had somehow become women were using their formidable sexualities to end the men's long, long war. They were standing up to the men at last, and the room sat at attention. A female voice from the balcony—someone young—called out, "Show them, girl!" There was some laughter. One row in front of the Langs, two audience members began to argue, and the people around them began to shush them. The arguers, Dory realized, startled, were Ruth Winik and Henry Spangold. Henry's voice was deep and urgent, barely a whisper. Dory heard, "Not exactly fair," and "Maybe a little *too* relevant," and "So I just have to sit here and *listen*?"

"Keep it down," warned a woman nearby, and activity bloomed in that little front section of the auditorium. Henry, in shadow, stood up as if he was going to leave. Then he bent and said something furiously to Ruth. Henry, big and broad, lumbered past the other people seated in his row, and then he stood in the aisle, pausing there. All the while, the actors onstage kept talking, valiantly trying to remain unconcerned by the squall in the audience. But then Henry Spangold turned and leaped up the three steps onto the stage.

"Oh my God," said Señor Mandelbaum's sister from the wheelchair tilted and braked in the aisle.

Dory took in a hard breath as she saw Ruth's husband go from silhouette to fully textured human being under the stage lights. "Look at this," she whispered to Robby, and he shook his head slowly. She gripped his arm. Ruth's husband had wild, uncombed hair, as if he'd been tugging at it in his seat.

"What is he doing?" Robby said. Willa and the other actors had recoiled from the sudden, surprise presence onstage of a man from the audience. They looked at one another, panicking. "He's ruining the play," Robby whispered. "I'll kill him."

Henry, in profile, faced the actors. "It's not fair, this play," he said to them. "I was reading the stagebill before. Apparently we're all supposed to think that men are so warlike that they sometimes have to be *denied*. And someone out in the audience was cheering a little while ago, like everyone knows this is the truth about men—that we deserve what we get. That we're just these violent, lusty animals who need our horniness placated. But it isn't true. We're not all disgusting, sex-crazed warriors. And what's wrong with what we do want? Urges are normal. What's so bad about them? I resent this whole play."

Willa and the others said nothing; they stared at him, and the whole audience did too. Now Robby could no longer sit in his seat and let Willa's moment be destroyed. He stood and pushed his way out of the row and into the aisle and then onto the stage. A few people clapped when he appeared, but mostly everyone watched in excitement. "This is my *daughter's play*," he said quietly to Henry Spangold, poking his chest with a finger. "And I'm going to have to ask you to leave."

There was applause. The sculptor backed away, but then he didn't move. "Am I wrong, Robby?" he asked. "You don't think everyone's sitting here thinking, yeah, it's true about men; I agree with the play. But maybe you don't know what I'm saying at all. Maybe no one does. Maybe it's only me whose marriage has gotten—" His voice broke off. "Oh, why am I going on about this?" Dory thought Robby would run him into the wings.

But Robby said to him, "No, you're not wrong."

His voice was a rough stage whisper. The other actors had by now retreated to the sides and rear of the stage, leaving the two men to face each other. They looked so young, Dory thought; they appeared like actors in a high school play. Dory watched as Robby turned and said, "Willa, just let me have a second, okay? Then you can go back to your play."

As if.

Willa didn't even want to look at him. She turned away, and her friends, who had been there to buck her up before the performance, tried to comfort her now. Robby looked out over the auditorium and said, "I've read this play, and I've seen it performed. It's not my favorite Greek comedy, but I actually like it. I don't mind it at all. What I mind, though, is that apparently something can happen inside someone you love—it can just *happen* somehow— and like magic she thinks that she's had enough, and that the way the two of you have been for a really long time is no longer worth the effort. Does that sound familiar to anyone?"

Dory closed her eyes and tried to stay conscious.

"I want our life back," Robby said to her from the stage.

She put her head in her hands. But then there was movement to her left, and the man sitting there—the husband of Gavin

McCleary's secretary—stood up too. He pushed past Dory and then there he was onstage beside Robby. He was squat, sweating. "Okay, fine, if people are taking this opportunity to say something, then I will too. Beth," he said. "I know I can be such a schmuck. Please forgive me. Please, please come back to bed."

The actors had fled the stage completely. Willa had been shepherded off by her friends, and surely she remained distraught; surely the kids were all in a huddle in the wings, talking about how these few men had gotten obnoxious and ruined the show. How her father, that beloved teacher, had been part of it. Where was Fran Heller in all this? Dory wondered. Surely at about this point, the drama teacher should be ordering someone on tech crew to close the curtains, and the house lights would go up and everyone in the audience would stand and say to one another, "What was *that?*" But Dory didn't see Fran, and no one moved to close the curtains.

Then, rising up one by one and gathering courage, several other men quietly stormed the stage and the Acropolis—fathers, teachers, local merchants. Some of them were there to get the other men to leave—"You are ruining my son Zach's play," a father said sternly, taking another father by the lapels. But some of them were there to make pronouncements to their women.

"I feel bad about that lamp, Marie," said a man.

"Will someone explain something to me?" asked Ron di Canzio. "How can the women of Greece actually 'stop sleeping' with the men, if all the men are away at war to begin with?"

Boys came up onstage as well, and they said their tender and sometimes inarticulate pieces, some with a swagger, some with tears, begging the girls to make love to them once more, to let them be together in the way they used to be. "This thing we had," said

Max Holleran to Chloe Vincent. "It was un-fucking-believable. Sorry, sorry," he added, as if just now remembering where he was, and who would be listening.

Everyone was listening. The people who remained in their seats listened. Children turned to their parents in disbelief. "Is this part of the play?" a six-year-old asked his grandmother, who said she really wasn't sure. The actors who had walked offstage had begun to gather together in the wings, or to return to the stage itself again, confused about what was happening here. Maybe the play hadn't been ruined? Maybe it was some sort of postmodern success that Ms. Heller had planned all along? They didn't really know, but they started to see that what was happening was very watchable.

Principal McCleary now approached the stage, clambering up awkwardly, and he adjusted his tie and looked out over the audience. Dory, who could barely think, felt relief knowing that Gavin was going to bring order. He was the principal, and that was what principals did. He had given a somber and surprisingly reassuring speech on 9/11, though that was already such a long time ago.

But when everyone both onstage and in the auditorium seats grew silent, McCleary announced, "I'd like to say tonight that I too am also in love with a woman who has been indifferent to me for quite some time. I need to say it now, despite how it looks. I cannot go on like this any longer. I need her to know I love her so much, and that I am sorry. I am sorry I am stiff and maybe unspontaneous. I just have to say it. Thank you, people."

Dory put her hands to her head, as if ducking from a boom. Where was poor Leanne? Had she already died in her seat in the back? Suddenly a small woman came up onstage and joined all the men. It was Wendy McCleary, the principal's wife, and she strode up to her husband, putting her arms around him. She was as tiny as a little girl.

"Gavin, I never meant for any of that to happen," Wendy said. "I didn't know it caused you such pain. I am here now, Gavin. Don't worry anymore, I am here."

The principal was briefly confused, but he bent down and let his wife hold him, and within seconds he had relaxed into the embrace. Soon he was looking into his wife's eyes as surely he had done twenty years earlier, when they had first fallen hard for each other in their own way, somewhere, somehow. Everyone's story of love had its own catchphrases and props that the couple would always remember and refer to tenderly. It was as if the principal was suddenly remembering now. He closed his eyes as he leaned against his wife, who held him steady. He let her take him, and he was relieved.

His example caused a few more men to climb the stage and publicly ask women to take them back. Some of them climbed up onto the Acropolis to get a better view of the audience and make themselves seen and heard. The structure, not built for this many people, began to split and crumble a little. There was Ed Cutler onstage, saying that he adored his wife more than she would ever know, and that he needed her. And there, almost immediately, was Bev Cutler. And Mr. Evans the old janitor, and his wife Mrs. Evans. "I don't want to fight anymore. I'd like to be the way we used to be, Adeline," he said to her in a slow, deliberate voice, so that the whole school finally heard the cafeteria lady's first name. And there was Abby Means along with her boyfriend whom no one had ever seen; and, wait, Malcolm Bean, the foreign-car dealer, who had come to the play tonight hoping that he could get a glimpse of Leanne. And various teenagers, all of them reuniting in a heap, some of them starting to make out and grope each other. Lioness on the Cheese Grater? Maybe that would be enacted here, if someone didn't stop it. Eli wasn't anywhere to be found, Dory noticed momentarily.

They were all out of control, she thought as she looked at the mash onstage. It had been a long couple of months, and now they were desperate enough to interrupt a high school play. The people onstage argued with one another or embraced. Robby Lang had been trying to let Dory know how he felt during these two months, but she hadn't been able to be responsive. Now she got up from her seat in the rapidly warming room and entered the aisle, then climbed onto the stage too, where she put her arms around her husband and kissed him, and kept kissing him, and wanted to, experiencing the mysterious pull toward physical love again. All winter she'd let them fall into quietude, into lassitude, into comfort. Wasn't one of the goals of life to be comfortable in your own skin and in your own bed and on your own land? But as soon as you achieved it, you felt an immense sadness, and then you wanted to wreck everything around you, just because you could. Comfort was the best thing, and maybe the worst.

Another spell had been thrust upon her so long ago, in the big hotel in Minneapolis, looking at the very young Robby Baskin in the lobby bar. She hadn't been able to see it, but it was real. Otherwise, why would you rise up from your enclosed and well-defended self and go be with that other person? Why would you open your life, the most secret entries into yourself, to someone you didn't really know? Who would do that unless she had to?

Over his shoulder as they kissed on the stage in the warming auditorium, Dory Lang looked out at the audience to see who were the holdouts, who remained—not that she could see much of anything anyway, what with all that light.

Backstage, Fran Heller leaned against a cinderblock wall with her eyes closed, listening to the sounds of commotion and ruination and love. She seemed to be in a stupor, obviously overwhelmed by the interruption and destruction of her play, which had been in rehearsals since December. Now, at the start of February, it was a lifetime later. She kept her eyes closed, and the kids on the tech crew and some of the actors in their bedsheets looked at her with anxiety, not sure what to say or do. They realized that she seemed almost serene.

In the middle of the madness, Lucy Stupak left the stage and ran to find her. "What *is* this, Ms. H?" Lucy asked. "Should I call someone?"

The drama teacher opened her eyes and regarded the girl. "There's no one to call," she said. Lucy's mother and father were onstage kissing as their daughter had never seen them kiss before. Even they couldn't help her now.

"But there has to be someone," said Lucy, and in desperation she grabbed the drama teacher's arm and pumped it. Ms. Heller shook her off, but the girl whirled around her, and Ms. Heller had to take her by her shoulders and hold her steady.

"Lucy," said Ms. Heller. "Lucy, look at me." Lucy Stupak's eyes were two little pools of swirling water. Displays of anarchy and expressiveness apparently terrified her. "Someone," said Ms. Heller in her teacher-voice, "please take her somewhere to lie down or something."

Two kind boys from the lighting booth put themselves in charge of Lucy Stupak, shepherding her out. By now the set had partly disintegrated. One of the columns lay on its side, and a teen-aged boy and girl sat on it, kissing, as if it were an old log by a country creek.

The spell had apparently been broken. All of a sudden, the heat in the auditorium kicked in, and a warm wind pushed its way through the wings and the vents and down the ladder from the lighting booth and elsewhere. It was as if the cold draft that had been in the auditorium earlier was reversing itself and disappearing back into its own unseen channels and flumes of air. The spell was done here. Those other spells—love, passion, resistance, a desire for life to return to the way it once was—had overtaken it. The auditorium grew as warm as a steam room.

The scene onstage broke up and couples walked up the aisle, arm in arm, as if at a mass wedding. Someone on tech crew pressed a button on the sound board so that the bouzouki music from *Zorba the Greek* came blaring over the sound system, and a couple of people gamely began to dance their way offstage and up the aisle. The doors of the auditorium were propped open and light from the lobby poured in, and everyone moved toward it.

By the time Willa appeared in her street clothes in the lobby, some of the other actors surrounded her, all arms, everyone happy, and happy for her, all of them at a high emotional pitch. It was as if they knew something big had happened tonight, but already they were a little vague in their minds about what it had been. Someone had floated the idea that Ms. Heller had possibly arranged this whole audience-participation thing in advance, and had decided not to tell the cast and crew about it. They said that she had apparently wanted it to lend the production a chaotic, magical, surprising, life-at-its-extremes quality. And so it had, if that was true. The performance was unusual and emotional; it was all that everyone had hoped it would be. Dory and Robby watched as these teenagers held Willa in a loose web of affection and congratulation.

The spell had come in cold, and tonight it had been diminished and finally overwhelmed. At its height, it was a knockout of a spell, fortified by a classic work of literature—a play that had lasted since it was written, and which lasted even now, in this age of very different gratifications. Like any really good book, the play had held the people who ventured into it, and then, when it was over, it had released them. The play was done now and the audience returned to themselves and their lives and the brightness and chatter of the lobby. They remembered only some of what had happened onstage, and they were starting not to feel it so acutely anymore. What stayed with them was a sense that the night had been a great success. Everyone felt generously and ardently toward spouses, partners, lovers, and everyone blinkingly returned to the real world.

Dory and Robby congratulated their daughter for her excellent performance, and Robby handed Willa the bouquet of yellow roses that he had earlier stashed in a supply closet down the hall. Other people gave Willa roses too, and she was like a pageant winner, her face beyond happy. There was to be a cast party tonight at the Petitos, one of those teenaged all-nighters, and Willa had told her parents she would sleep there and come home no sooner than tomorrow afternoon.

"Be careful," Dory had said to Willa, whatever that meant. But Willa was already looking past her, and thinking of something else.

In the car going home, Dory yawned and leaned against Robby's shoulder in his parka. He blasted the heater, and she said again, "Willa was terrific."

"She was," said Robby. "The whole thing was really good, wasn't it? I give Fran a lot of credit." Their memories of the evening were already shifting, blurring, sliding a bit so that they all made sense. It had been a strange production, and yet strange could be good. And what, they wondered later, had been so strange about it anyway? After a while they weren't sure. The details of the night no longer mattered, but the outcome still did: a moving, brave daughter; a partnership that had the ache of possibilities restored to it.

"I hope the Petitos keep close watch tonight," Dory said. "You know what goes on at cast parties. You remember the parties when you used to direct the play. Drinking. Weed. That kid who put those things up his nose. That couple in the hall closet."

"Eli won't be there, will he?" Robby asked, and Dory said no, she didn't think so; he hadn't been at the performance tonight. They were silent, weighing this and trying to decide whether his absence was good or bad.

They didn't know that Willa, now released from the spell, surrounded by friends, and being complimented to the point of overstimulation, was preoccupied by how to find Eli and tell him that she had been wrong. To say that it didn't matter how long they lasted as a couple. She'd called his cell, but it had gone straight to voice mail. She'd started texting him then, simply writing:

?

?

?

But her parents didn't know any of this. They also didn't know that Eli was at that moment in the Port Authority Bus Terminal in New York City with his phone turned off, waiting for a bus that would eventually take him to Lansing, Michigan, where his father lived. He sat in a molded plastic seat and tried not to make eye contact with a disturbed-looking man who was trying to make eye contact with him. Finally, Eli just closed his eyes. The bus wouldn't leave for another half hour, and he would be traveling all night. He'd called his father earlier and said, "Hey, Dad, it's me. This has not been preapproved by Mom yet, but I am wondering if it's possible for me to finish up the school year in Lansing."

"Did you and Mom have an argument?" Lowell Heller wanted to know, and Eli had assured his father that no, there had been no argument.

"It's other things," Eli said. "I'd rather not talk about them right now, if that's okay with you. I'd rather just come."

His father, to his credit, did not push. He finally said yes, Eli could come to Michigan, at least for a little while, and they would see what was what. He couldn't make any guarantees about the rest of the school year; that was a tall order, and it wasn't the way this family had been set up. But he said of course sometimes in life there were emergencies and you had to adjust. He told his son he missed him very much, and that he hoped he could help. And he said that when Eli arrived in Michigan, he would be waiting.

Eli had some cash, a backpack of freshly laundered clothes, three novels with bookmarks in them, his textbooks just in case he ended up coming back to Stellar Plains this school year, and his cell phone and laptop. As he sat in the bus station, he didn't know what had really happened over the winter or the course of the evening; and he had no idea that Willa had been trying to reach him. She hadn't tried to contact him in so long; why should he think she would try tonight? He'd shut off his phone because he didn't want to hear from his mother, who, when she eventually read his e-mail telling her he was gone, would flip out and definitely demand that he return home. He just didn't want to have to think about her feelings or needs right now. He didn't really want to think about anyone at all.

In the parking lot outside the high school, someone pulled Willa into the caravan of cars driven by newly licensed senior-class drivers, and they all headed for the cast party. Soon the actors and crew were lying around the Petito house with their heads in one another's laps, stroking one another's hair. As they played guitar and sang songs and drank warm beer and smoked joints and cried and kissed and felt one another up and did whatever they did, Willa told herself not to think of him, because it would ruin the night for her, but she couldn't help herself.

The drama teacher never showed up at the cast party, and no one could imagine why. "Ms. H should at least have put in an appearance," someone complained. "That's what Mr. L always used to do. He'd come at the beginning, and then he'd make a toast to the cast and crew, remember? And then he'd leave after a little while, and the party would go on all night. That's what the director is supposed to do. *Lysistrata* was a *hit*. Why didn't she come?"

"She's a freak," the props master said, and no one disagreed, but it wasn't really a criticism.

"Maybe we can get her to do *A Streetcar Named Desire* next year," said Carrie Petito. "Some crazy, improvised version. Willa, you'd be great in that. You and Marissa both. There are two great female parts in that play."

At around one in the morning, Marissa Clayborn came to the Petito house; beside her was that boy blogger from *The Campobello Courier*. He had been sitting faithfully beside her bed, and he was there when she suddenly sat up at some point early in the evening, and said, "Alex, this is absurd."

"What?" He'd been blogging, typing very fast.

"My sex strike isn't taking off," she said. "I'm just one obscure person in suburban New Jersey. News Eight made a video of me in the bed, but it hardly went viral. I'm not like those women in Kenya who got worldwide coverage. I'm just one teenager, and basically no one else seems to be joining this sex strike. Maybe they don't want to give up sex, or maybe they don't know enough about what's going on in Afghanistan to be as outraged as they should be. Whatever it is, it's not getting attention. I think I'm going to call it a day."

"But what about the war?" Alex asked.

"I'm planning to attend an international war resistance conference for high school students over spring break," she said. "It's in Helsinki, and I'm going to have to get the school district to pay for it somehow. But the first thing is that I feel like I need to leave this bed."

"Oh," Alex said, and she could see that he looked very upset that she was going to get up and go, and that their time together was about to end. He looked like he wanted to lunge forward and smother her face with kisses, and she didn't want that at all. Even with the spell lifted, Marissa Clayborn did not want to have sex with Alex or anyone at the moment. But she didn't have to; no one would make her do that now or ever. She would have sex again exactly when she wanted. She didn't know if it would be because someone smiled at her across a room at a party, or because she admired his big brain or his shoulders. She had no idea what would precipitate sex or love; all she knew was that she wanted to experience desire, however brief.

A cross town, parents and teachers and assorted other adults were coming back together, picking up where they had left off earlier in the winter, or even earlier in the night. Men and women threw themselves upon each other. Laughter bounded around rooms. Wine bottles were opened, buckets of spicy chicken wings were eaten, candles were lit, and meaningful music was played. It wasn't all giddy and easy, however. Over at the Cutlers' big house, although glad to be reconciled, and lying on their backs in bed side by side, holding hands, Ed and Bev were silent. It had been a long time not only since they'd touched, but also since they'd talked about themselves with any seriousness.

"That thing you said," she suddenly said to him. "It hurt me so much, you know." She kept looking at the ceiling, not at him.

"Please look at me, Bev."

She didn't want to, but she did. Their heads were close, and there was his handsome face, a few capillaries broken in the nose—each one perhaps representing some vicissitude in the stock market—and the strong chin. He put a hand on her face, which felt to her as if she was being given a glass of water after a fever: relieving, but almost too much.

"It was stupid of me," he said. "It just came out. What can I say? You'd changed. But hey, who was I to talk? I had no hair anymore. My ass sagged like an old man."

"But Ed, this was building up. You were obviously not all that interested in me anymore. Your heart wasn't really in it; I could tell."

"What was I going to do? So many times you turned the other way. You faced away from me."

"I did?" she said. "I didn't realize. You could have said something."

"I probably should have. I figured that this was what you wanted, that it was easier for you. I wasn't going to beg you, Bev. And," he added, "I was distracted too. I had things on my mind. The numbers were horrific. Everything was out of my control."

And for the first time in a long while Bev could imagine finding some way back, though the particulars of how that would happen remained obscure. She knew that Ed had always been a little bit *dickish*; that was the word she'd heard a couple of students use, and it had stayed with her. He couldn't just cast off this quality when he was at home with her. It was part of him, though the world no longer supported it in him, or cared about him very much. The world now cared only about the *young* and dickish. He was an aging, fairly aggressive man who was also a decent person, she knew, and who had been partly misunderstood, and humbled, and loved her.

Maybe she would always be fat, and if that was the case, then at least, she thought, she could try to use her body for the things she'd always liked doing. She could move around more; she could start walking. They had so much property, and Bev could ask Ed if he would go walking with her; and while they walked they could talk about whatever bothered them—all the slights they'd felt, the betrayals—as well as what they still liked, and loved. But she wasn't sure yet how to be in this version of her body, how to inhabit it and have sex in it; how to feel that it was hers, regardless of whether it was the one she wanted, or would ever have chosen.

She thought about how she had let herself go. *He* had let her go too, though he hadn't meant to, or wanted to; and then she had let him go as well. Tonight, in bed, Bev had talked to him, and it was a kind of foreplay—almost as good as talking dirty in their bed, which they used to do, and which maybe, at some point, they would do again. She remembered once talking this way to him, and how his whole head—already balding at the time but still with some silky light brown hair—had responded by blushing, glowing. Now he rested his head against her, and they stayed like that for a long time.

hree miles away, in the Winik-Spangolds' house in the middle of the night after the play, Ruth and Henry lay poised, waiting for a child to cry or need to be held or brought into the bed. But for some reason, as though they'd been given knockout drops, the children slept, while the adults were both wide awake. "Listen to me, Henry," said Ruth. "The problem, for me, was that I was never very protective of myself. I thought I didn't need that, but apparently I do."

"Okay," he said. "Go on."

Their baby boy stirred and banged in his bassinet, and Ruth half sat up, but it was a false alarm, and she lay back down. "I may get a lock on the bathroom door," she said.

"I could install it tomorrow."

"And when the boys are older, a lock on the bedroom door too."

"Wouldn't that make it like a prison?"

"*Our* door," she said.

"Oh. I see."

"I am not interested in women," she said. "I mean, sometimes I see one who I think looks sort of androgynous and cute, and that's nice. But it doesn't pull at me now, because I'm not available. I'm not. The problem is that I never really parceled myself out properly to all of you. I gave everybody everything. I know it won't always be like this," Ruth told him. "With everyone all over me, touching me; I know that. One day it will be much less intense. But I just don't want to wait it out. I don't want to have to *tolerate* my home life. That's not something I ever wanted."

The silence continued; the boys slept on, which was a miracle. "What about me?" Henry asked.

"You. I am here for you. But I have to say—and I mean no offense by this—I don't think these dates you keep asking for are exactly up to par. For you either. They're always so rushed, Henry, aren't they? I don't want us to rush like that. I don't want to miss so much."

Henry Spangold threw a thick, hairy leg across his wife, and she lifted herself up on her strong arms and towered over him, smiling. And soon, somehow, their war was over.

. . .

Leanne Bannerjee left the school after the play, and behind her in her rearview mirror she could see the lights of Malcolm Bean's low-riding car. He flashed his brights at her, which seemed to be the equivalent of winking. As she headed toward her home, she thought one final time about the scene she had witnessed in the auditorium, the way the principal's wife had reclaimed him publicly, and how he had willingly gone with her. Leanne would be fine with this; she wasn't in love with Gavin McCleary. But still she didn't want to change her life and become one of the married women of Stellar Plains. She was glad to be seeing Malcolm tonight; she felt *crisper* knowing he was following her home. She hummed and bristled and stepped a little harder on the gas, thinking of what they would do.

Briefly Leanne imagined telling her friend Jane that she would quit her job at the high school and come to New York City and join Jane's practice of teenologists. There were three of them in the suite of offices on Park Avenue and 80th, and they even had a receptionist. All of the women were young and fashionable; that was part of the point. Teenagers related to these therapists and were starryeyed about them, and somehow some kind of therapeutic transference took place, but it was all dubious to Leanne. No, she wouldn't leave this town, not yet. Plus, the idea of appearing on reality TV with her clients, which was about to happen to Jane—some show called *Families in Freefall II: The Kaplans*—was too appalling to consider. Did everybody have to be famous? Wasn't it enough to be excited by your own life; by, say, sleeping with a few different men, enjoying each one for the pleasures he could give you, and not caring about whether or not other people had judgmental thoughts about you?

She loved men, that was the whole of it; or anyway, she loved the complement of them, and the way one gave her something that another did not, and still another gave her something else. When she was by herself she could think about all of them, or one of them, or none. Leanne didn't want to be without male involvement and envelopment, or without *action*—without screaming in bed with a small rotation of men who each offered something, in concentrate. Who each brought her sharply up toward the rim of extreme excitement, where she could peek over the edge. She wanted all of that, and could have it too; but she didn't need to be involved with a married man; that was obvious to her now. She could draw the line there.

And when a girl like Jen Heplauer came into Leanne's office during the school day and said, *Dr. Bannerjee, a blow job isn't sex at all, it's just a blow job*, Leanne might tilt her head in that bird-on-a-branch way, but she really hoped to be able to say, *Well, it depends on the blower and the blowee. It depends on the light in the room. It depends on the kindness of the guy.* And so on and so on.

So do you think the Cumfy will burn to a crisp if I set it on fire?" Dory asked Robby after they walked into the house.

"What? Oh, that's funny," he said. "I see. A symbolic burning."

"I really want to try it," she said. She was all charged up tonight. The play had been wonderful, and Willa had been brilliant in it, and through the overwhelming, now only partly recalled experience of watching the actors and hearing Robby talk to her from the stage, and then joining him up there, she had come around. They were alone together in the house now, while Willa was off at the cast party for the rest of the night. They both knew that something was about to happen between them, and the anticipation had a highly stimulating, nearly teenaged quality to it. Something was about to happen, and it was inevitable, and they were heading right toward it. Robby wore the soft blue shirt that he'd been wearing forever; it never went out of style. He could wear it to school and he could wear it to bed. It was not new, and he was not new to her either, but his long arms filled the sleeves, and there at the ends were his hands, which weren't a woman's hands at all. They were his. Onstage she'd held them, and had kissed his mouth, and kissed it more and more easily. One of the kids in the audience had called out, "You go, Mr. and Ms. L!"

You go, she thought now. She took the Cumfy out into the yard along with a pack of matches, and Robby followed her. He told her he thought this plan of hers was dopey and unnecessary, but still he accompanied her outside, and the dog came too. Snow was melting in the yard; Hazel peed on the curled, unfrozen palm of a leaf that had been preserved all winter in the ice's amber. On the patio, near the barbecue in its plastic winter apparel, and near the white metal chairs that were speckled with rust and lacking cushions, Dory tried to light the edge of the yellow blanket.

Nothing happened. The blanket, even with the match cupped in her hand, would not catch. She tried match after match, but the Cumfy was apparently nonflammable. "Let's go in," Robby said. "It's cold out here." But this was just a reflexive response; it wasn't that cold out anymore. The winter had softened. The Langs went into the house, and she carried the Cumfy upstairs in her arms, and then Robby lay down on the bed, and she did too. They took off their clothes and slipped under the Cumfy, which looked to Dory like a big, garish American burqa. Clicks of static could be heard and felt as they turned beneath that yellow, chemical, indestructible piece of cloth.

They had roared through sex and childbirth and their child's childhood, and now they were different, and they couldn't go back there. Or maybe they could go back there, but it wouldn't look the same. Sometimes they would still want this, just not necessarily frequently. Stirrings would take place, and they would arrange themselves accordingly. Sex wasn't everything, but it was something. It was something to them.

She thought of the thing he had been saying when they had first met in the hotel at the conference. He'd been quoting that ridiculous student paper: "'At the time that Virginia Woolf and James Joyce were writing, the world was very much as it is today, though to a lesser extent.'"

Which somehow was even a little true if you applied it to your own life, your own history, because what you knew and felt and wanted now, and the way you could love now, had a long valley of seriousness running through it that had perhaps always been there, though to a lesser extent.

16.

On Monday morning, *The Campobello Courier* described the performance of the Aristophanes comedy *Lysistrata* as "heady and almost breathless," and the reviewer complimented Ms. Heller for her decision to go with "a po-mo angle that everyone seemed to love. My parents loved it too!" The review didn't get into specifics, and nobody really remembered that much from the play anymore. "Ms. Heller did a great job," the reviewer went on, "even with all the graphic material that she had to remove." He called sophomore understudy Willa Lang "fantastic—a performer who compels us with her urgency, integrity, and beauty." For weeks Willa would enjoy thinking of those three final nouns. But now, before the review had come in, late Saturday afternoon after the cast party—that long, weird night—Willa Lang couldn't stand that she had let Eli go for reasons that no longer seemed reasonable.

At the party, a boy on tech crew had gently told her that Eli had texted him and said he'd decided to leave New Jersey and go live with his father in Michigan. When Willa heard this, she felt certain that Eli was gone for real; this wasn't going to be just one of those brief, moping teenaged sojourns, from which the sojourner returns in a few days, eager for a hot meal and his own soft bed. After she heard he was gone, she drank a lot of beer at the party, and got very drunk, and cried, and was sick in the Petitos' downstairs bathroom, where not too long ago Carrie had secretly jabbed a sewing needle into her navel and hissed, "Fucking fuck fuck fuck," as the pain sped through her with its own elaborate stitch. Willa, in her own pain, allowed herself to be helped onto an air mattress in the living room, and she lay on her back and stared at the ceiling and listened to the soft sounds of her friends in the other room, and she did not sleep for a very long time.

The next afternoon Willa came home from the cast party and found that though she was ill from love and overwhelmed by the lurching stops and starts in her life, and though she had apparently been such a triumph in the play, such a star, her house was maddeningly the same as ever. Hazel lay asleep. Her parents were probably in the den grading papers. Her father had put one of his cheese bakes in the oven for dinner. It had been just too much for her to find out that Eli had left. Too much to have been the lead in the play after one day's rehearsal, and then have everyone swarm her afterward. Too much to have gotten so drunk, and then so sick. Too much, perhaps—though in a supremely good way—to have had actual sex this school year, complete with real orgasms, and joking around afterward, and occasional flute playing. All of it, now, too much.

So, how wrong it felt then to come home and find her little

white house and her family right here, the same as always, along with all the objects that had been constant in her life over the years—the upright piano, the dog—and yet somehow not be able to take them in, because she was different, and something she now needed wasn't here. She bent down and kissed her dog, who raised her head and breathed on Willa with meaty but delicate breath, as if she'd just eaten a sparrow. The dog was elderly, and would not live too much longer, and Willa was so emotional right now that she could easily, self-indulgently have flung herself down beside Hazel and wept as if the dog had already died. But Hazel, after a moment of affection for this girl who used to tie party hats onto her smooth golden dog-head, and run with her around the yard all summer, returned to her own slow bout of self-love; she knew what she liked best.

Willa went upstairs to her pink bedroom. At her desk, she lightly touched the space bar on her computer and watched it spring awake. She immediately saw that Eli had written her a short note, explaining that he had left, and where he'd gone: "if u feel like it find me on farrest," he wrote. "i will be there a lot i imagine."

She went straight to Farrest then, even though she hadn't said hi to her parents yet, and she still smelled like beer, and vomit, and she needed to wash, and then sleep. The uncomplicated green forest awaited her after log-in, and it was crowded now, since it was a weekend and no one was in school. There was Marissa the hawk, Marissa who had only just gotten home from the cast party herself, where she had reassured Willa that she was very happy for her that the play had gone well, and that she wasn't sorry she'd made the decision not to play Lysistrata. Willa said hi to Marissa again now, then spoke for a second to a few other people she knew, some from school, a couple from Farrest. Several of them were aware she had just starred in a play; others had no idea she was even a high school student in New Jersey. To them she was just a purple female ninja in a crowded forest.

She had to find Eli, though she had no idea if he was here right now. She looked and looked in the usual quadrant, past pirates and wraiths and little children with enormous eyes. The centaur was pulsating under a tree.

"there u r," she said. "r u ok?"

"yes. how was the play?"

"isnt that beside the point now? u LEFT."

"i couldnt stay. i hope u understand."

Willa thought about asking him to come back, but she didn't want to seem to be toying with him, and he was already so far away now, and she was too tired to think. She waited for him to ask her again if she would reconsider their relationship, but he didn't. For now, at least, they would be together only here on Farrest. A creature that she had never seen before—a spider—kept circling them and scuttling up to the centaur, for some reason wanting to ingratiate itself.

"please," the spider said to Eli. "please."

The centaur and the ninja instinctively strode away from it, moving faster and faster together through the grass.

That night, alone in her living room, Fran Heller made the decision to resign from Eleanor Roosevelt High School on Monday. McCleary would be shocked, of course, because he'd expended

great effort bringing her into the district. But Fran would resign on
Monday because, really, what was the point in staying here now?
She'd done what she'd planned to do, and the most relevant and
enjoyable part of it—the big climax, the reason she'd done it in
the first place—was over. This was the way it always went. You
worked and worked to get the play into shape, helping the actors
breathe feeling into those ancient lines. You designed the lighting,
you drew sketches for the Acropolis, you assembled the cast at
your knee and got them motivated for a long season of rehearsals.
"A comedy, yes," you told them. "But what it's about is something
quite serious." And on the night of the performance, you had them
all join hands, and you let them know that they were a part of
something significant, and then you sat back and watched.

The drama teacher was alone in her adobe-painted house at
the far end of Tam o' Shanter Drive; the paint choice had seemed
like a good idea in the summer, when she and Eli had first moved
in, but at some point in the late fall, when the sun had set before
dinner and the bright house looked a little desperate in the dying
light, she had regretted it. She could also admit now that she
regretted causing the women and men in this town so much pain,
though it had been a necessary step toward making everything
better for them. Their pain was gone now, alleviated in the way
she had known it would be. All except her son's pain, which she
had never anticipated. Nor had she anticipated that, because of
what she'd done, he would end up leaving her. That she would
lose him.

No matter what town you were in, Fran had found, people
fell into a rut when left to their own devices, or else they let themselves stray so far from their original desires, or they were sexually

reckless, or needy, or built their love lives on a faulty foundation. You could see it again and again wherever you looked. The most well-meaning and loving couples in the world started to let everything get too familiar and *erode*, or forgot to plan for the future, or made sexual choices that would clearly lead to disaster. Again and again people were mindless or erratic when it came to matters of love and the bed.

Decades earlier, at the beginning of the great and wondrous bliss that was Fran and Lowell Heller's marriage, the couple had agreed that they would never allow themselves to become overwhelmed by their domestic life. This, they suspected, would have been their sensual and sexual undoing. They loved to be together in the mornings after spending the night together. They lay in bed, listening to Bach or the Velvet Underground. They walked around the house proudly naked. But how insidious it could all be; familiarity could steal away everything exciting. They swore one night that they wouldn't let this happen to them. A year and a half after Eli was born, Lowell found a job in Michigan, and the specific arrangements were worked out. Lowell would move to Lansing, and Fran and Eli would stay behind in New Jersey. Lowell would miss them horribly; he adored his wife and his baby boy. He would visit his family a few times a year, and Fran and Eli would live with him in the summer.

Every night they talked. Sometimes Fran took the phone into her bedroom and spoke to her husband about what she would like to do to his body that very minute, and he responded in kind. He was a compact, sandy-mustached man who did not look forty. But had they lived together, he might have easily looked forty now, even fifty. The limited time they spent together was life-enhancing, because domesticity hadn't diluted it with its liquid detergents and its conversations about car inspections and the like.

These people here in Stellar Plains and in other towns, they'd had no idea how to conduct their love lives. They let everything fall into comfort or indifference or chaos or disrepair. They'd had no innate sense of how to protect the thing they claimed to care about above all else—and instead they'd found many, many ways to let it rot. Some people *seemed* fine, *seemed* happy and contented with each other, and for the moment they actually were. But you knew that it was only a matter of time—months, years, it depended on the individuals—until their relationships began to erode just like everyone else's.

So Fran Heller saved them all from themselves. She had done this in Ferndale, New Jersey; and then in Cobalt; and now here in Stellar Plains. She herself had no unusual gifts in this direction, no supernatural "abilities," of course, and she had never known anyone who did. Such people probably didn't even exist. She'd only learned about the spell accidentally back in Ferndale, where she'd been the drama teacher in the mediocre high school for a number of years before choosing the play for no particular reason. She'd been in the mood for something classical, and *Lysistrata* had a lot of parts for girls, and she could easily eliminate the racy material.

But right after rehearsals began in that high school in Ferndale, Fran noticed that some of the women and girls suddenly started turning away from men and boys. Relationships broke up entirely, or were simply desexualized, and Fran Heller started to hear about them through the school grapevine. And though no one understood why this was happening to them, Fran began to figure it out. She was open-minded about cause and effect, and she had always intuitively believed in enchantment, and in the powers of literature and performance.

So an amateur high school production of *Lysistrata* apparently could cast a no-sex spell upon the females in its midst. This seemed, on first glance, as random, say, as the fact that bread mold could be used to cure disease. And yet it made a kind of perfect sense. The idea of a sex strike, of saying *no*, was powerful and suggestive, and not just necessarily saying no because of a war, but for a hundred different reasons.

Fran couldn't get over it; she sat quietly, thrilled, chewing on her nails as she watched the effects of the spell that first year, having no idea what would happen next, or how it would all end. But on the night the play was finally performed, the men and teenaged boys of Ferndale had started getting worked up and arguing in the audience about the message of the play—was it insulting to men, was it fair, was it a little too close to their own lives—and one of them had popped up onstage, and another had gone up to bring him down. There was some kind of theatrical scuffle, and then finally a few go-for-broke men had stormed that Acropolis, asking their wives and lovers and girlfriends to take them back, and they did.

After Ferndale, Fran Heller decided she would go elsewhere and see if she could do it all over again with the same results. She had been made to see that nature was sometimes out of balance; she had always viscerally understood this to be true, and had felt it in other moments in her life, such as once, when she saw a baby dressed like a stripper, or another time, when she saw mushrooms growing in a shower stall. But nature could frequently get out of balance in bed, and now she thought she knew a way to rectify this.

It was overwhelming to be able to sense, roughly, what would happen as the cast rehearsed and the spell moved through a town—yet still not know the exact people who would fall under it. All of the susceptible ones seemed to be in some sort of relationship with men; all of them also had some proximity to the play, or to someone in the play, but it didn't seem to strike them in any particular order. Fran and Eli had landed next in Cobalt, an innocent, not-bad New Jersey suburb. She put on *Lysistrata* again, and, sure enough, it happened; corrections were made in various people's sexual lives. Fran told no one about the spell, or about being its conductor, administrator, practically its impresario—no one except Lowell, to whom she told everything, though almost never in person.

The drama teacher realized that she could keep putting on *Lysistrata* all over New Jersey, or even all over the eastern seaboard if she wanted, working with bright-faced adolescents, teaching them to act, getting their parents to donate sheets for use as chitons. Causing couples to fall sharply away from each other, and then, in the middle of the performance, to fall sharply back. Just as it had done last night, here in Stellar Plains—despite that heart-stopping panic about the *lead* needing to be replaced, of all crazy distractions—a combination of other, ardent spells always overtook the *Lysistrata* spell at the very last minute.

She picked up the silver loving cup from where she had placed it on the coffee table, and ran her hand across the inscription on the curved, tarnished surface. Fran had gotten in the habit of taking a small memento from each school, and this one had been a no-brainer. After the kids were all off at the cast party, and after the tech crew had finished striking the set, she had been the last one in the silent school. She'd opened the glass showcase in the hallway outside the auditorium with the tiny key she'd been given at the beginning of the school year, and removed the loving cup from where it had probably been since 1969.

As she sat touching it now, she looked at the words "*You Can't Take It with You,*" and she laughed aloud, once, at the fact that, in this instance, oh yes you could. After she'd removed it, she'd rearranged all the photos and objects in the dusty showcase so that no one would notice something was missing, not that anyone ever really looked in there anymore. She almost imagined for a moment that the silver cup had been given to her and her cast, in honor of this wonderful production tonight. "Thank you," she heard herself saying, and the memory of the entire play from start to finish should have been deeply satisfying to recall right now, except that she could not stop thinking about her son.

It just hadn't occurred to her that Eli could be a casualty of her actions. In the past he had been too young, or not interested enough in girls, and the play wasn't relevant to him. Fran had assumed it would always be that way; why hadn't she realized that one day he might get involved with a girl in the school where she taught; even a girl in the play? And that by entrancing a girl he loved, the spell would bring him heartbreak, even the temporary kind. And then—what were the chances—that the love between him and this girl might be the rare one that didn't recover.

Eli was independent and intense; he'd always had his own mind, and that was still true now. When Fran had returned home after the play with a do-gooder's feeling of accomplishment, and the loving cup pleasingly heavy in her shoulder bag, she had sat at her laptop and read her son's e-mail, in which he told her he'd left. Her head had pounded as she read it. "I'm not running away, per se," he wrote. "I just want to get on with my life w/o Willa, ok?"

She understood that he had left before the moment of Willa's dis-enchantment, and before the reunion that Fran had always intended. "Don't take it personally, Mom," Eli wrote her, but of course she did. She had raised him alone, basically. They had been incredibly close, and she wasn't ready to turn him over to Lowell full-time. She simply couldn't bear it.

But maybe she wouldn't have to, she thought. Once Eli found out that Willa now wanted him back, he would come home. "I just know that you and Willa will work things out," Fran wrote back to him. "I can tell she has changed her mind." But Eli didn't write back.

Fran had panicked. She'd called his cell, and the voice mail picked up immediately, so she left a message saying, "Please, Eli, take the next bus home. Your dad will pay for your ticket. Call me when you get this. Please, honey, give a call." When he didn't call back within ten minutes, she left a second message, feeling ill from the stress of it. God, she thought, she'd become as needy as one of the men who'd been begging the women that winter.

Above Fran Heller on the wall of the living room, the ceramic masks of comedy and tragedy grinned and frowned, just as they had done that night in Cobalt, when the production was over and everyone had scattered, and she'd pulled the masks with pliers from the wall of the auditorium for another keepsake, then put them in her bag and kept walking.

Listen, fair woman, she imagined the masks saying as one voice, as one chorus. *Do you really think so many men and women benefit from the extreme intervention that the play brings?*

Yes, Fran would have replied, *I do. Not everyone is enlightened; not everyone knows how to live.*

But what about the young man sprung from your loins? How did he benefit? He is suffering, isn't he? And he is alone.

But Fran Heller didn't want to think about her son anymore tonight. She had figured out how to adjust and correct the couplings of virtual strangers, but when it came to her own teenager, she didn't know what the hell she was doing. No one ever did. Always, he would be one step beyond her; this was how it was supposed to be, but it was as sad as anything she could think of, as sad as the saddest tragedy. Fran Heller made her way down the hallway to her bedroom, and dialed the house in Lansing. Lowell answered, and she said to him, keeping her voice casual and light, "It's me, babe. Everything okay over there? Yes, yes, good." She lay down on the bed, for she hadn't slept in a full day, and she was so tired. Her husband's voice spoke to her from across a great distance, but he might as well have been right there beside her.

In the weeks to come, she would circulate her résumé, hoping that a drama teacher was needed somewhere not too far away. And when she was hired, she would move there and settle in, and it would all begin. Some of the women who lived in that new town, both the younger ones and older ones, would begin to feel puzzled that desire had fallen away from them so suddenly and easily. That for reasons they didn't understand, they had given up what they'd loved. That everything was different now. But they wouldn't know what to do about it, and for a while at least, they would just have to let themselves remain suspended and powerless—waiting, as we all do, for the spell to lift.